CORDYCEPS RISING

JE GURLEY

ISBN: 978-1-925047-42-4

1

June 26, Chiquibul, Belize –

Roger Curry clambered up the rugged rocky slope, little knowing that each step brought him closer to death. Even if he had known, he would not have retreated. Roger was no adventurer, but his friends were missing and it had fallen on him to find them. The oppressive heat and humidity of the Belize jungle didn't help matters. Roger, used to milder Tennessee summers, stopped frequently to wipe the beads of sweat from his face before they rolled stinging into his eyes with his already soaking wet handkerchief. His shirt was plastered to his clammy skin, and his damp underwear chafed his crotch. He resisted the urge to reach down his pants and scratch his scrotum. He moved with slightly less agility than did his guide, Chiri Hutapec. The young, diminutive Yucatec Mayan scampered over the loose boulders and sharp limestone scree with the agility of a New World monkey.

Juan Saldo, his interpreter, smiled down at him from his boulder perch, as he pointed ahead. "The entrance is on the other side of this ridge."

Saldo was at home in the jungle, naming almost every bird and creature they had encountered on their long trek through the wilderness. Roger envied Saldo and his composure in the withering heat. Saldo looked as if he were walking home from a tavern after a few cold *cervezas*, while on the other hand, Roger was ready to collapse.

"I hope you're right," Roger replied.

The Chiquibul Cavern system lay deep in the heart of the Chiquibul National Park on the western slopes of the Maya Mountain Massif region of western Belize and eastern Guatemala. It was inaccessible in the rainy season and difficult to reach at any time of the year. This was Roger's first trip to Chiquibul, or to anywhere outside the U.S. for that matter. The Tennessee Conservancy, in a joint venture with the Belize government, was performing a thorough study of the 540,000-square foot cavern system to determine the number of visitors the cavern could safely accommodate without damaging its fragile ecosystem. More administrator than spelunker, his journey was to determine the fate of the last expedition, now over two weeks past due. No word had reached any settlement since the expedition had first entered the jungle two months earlier.

The expedition's leader, Michael Harris, was a thirty-two-year-old-veteran caver with spelunking credits from twenty-five caverns around the world. It was unlike him to remain out of communication for so long. The area's native Indian tribes – the Garifuna, the Kekchi, and the Yucatec Maya – had heard nothing of the missing team. Roger had hoped to question natives in San Antonio, a small city upriver from Punta Corda where they had arrived by boat from Belize City, but Saldo inexplicably had suggested bypassing the city. "Trouble," was all he replied when questioned, leaving Roger to ponder what kind of trouble – drug smugglers, or an uprising of the indigenous population over newly imposed strict hunting and fishing laws.

Standing atop a fallen tree, Hutapec waved Roger to stop. The diminutive guide shaded his eyes as he scanned the terrain around them, and then pointed higher up the slope.

"*Il Xiib*," he called in Mayan.

Roger turned to Saldo who had waited for him to reach his position. "What did he say?"

"He said he sees men," Saldo replied.

Roger's pulse quickened. Had they found Harris? "What men? How many men?" Roger asked eagerly.

Hutapec held up five fingers and yelled, "*Ho*."

"Five men," Saldo translated.

Roger pushed past Saldo, but Saldo reached out and grabbed his arm as Hutapec said something more. "Wait," Saldo warned.

"Wait for what?"

Saldo shook his head. A look crossed his face that Roger recognized as fear. "Hutapec said '*Hook'ol*', leave."

Roger was livid. "Leave," he snapped, "after coming all this way? If he sees men, it must be some of Harris' group."

"Something is wrong, *senor*. They do not move. They stand as still as statues."

"I must see." He shook free of Saldo's grip and climbed higher up the slope. He quickly spotted the five men standing in a group at the edge of a cliff. "Harris," he yelled. His voice echoed across the valley, but none of the men moved. Were they deliberately ignoring him? Then he noticed vines growing around them, up their legs and across their faces, as if binding them to the cliff. "What the fu ..." he moaned.

Saldo joined him.

"Are they dead?" Roger asked, knowing no other reason men would stand silently as vines encircled them.

"Hutapec says they are." He pointed to vultures circling overhead. "He questions why the *buitres* do not land."

"I must go to them."

Saldo sighed, clearly against the idea. "Let Hutapec go first to see if it is safe. Then we follow."

Roger chaffed at waiting, but after arguing briefly, couldn't persuade Saldo to change his mind. "Oh, very well," he finally conceded.

He sat on the ground and waited as Hutapec climbed the slope, disappearing into the trees for fifteen minutes before reappearing beside the motionless men. He waved Roger and Saldo forward. Roger's heart pounded both from the exertion of the climb and from a sense of dread that mounted with each step that he took. It soon became apparent that Harris and the others were indeed dead. The stench of decay surrounded them, along with another odor, reminiscent of overripe bananas.

As he climbed over the last boulder and got his first close glimpse of Harris, the manner of the men's deaths became apparent, but still unbelievable. What he had first mistaken as vines anchoring them to the ground, was a network of finger-thick mycelia from a strange fungus growth covering the men's bodies, almost completely enveloping them. Their desiccated flesh sprouted tendrils with dark purple bulbous tips that swayed ominously in the breeze. Similar bulbs emerged from their ears, eyes, nose, and cracks in their skull, as if their brain had exploded from within. As he watched in horror, one dark bulb burst open, spewing tiny spores that drifted with the wind toward him. The smell of rotten bananas increased. Hutapec, who had remained cautiously upwind of the men, scampered higher up the slope away from the scene of death.

"What ... what is this?" he asked Saldo.

Saldo shrugged. "A fungus, maybe, but I've never seen it before." He spoke to Hutapec, who barked out a one-word reply. "He calls it *Black Death,*" Saldo said. He shrugged again. "I don't know what he means. He is afraid to speak more of it."

Roger was puzzled. "Why did they just stand here and let the fungus grow on them?"

"*Quien sabe*. Who knows?" Hutapec pointed to a nearby ravine and spoke. "Hutapec says six others, all native guides, are also dead, mauled, as if by a jaguar, but he thinks these men did it. Look at their hands."

Roger saw that three of the dead men's hands were crusted with dried blood. He refused to believe civilized men could do such a thing. "They wouldn't kill anyone. They're scientists for Christ's sake." He glanced down at the Chiquibul River flowing westward into Guatemala after emerging from the caverns. The late afternoon sun glinted off its surface like a ribbon of glass stretching through the jungle. "Where are the caves from here?"

Saldo pointed below and to the east. "There, but Hutapec will not go, nor will I. The natives think the caverns are the entrance to hell."

"You don't believe that?"

"Hutapec does, and he will not go," Saldo replied, as if it were explanation enough. He glanced at the bodies and made the sign of the cross. "After seeing this, I will not go either."

"We have to bury them and call the authorities."

"We must go back. It will be night soon. Hutapec believes the moon, *Uh*, will be an evil one. Bad things are happening in the land."

At this, Roger turned on him. "Why did we avoid San Antonio?"

Saldo paused as if reluctant to speak. Finally, he said, "There were mobs of men, violent men who killed like animals." He glanced with revulsion at the ravine where the dead natives lay. "Like them."

Roger was appalled. "You can't be serious. Men killing like animals."

"It is so," Saldo insisted. He pointed to the river below them. "The river flows through San Amelia in Guatemala. There are rumors of much violence there as well." He crossed himself. "It is a time of much evil."

Looking at the erect corpses of his colleagues, sent a shudder running through Roger's body. "We have to bury them," he insisted.

Saldo nodded. "I will help you, but Hutapec will not touch the dead."

Two hours later, Roger and Saldo had managed to scrape five shallow graves in the hard earth of the slope and cover the bodies with rocks. Neither Saldo nor Hutapec offered to bury the natives, so Roger ignored them. The jungle would quickly reclaim their bodies. Roger started at the five cairns of stone and the small pile of personal effects he had removed from the bodies. One item was Harris' journal, slightly moldy and smelling of death. He was loathe to touch it, but hoped some clue to the men's bizarre deaths lay within its crumbling pages.

After they had interred the bodies and he had intoned a few words of parting over his friends, Roger was eager to read the diary, but Hutapec refused to linger in the area. The guide set a quick pace back down the mountain toward Punta Corda where a boat waited on the coast to transport Roger back to Belize City. From there, he would alert the authorities about the deaths. The authorities, he assumed, would exhume the bodies so they could have a proper burial in the States.

The jungle, normally thriving with wildlife and filled with the sounds of predators hunting prey and with raucous territorial calls, was eerily silent. Hutapec remained silent as well, refusing to speak even to Saldo. As they hacked their way through the jungle, Saldo kept his eyes on the surrounding trees. He, too, was strangely reticent, speaking only when Roger initiated conversation, and even then, he answered succinctly, ignoring any of Roger's attempts to draw him into any discussion pertaining to what they had seen. His nervousness fed Roger's growing apprehension.

At dusk, they made camp in a small clearing beside a quiet stream. Neither Hutapec nor Saldo laid out their bedrolls for the night, choosing instead to remain awake and watchful through the night. Saldo kept the campfire banked low, as if afraid of attracting unwanted visitors. He kept his rifle across his knees. After a hurried meal, Roger opened Harris' diary and began reading by flashlight. He skipped the first part concerning the journey and began at the point where Harris had reached the cavern.

* * *

June 6 – Chiquibul

"The caverns are spectacular, true wonders of the world! I have delved the depths of many systems in my lifetime but none as beautiful as these. They remind me of Cumberland Caverns in Tennessee. I hope we will find unplumbed depths."

June 8 –

"Mapped out a great deal of the cavern. We discovered a new grotto deep within the caverns hidden behind an ancient rock fall. It proved a dead end, but inside, Louis Masters found a strange fungus growth which he claims should not survive in total darkness. Since his field is biology, I don't doubt his word. He has taken samples for further analysis."

June 10 –

"I am feeling feverish and exhausted, but perhaps it is due to the rapid pace I have set for our expedition. There is much to be done and little time in which to accomplish all our goals. Masters is complaining of chills, and Doug Seals is coughing incessantly. Perhaps my fatigue is related. I issued aspirin and Chloroquine for all of us, just to be safe. I hope we will not have to cut our survey short."

June 11 –

"Seals has gone insane. I can think of no other word for his state. We awoke to find him missing from camp. We later spotted him rushing through the caverns in complete darkness, screaming like a wild man. He attacked us when we attempted to subdue him. We finally managed to sedate him. The chase weakened me severely. I must rest.

"Masters says he has identified the mushrooms as an unknown species of the genus *Orpicordyceps unilateralis*, known as the 'zombie fungus' because of its bizarre effect on some ants. It produces cyclosporine, an immunosuppressant. Perhaps that is why we feel ill. The jungle is awash with insect-borne diseases. In our weakened condition, our bodies cannot fight them off. I am gravely concerned."

June 12 –

"My mind reels with insane thoughts. It burns as if on fire. Seals has escaped and I cannot rouse Ellis to help me search for him. I believe this fungus we have discovered is to blame. I found tiny strands of mycelia in my sputum. We are all infected. The native workers are frightened and threaten to abandon us.

"I have been wondering if the presence of this strange fungus is the cause of the sudden disappearance of the ancient Maya from the nearby ruins of Lubaantun and Cahal Pech. Their abandonment was rapid and mysterious. Perhaps, I'm wrong, but the coincidence is frightening. We must leave this place."

June 13 –

"Now Masters is missing. I feel I am going insane. I can feel this fungus coursing through my body, devouring it bit by bit. It's in my head. My thoughts are wandering, boiling into bouts of barely controlled rage. It is difficult to concentrate on this journal. I am very ill and I anger easily. I lashed out at McNeil for no reason. We almost came to blows. The damned natives are in the jungle singing some screeching gibberish that is grating on my nerves. I must stop them."

The journal ended at that point. The last few entries were almost illegible, hastily scribbled in a trembling hand. Roger closed the book with a sickening feeling. An intense sense of dread swept over him. If the fungus had escaped the cavern system, it could even now be flowing in the waters of the Chiquibul River into Guatemala, or riding on the winds into Belize. He wondered if he was infected. He tried hard to convince himself that his aches and pains were due to the hardship of the journey and not the first signs of infection. Sleep did not easily come to him. Instead, dire visions of the end of the world and quivering mushroom men stalking the streets of Nashville played like a horror movie through his head. He awoke exhausted an hour before dawn. Hutapec and Saldo were already breaking camp. Their haste fed his trepidation.

"Leave the equipment," he snapped at them, "I want to reach Punta Corda as soon as possible."

Neither man argued. Hutapec dropped the supplies and plunged into the jungle with his machete breaking a trail. Saldo left his pack but cradled his rifle in his arms as he followed Hutapec. With a final glance back toward the Chiquibul Caverns, Roger followed them.

* * *

June 29, Miami, FL –

Roger knew he was infected. Each spasm of coughing racked his chest. His skin itched and burned. He was surprised the TSA people had allowed him through the airport in his obviously ailing condition. The bright lights blinded him through his shades, and the hordes of noisy people punished his eardrums. He couldn't spend another hour in the confines of a jet or in a crowd. He was weak and feverish. He needed to rest before continuing his journey to Nashville where he would see his doctor.

The desk clerk at the Miami Hilton Airport smiled congenially at him as he staggered through the door, but he knew that her smile was a lie. He could hear her heart beating out blood to each forced muscle around her mouth. She resented his intrusion into her busy day. He stumbled into the red velvet rope separating the desk from the lobby and cursed loudly.

"May I help you?" the receptionist asked.

"I need a room," he replied gruffly.

"We have ..."

He cut her off and thrust his credit card at her like a weapon. His hand shook uncontrollably. "Here! Just give me a damn room."

She dropped her smile but complied with his request. It seemed an interminable amount of time passed as she entered his information in the computer. He ignored the curious stares of the other people in the lobby, suppressing his desire to lash out at them. Finally, she handed him a keycard in a small paper cardholder.

"Room 517, Mr. Curry. I hope you enjoy ..."

He snatched the key from her hand before she could finish her statement, stumbled with his bag to the elevator, and stepped inside. The bright overhead light of the elevator drilled into his brain like a laser. His eyes barely focused long enough to see the numbers as he punched the twelfth floor button. Leaning against the rear wall, swiping at the beads of sweat dotting his forehead, he pressed his hand to his aching stomach. It had been hours since he had eaten, but he feared its rumblings were not from hunger. He watched an obese woman, matronly and stern in a high-collared, pale blue dress, approach the elevator. She entered the car, moving to the opposite wall as far away as possible in the small space, and stared at him. He tried to ignore her, but her mere presence annoyed him. He suddenly doubled over in pain, as the convulsions in his belly sought an outlet. He farted loudly. The woman wrinkled her nose at the cloying stench and shot a reproachful glare at him as the doors began to close. She stopped the door with her hand and stepped out saying, "How rude." He resisted the urge to wring her fat neck.

In his room, he dropped his bag on the floor and yanked the curtains shut to hide the offending setting sun. The room was stifling. He spun the thermostat from 72 degrees to its lowest setting. His tongue was too thick for his mouth and his throat ached. He gazed at his reflection in the bathroom mirror as he poured water from the tap into a glass. It was like looking through a veil. He removed his sunglasses. A fuzzy growth protruding from the corner of his left eye had sent tendrils across the pupil. He tried to extract it with his finger but only succeeded in mashing the tendrils and making a mess. He ignored the pain. His skin was sallow and clammy.

Disturbed by his stark image, he backed away, crashed into the door, and, in a fit of rage, threw the glass he was holding at the mirror. Tiny shattered images of him cascaded into the sink from the broken mirror. The sound of breaking glass thundered in his ears, echoing as if in a cavern. He clamped his hands over his ears, but the sound didn't diminish. He raced around the room clawing frantically at the floral-print wallpaper, tearing it off in thin strips with his fingernails. He jerked a picture of an ocean scene from the wall above the bed and smashed it to the floor, grinding his heel into the broken glass. Exhausted, but not satiated by his orgy of destruction, he collapsed on the bed, panting. His brain was on fire, threatening to spill out through his ears. He pressed his hands to each side of his head and screamed.

He didn't know if he slept or if his mind had simply stopped functioning for a while. When he opened his eyes, it was full dark outside. The room, though spacious, closed in on him, smothering him. He needed air, open space, some place high above the din and the light. He threw open the door to his room and raced down the corridor, banging on doors and yanking pictures from the walls. At the elevator, he overturned a marble table, smashing a large flower-filled oriental vase on the tiled floor. A rage rose in his gullet like bile. He bit back on it but could not stop the scream that ripped from his throat, a wail of anguish and anger that echoed down the corridors.

The elevator door opened. Two men dressed in business suits stepped out. Engaged in conversation, they paid him no heed, brushing by him as if he did not exist. One glanced at the overturned table and the pool of water from the shattered vase, but quickly turned his attention back to his companion. Roger growled at him. A blind fury born of dark images moved him to action. He leapt upon the man and beat him savagely with his fists. When the man's companion tried to help, Roger bit his arm, grinding his teeth in the man's flesh until blood sprayed them both. The man screamed and fell. Roger kicked him in the head until he no longer moved. He then chased after the first man who had used Roger's attack on his friend to try to escape.

He caught the man outside the room containing the ice machine. The man's high-pitched screams drilled into Roger's befuddled mind like burning augers, searing flesh and burning away who he was, what he had been. He was no longer human, but an animal. He clamped his hands to his head and moaned, but something inside drove him back to the creature in front of him. The man pleaded, but the words held no meaning to Roger, just more noise pounding in his head. His hands throttled the man's neck and twisted. He continued to twist long after the man's face had turned blue and his jaw had fallen open. His lust for blood still not satisfied, he pounded the man's head against the ice machine until blood, pieces of bone, and bits of brain dripped down his arms. Ice, summoned by the pounding, filled the recess for ice buckets and spilled onto the floor around his feet, joining the blood staining the tile.

Curious heads drawn by the screams thrust through opened doors. He ran from their stares. His body burned from within. He felt as if he were going to spontaneously combust; become a human torch. He shed his clothes as he stumbled down the corridor. He opened the door to the stairwell and ran upwards, yearning for some place high above the clamoring din. He kicked open the roof door and walked to the edge of the roof. Standing there, staring down fourteen floors to the swimming pool, he wanted to jump, to end the pain, but found he couldn't; not from fear of dying, but because his mind, no longer his own, wouldn't allow it. A tear trickled down his cheek, followed by a tiny tendril of mycelium fiber licking at the moisture. Frozen to the spot, unable to force his muscles to move, he wept. Tears ran unfelt down his cheeks, their moisture feeding the tiny growths pushing through his pores. He knew he was dying. He would soon become food, a host for the monster growing inside him. Remembering the horribly grotesque bodies of his colleagues in Belize, he wanted to shudder, but his mind denied him even that small release.

2

July 1, Miami, FL –

Dead Man Standing. That was something Detective Kyle Bane didn't see every day, and in his job with Miami's Special Investigation Squad, he had seen some bizarre things. During his six months with the squad, they had taken down a Haitian drug lord with a penchant for voodoo, busted a money-laundering scheme involving two college freshmen, and solved a kidnapping case where the husband had locked his wife in a secret basement room to prevent her from leaving him. It was more rewarding than his first five years on the force, busting pimps, hassling two-bit drug dealers, and chasing purse snatchers in Hialeah. However, phrases like 'Dead Man Standing' made him realize what a rookie he was.

Two uniformed officers had been first on the scene, but what they found had stymied them. Never having witnessed such a bizarre death, they contacted the SIS. By the time Kyle had arrived, the roof of the Airport Hilton was swarming with white-clad CDC people, led by a woman wearing a red hazmat suit that set her apart from the others. So far, she hadn't been very communicative. Since his own experience with naked dead men sprouting what looked like mushrooms from every orifice in their body was severely limited, he allowed the CDC people to do their jobs. From his brief glimpse of the corpse, he was glad that had not eaten breakfast. Even so, his stomach grumbled.

Two men in white hazmat suits scurried around the roof spraying every surface with a chemical from pressurized backpack canisters. He didn't know what was in the tanks, but he was glad the wind was blowing away from him. If they needed protective gear, it had to be some serious stuff. He frowned as four others placed the corpse into a hard plastic cadaver transport container.

Once they had secured the lid, they lifted it by its recessed handles and carried it to the stairwell. He didn't like anyone interfering with his crime scene.

His mind was still fuzzy from lack of sleep, but not too dead to question how the Centers for Disease Control people had arrived so quickly and taken control of the scene.

"Where are you taking my body?" He posed his question at the woman in red.

She cocked an eyebrow and glared at him through the clear plastic visor of her hazmat suit. The loose suit draped over her body like a potato sack, but bunched up in enough places to indicate a few curves beneath it. It was an old habit, sizing up people he met by judging their potentials as adversaries. He pictured her as svelte, athletic, and able to stand her ground if push came to shove. Her nametag read 'Marli Henry, MD – Epidemiologist, CDC.'

"Your body?" she asked. Her voice, filtered by the hood, was tinny.

"Yeah, my victim, or whatever the hell he is," he said in his cockiest tone.

Doctor Henry jotted a few notes on a laptop ensconced in its own mini-hazmat suit before answering. "We're taking him to a CDC quarantine site at MIA, and then we're transporting him back to Atlanta."

"Before you whisk him off to Miami International Airport, I need some information."

Her condescending look immediately set his hackles rising. She might rank higher than he did, but he didn't like to be ignored or dismissed, especially by a woman wearing a giant red condom. "Any information you need will be provided by your superiors through the proper channels. This man was not murdered; therefore you have no jurisdiction."

As she turned to leave, he stepped in front of her. "Hold on a minute, lady. You don't know what happened to him. Unless he tried to smuggle mushrooms into the country in his ass, I don't think this could be classified as death by natural causes."

She placed her hands on her hips. "I am not *lady* anything." Her chilly tone almost gave him frostbite. "My name is *Doctor* Henry." She sighed and relaxed her stance. "Look, I understand your concern, Detective Bane. Now, try to understand mine. You, the two officers who were first on the scene, and everyone else who had contact with this man will require quarantine until we can determine if what he has is infectious. That means tracing his movements since his arrival two days ago from Belize. If he is infectious, how many people do you think he might possibly have infected since then?"

He understood her dilemma, if not her attitude. He suspected she was trying to lull him into feeling sympathy for her plight, just to shrug off his demands. It wasn't working. Instead, he saw an opportunity to insert himself back on the case she was trying to steal from him. In addition to the corpse's fellow passengers, she would have to access the manifests of every flight in MIA during that same period, crosscheck their destinations, and determine what visitors might have met any passengers at the airport. It was a monumental task.

"I can help. I'm familiar with the procedure."

She stared at him for a moment before nodding. "All right, but you'll have to do it in quarantine." She motioned with her hand, and one of the men in a hazmat suit hurried over carrying three more suits. "You and the two officers will have to put these on."

He stared at the white suit with disdain. It looked like a pair of hooded pajamas with feet. "You're kidding me."

"Do I look as if I'm in the mood for humor?" She narrowed her eyes at him, an intimidating look she had probably practiced in front of a mirror, but he had witnessed such a look by men who had no qualms about cutting off your head and spitting down your throat. Still, it conveyed her meaning. "Now, put it on or I'll call for three more quarantine containers."

The idea of being sealed into a hazmat suit seemed less claustrophobic than traveling in an oversized coffin. Besides, the two officers were watching him to see how he handled the situation. He had lost the argument and she knew it. Better to give in gracefully. He shrugged his shoulders. "Okay, you win."

He struggled into the suit, and one of the men in white helped him secure the hood over his head. He was a little annoyed that the two uniformed officers had less difficulty than he did. He felt a little like the deep-sea diver in the bottom of his small aquarium. He moved his arms and legs experimentally.

"A bit tight in the crotch," he complained.

He caught a brief smile on Doctor Henry's lips before she quickly replaced it with a more serious look. "You won't need to wear it very long, just until we reach the quarantine unit."

"By what skullduggery did you people find out about this man and arrive so promptly?" he asked and watched her face for a reaction. Sure enough, a slight twitch of her lips and a furrowed brow gave her away. "And while we're on it, how did you know that he arrived from Belize? What am I missing? His luggage and passport is still in his room. I checked before I came up. The desk clerk just supplied his name from his discarded clothing and wallet."

She glanced at her laptop, buying time as she tried to formulate a plausible answer. "Someone in your office informed us."

An obvious lie. "Oh, I doubt that. We're efficient, but we don't work that fast. No one had a clue about the condition of the body except ..." He paused as his mind worked furiously. The pieces began to fall into place. "You were monitoring calls. You were expecting this," he accused.

"Don't be silly. I ..."

He quickly cut her off. "Don't deny it. Something happened in Belize, something that reached your attention. You were looking for this man, or at least someone from Belize."

"I can't answer that."

"You just did."

"Detective Bane, I don't have time for jurisdictional squabbles. If you wish to help, you may, under my direction, of course. You may prove useful. If not, we'll determine whether or not we can release you from quarantine and allow you to return to your job of pummeling drug lords."

How had she known about that? Kyle straightened his stance and looked at her defiantly. "I merely defended myself. He had a knife."

"I understand the knife ended up protruding from Mr. Santiago's buttocks."

He tried to suppress a grin. "Well, he should've been more careful where he sat."

This time she smiled and allowed it to linger. The smile softened her features. He could see the woman that she probably was when not investigating fuzzy dead men standing, or trying to slice the balls off overly inquisitive detectives. "Perhaps so." She turned and looked out over the city. The gray, early morning skies added a touch of gloom to her words as she said, "I hope we're not too late."

"Too late for what?"

She ignored his question and began walking to the roof exit. He grabbed her shoulder and spun her around to face him. He pressed his facemask against hers.

"What do you mean?"

She shook her head and pulled away. "I can't tell you yet. Please be patient. We might need men like you."

He was confused. First, she tried to brush him off. Now, she needed him. "Need me for what?"

"For the end of the world."

He searched her face for some hint of humor, some indication that she was playing with him, but he saw only intense dread.

"You can't just say something like that and walk away," he said.

"I'll explain later, after your quarantine."

"You mean, if I don't turn out like Mr. Curry."

She nodded. "Yes."

He followed her to the door, his stomach churning like a volcano ready to spew its load of lava. Puking in a hazmat suit was not a good way to begin a day.

* * *

17

He had once visited the quarantine area at Miami International Airport during a drug case. It was a small, unadorned room on the third floor of one of the terminal wings, and he envisioned beating at the shrinking walls with his fists after a couple of days of confinement. He was surprised when after whisking him through the guarded northeastern gate of the airport, the van pulled up beside two large white tents. The area around the tents was a beehive of activity, but the airport was not. The runways lay silent. No jets taxied for take-off or circled the skies above the city awaiting permission to land. Jets parked at terminals were empty, baggage carousels motionless. The silence was ominous, disconcerting. The busiest international airport in the country was closed.

"You shut down MIA?" he asked, incredulous that such a thing was even possible. Miami International handled almost 73,000 flights per year, nearly 40 million passengers. The logistical nightmare created by shutting it down would send ripples throughout the flying world.

"We had to," she answered almost apologetically. She waved a hand toward the nearest tent. "We're observing sixty people that had close contact with Mr. Curry."

"Sixty people? That's …"

She nodded. "Yes, that's pathetic. I'm afraid we're just scraping the tip of the iceberg. The local customs people failed to do their job properly and allowed Mr. Curry simply to walk out of the airport. Hundreds more are probably moving throughout the city infecting others. Maybe thousands more left before our quarantine took effect. God knows how many they might infect."

"But it's a fungus, a mushroom. Isn't fungus easy to kill, like ringworm or jock itch?"

Her smile was weak, meant, he thought, to dull the depth of his ignorance. He felt like a schoolboy failing an exam.

"Fungi are among the most prolific species on the planet. Early man depended heavily on fungi for making bread, beer, and cheese. We eat them for food. Some are even delicacies. We develop antibiotics like penicillin from them. Without them, nothing would decompose. Our own civilized wastes would bury us. On the negative side, some fungi are also parasitic and difficult to control. Some are deadly."

"Like this one."

She nodded. "Some Cordyceps species are mildly parasitic to insects, but have never before posed a risk for man. This new species is different. It's highly infectious and kills quickly in a gruesome manner, which you witnessed firsthand." A little color drained from her face. "I've never seen anything like it."

He took a deep breath and asked her the question that he had been dreading. "What if I'm infected?"

She glanced away for a moment, realized what she was doing, and focused on his face. He liked that. It made her pronouncement more personal when she said, "If you are infected, then I'm afraid you'll die. As yet, we have no cure."

He released his breath, surprised at the calmness in which he accepted her sentence of death. It wasn't that he was eager to die or that he was unafraid of death. It was just that he had faced death many times and had somehow managed to survive. His sixth sense told him that he would squeak by this one as well, or maybe it was simply his stubbornness refusing to accept the inevitable.

"We'll see," he replied.

"I admire your courage, Detective. I hope you do make it. I need an investigator that isn't afraid to make the hard calls."

He glanced at the tent and scratched at his chest. "I want to get out of this hot air balloon. I suppose your men will want to scrub me down."

She nodded. "Thoroughly."

"Well, the sooner I get started, the sooner I'll get out of here."

Two suited men led him into a small tent behind the larger one with a high-pressure hose and scrub brushes on long poles. The scrubbing they administered was as thorough as she had promised. One man sprayed the exterior of his suit with chemical foam, while the second attacked it vigorously with the brush. They rinsed him with cold water, stripped him naked, and repeated the procedure on his skin. The brushes were coarse and felt as if they were stripping his skin from his bones. The chemical got into places he viewed as private, but which the technicians merely deemed a challenge. After fifteen minutes, he was allowed to towel dry and don a thin, white, one-piece jumpsuit that reminded him of the sterile suits the police forensics teams wore. They passed him through the clean room into the main section of the tent. He was surprised to see individual transparent plastic cubicles instead of a single open dormitory, but it made sense. If he wasn't infected, keeping him apart from the others ensured that he didn't inadvertently become infected. Each cubicle held a cot and a small nightstand. As the technician ushered him inside, he felt a sudden rush of claustrophobia. He fought it down. He tried not to gawk at his fellow roommates, hoping they afforded him the same courtesy.

"Hey, don't I even get a comb for my hair?" he demanded of the technician. He ran his fingers through his tangle of curly brown locks to make his point. The technician ignored him and secured the door with a heavy zipper. Kyle noticed that the zipper couldn't be reached from the inside. "It's going to be a long couple of days," he said, and sat down on the edge of the cot to wait.

The first few hours of his quarantine were the hardest. He paced the small cubicle until he tired, and then yelled at his keepers until he was hoarse. They ignored him as they did the other clamoring patients decrying their forced confinement. His hosts had taken his cell phone and his notebook from him, along with all his personal items. He passed the time counting technicians, trying to identify them individually through their sterile suits from their walk and their mannerisms, but quickly became bored. He was too keyed up to sleep, and the tasteless meal they finally provided, did little to satisfy his appetite. He tried to identify its contents, but finally gave up, deciding that the CDC had an entire department dedicated to creating tasteless cuisine from inanimate objects, rather than from meat or vegetables. For all he knew, the food and his itchy jumpsuit had come from the same source.

Time seemed ethereal. He had difficulty distinguishing night from day. The banks of bright lights remained on continuously. His internal sense of time failed him. With no watch, he guessed at the time, dividing it arbitrarily into days and nights by periods of sleep. He knew it was an inaccurate system since he slept only when the urge overcame him, and then only for a short time. His hosts served bland meals at irregular intervals, delivered through a small airlock in the cubicle wall. He ate the nondescript food despite its lack of taste, simply to occupy his time. There was no privacy. All bodily functions were performed in full view of any interested party. The humility of sitting on a cold metal chamber pot curtailed his bowel movements. Once each arbitrary day, he passed the container of wastes through a small double-sided partition at the rear of the cubicle. He felt the urge to fling feces at the sterile plastic walls like a caged monkey, but imagined his keepers would not look kindly upon such a wanton display. A container of water arrived at irregular intervals, which he used for drinking and for washing his face. His keepers did not allow him to shower. Luckily, the filtered air in his cell kept the odor to a minimum.

His forced isolation deepened his foul mood. He was stuck inside a plastic bubble while the city outside might be tearing itself apart at the seams. His life had been placed on hold on a whim of the CDC. With no one to talk to but himself, conversation turned to introspection. Would his absence even make a mark on the world? His date with that cute lawyer's assistant, Saitha, would have to wait, but he doubted she would wait long before finding someone else to favor with her attentions. His fellow officers on the Special Investigation Squad tolerated him, but his frequent undercover operations and newcomer status had not garnered him any close friends. Even his old colleagues in the Midwest District office had broken off close ties, feeling that his transfer to the SIS was tantamount to abandoning them.

By what he assumed was the third day of his captivity, eleven of his fellow patients had begun to show signs of infection, pacing their tiny cubicles while screaming, or tearing at the thick plastic with their teeth and fingers. Their face, which had previously been muted with fright and suppressed anger, became masks of wild rage, instantly attacking the suited technicians with the ferocity of caged beasts. One-by-one they disappeared through a set of double doors at the rear of the tent, strapped ignominiously to gurneys. He didn't inquire about their destination, hoping that he didn't soon discover their fate firsthand.

He began watching his fellow confinees closely, searching for the first tale-tell signs of infection. Some paced their tiny cubicles like caged animals, constantly mumbling to themselves as if conversing with someone via their missing Bluetooth. He couldn't tell if this was one of the first signs of the fungus infection, or simply a withdrawal symptom of modern man's infatuation with constant instantaneous communication. A few sat quietly, as if meditating, submitting themselves to their confinement with stoic humility. These, he envied. He had never been an adherent to the philosophy of fate, that some things were preordained and man could do little to change them. Acceptance of his present condition and submission to it were two different things. He couldn't leave, but he didn't have to like it.

After a while, he began to distinguish the subtle point at which the fungus began stripping away the thin veneer of civilization to which all people cling, that façade of superiority that separates humans from the animals. In his profession, he had intimate contact with the scum of the earth and knew that veneer to be very thin. In some, the normal signs of agitation grew more intense, more uncontrolled, until rage burst to the surface. The quiet ones were the most surprising. There was no visible tipping point. They retained their serenity until exploding into violent outbursts. In the end, both types met the same fate, carted out through the double doors.

Slowly, his fear began to subside. So far, he suffered no symptoms other than restlessness. His mind remained clear. He restrained the urge to pace, to avoid a hypo of whatever drug the technicians administered to their unruly charges, though he knew they could easily administer any drug of their choosing in his food or water. He was familiar enough with Homeland Security protocol to know that in a crisis, his individual rights were nonexistent. He kept his mind from his plight by considering the facts of the case.

Fact One – the CDC had known about Curry's existence or someone like him before the manager had phoned the SIS. They had been searching for him or someone from Belize. The only way they could know this, was if something had happened in Belize to attract their attention. He had heard nothing on the news before his incarceration, which meant that officials were suppressing the information.

Fact Two – somehow, they had missed Curry at the airport. That meant that they weren't properly prepared. They weren't aware that Curry was Patient Zero. He had slipped through their hands and spread the infection to Miami, and through his contacts to other parts of the country. If not for the murder at the hotel, the police would not have even known of Curry's presence. As it was, they had lost two precious days.

Fact Three – the police had blown it big time. The first officers to arrive at the hotel had searched for the assailant unaware that it was Curry, but had failed to search the roof, a costly mistake, a two-day mistake.

Fact Four – he had to get back on the case. Curry had been his murder victim, even if his killer was a mushroom. There was something about investigating a crime, sifting through mounds of evidence, and apprehending the culprit that triggered an endorphin reward in his brain. It felt good to solve a crime. That's why he had become a cop. It certainly hadn't been for the pay or the social status.

Fact Five – Doctor Marli Henry was smoking hot. Even through her plastic facemask, the curve of her lips and her high cheeks marked her as sensuous. Her face, framed by the red of her suit, lingered in his mind during his captivity. He had little else to dwell on. He would enjoy seeing more of her, provided he lived, of course.

He got his wish when Marli, as he now considered her, rather than Doctor Henry, returned carrying an armload of papers and an I-Pad. She wore a skirt and blouse beneath a white lab smock, and a simple cloth mask covering her mouth and nose instead of the uncomplimentary red suit. He noted that he had been right about her curves. They were luscious. He was delighted to discover that she was a redhead. He liked that. Redheads had spirit. Her green eyes complimented her deeply tanned skin. Beautiful and intelligent, two characteristics that he had found in short supply in the low-life circles he had lately been traveling.

"Good to see you again, Doctor. Have you come to release me?"

She went to the rear of his cubicle and inserted the material she carried into the small opening. "Here is a list of passenger manifests and destinations. If you want to help, see if any of these names appear on multiple flights."

He noted the manifests. Most were flights from Miami to other hubs across the country and flights out of those hubs. "It's a little late for this now isn't it? I expected this two days ago."

She said nothing as he read her face. She hid her emotions well, but he detected a mixture of regret and shame. "You didn't want to bother me in case I turned," he said.

After a few seconds, she nodded. "I need your help."

"Okay." He walked the few paces across his cubicle and sat on his cot. "I'll see what I can do. How much longer will I be here, provided I don't turn fungus head?"

"Fungus head? Oh, I see. Not much longer."

She turned and left. It only took him a few minutes to realize that the I-Pad she had provided was a simple notepad with no internet connection. She wasn't ready for him to have contact with the outside world. It did allow him to learn that his incarceration had lasted fifty-six hours so far. It had seemed longer. Bored and eager to have anything to take his mind off his predicament, he began poring over the material. All too quickly, he discovered numerous names that appeared on two or even three flight manifests, potential carriers of the plague across the entire country. She must have known this already. He was familiar enough with make-work to realize that she was attempting to fulfill her pledge without letting any real information slip. He added a long, nasty note to her with his summary. He hoped she read it.

3

July 4, Little Havana, Miami –

Rita Hernandez lifted the edge of the pulled blinds and stared through the window at the empty street outside her home. It was eerily quiet now, but just a few hours earlier, a dozen mad people had raced through the neighborhood turning over garbage cans, smashing car windows, and attacking anyone on the streets. She had watched in horror as her sixty-one-year-old neighbor, Maria Domilo, had been savagely attacked and killed. The old woman's body still lay on her front doorstep. No one had come to move it. No one had dared leave the safety of their homes. There were no working streetlights. The power had been off for over forty-eight hours. She had no idea what was happening in the city or if the craziness was confined only to her neighborhood. The people she had seen were not gangs, or an invading army. By their clothing, they were ordinary men and women, postal carriers, waitresses, and mechanics, people she had seen and interacted with every day who for some unimaginable reason, had gone terribly insane.

A haze of acrid smoke drifted down the street from a burning auto at the end of the block, but Rita suspected the smoke came from more than one source. The skyscrapers on the eastern horizon were backlit by a reddish glow that was not the moon. She had never before seen the city so dark and silent. The skyline known as the White Wall was now a row of darkened tombstones. At a whimper from her one-year-old son, Tomas, she dropped the blinds back into place.

"Hush, Tomas," she whispered gently, "I'll feed you."

She took the last jar of baby food from the kitchen pantry, and she was almost out of canned formula. The milk and food in the refrigerator had spoiled when the power had shut down. All she had eaten in two days was cheese sandwiches and cold soup. The stove was electric and she was afraid to build a fire to heat the soup. The darkness frightened her as much as the uncommon silence, but showing a light to draw the crazies frightened her more. The batteries of the flashlight in her emergency hurricane bag were dead. She should have checked on them regularly. Ricardo would know where fresh batteries were, but she did not. She also did not know where Ricardo was. It had been a full day since he had left in search of help. After hours of waiting and staring out the window, she now feared for his safety.

Little Tomas sucked hungrily at the spoon as she fed him the last of the mashed carrots. She didn't know what she would do next.

"*Pobricito*," she cooed, "Papa will return soon." But in her heart, she wasn't as certain.

Before the power had gone off, the television had warned people to remain calm and to stay indoors, but had given no specific reason for the emergency. She had heard shots fired, seen the fires. Where were the police? Where was the army? Military helicopters had passed by overhead. Why had someone not come to rescue them? Her father would have said that the authorities didn't care what happened to poor *Cubanos;* that the rich white neighborhoods would come first on their list in times of trouble. He had arrived in Florida aboard a sinking fishing boat during the 1980 Mariela Boatlift, when Fidel Castro had emptied Cuba's prisons and jails. Her father had been an activist in Havana, and continued his attacks on Castro's regime in Little Havana, but he had soon grown weary of the economic disparity between *cubanos* and *gringos* in Miami and began a neighborhood employment agency. Her father was now dead, but his agency lived on. Rita worked there five days a week, or she had until a few days ago. She didn't know if anyone still manned the telephones or if anyone sought work.

At the wail of a police siren, she stopped feeding Tomas and raced to the window, but the patrol car did not even slow down. It continued down the street and around the corner, turning south onto 8th Avenue. The sound quickly faded. She spotted movement in the shadows across the street in Riverside Park and hoped it was

Ricardo, but it wasn't. It was two more of the crazy ones. They moved furtively, their motions jerky and exaggerated. They raced quickly from spot to spot, and then stood and turned in circles as they sniffed the air. She grabbed the baseball bat leaning against the wall, her only weapon, and held her breath as they crossed the street. To her immense relief, the pair disappeared into the alley.

The telephones no longer worked and she had no cell phone. She didn't know who she would call if it did. Her Uncle Manny? He lived in Hialeah with his wife and three children. He probably had problems of his own. Father Domingo? The church was two blocks away and the priest was an old man. A light flashed briefly in a window across the street, as if someone had peeked out. At least everyone in the neighborhood wasn't dead or had fled.

She returned to feeding her son, softly singing a tune from her childhood, *Arruru mi Nino*. The words and the melody of the children's lullaby calmed her nerves, just as it had as a child when the skies were stormy and her mother had sung it to her. When her son had finished eating, she held him tightly to her breast as she walked around the room singing to him. Soon, his eyes closed. She placed him in his cradle and resumed her watch by the window.

There had been no fireworks this Independence Day, no parades, just fear and confusion. For all she knew, it could be the end of the world. She brushed back a lock of long, black hair from her thin but attractive face. It hung limp and lifeless. She hadn't washed it in three days. She wished she could shower, but the water was cold, and she was afraid to leave Tomas alone. What had happened to Ricardo? A drop of water rolled down her cheek. She fought back the tears, but it was no use. She covered her eyes with her hands and sobbed deeply until her shoulders shook. She was twenty-five-years old, a new mother and a new wife. Her world was slowly unraveling around her. Nothing in her life had prepared her for this. If only she was frightened she could cope, but with everyone too afraid to leave their homes, the horror became unbearable. If Ricardo didn't return soon, she would have to take her son and seek help. To whom could she turn? Where could she go?

She fell to her knees beneath a wooden crucifix her father had brought with him from Cuba and began to pray aloud. Her prayers were earnest and from her heart. She trusted God and he would not let her down. Soon, a sense of solace fell over her. The fear fell away like a discarded shawl. God would see her through this terrible ordeal.

A pounding at the door interrupted her prayer vigil. She quickly rose to her feet and rushed to the door.

"Ricardo?" she yelled as she threw open the door.

It was not her husband. It was a man, his shirt soaked with blood, his face smeared with it. For just a moment, she thought that he was injured, seeking help. Then she looked into his eyes and gasped. He had none. He stared at her through a purple mass of wet filaments clinging to his face. His face was a rictus of feral anger and loathing. His chest heaved and his expelled breath stank of mold and rot. His breathing sounded as if he inhaled and exhaled through a wet sponge. He was no longer a man. He was a creature, a *demonio*, a demon from hell. A small squeak emerged from her throat. The creature cocked its head to one side as if listening, and then sniffed the air and growled. Her heart pounded so loudly in her chest that she imagined the creature could hear it. She eyed the baseball bat a few feet away. She took one tentative step toward it, and the creature cocked its head in her direction. From the next room came a whimper, as Tomas stirred in his sleep. The creature zeroed in on the sound and raced across the room. In fear, and with strength of will she did not know she possessed, she picked up the baseball bat and attacked the loathsome creature from behind.

Her first blow was poorly aimed, bouncing harmlessly off the creature's shoulder. Now, it focused its attention on her. It crouched, tilting its head from side to side like a bird. She had played softball with Ricardo. She was not very good at it, but she remembered what he had told her – keep a firm grip on the bat, keep her eye on the ball, and swing hard. The creature lurched at her. Her second swing was more deliberate, as she aimed at the creature's head. She positioned her feet slightly apart for balance, and put all the muscle in her arms and shoulder into the swing. The ash bat connected with a loud crack. The creature staggered sideways and fell against the wall. Before it could regain its feet, she rushed at it and fell upon it. Delivering a flurry of blows to the top of its head, she screamed in anger and in fear as her arms worked feverishly, rising up and down with the bat. When she stopped, exhausted, the creature's head was broken open like an overripe melon, its brains and another jelly-like substance coating the bat. The wall, the floor, her hands, and her face were covered in blood. The stench was overpowering. She gasped, dropped the bat on the floor, and staggered as her knees buckled. She caught herself on the sofa before falling over the corpse. She had not killed a man, she reassured herself, but a *demonio,* but her heart was still heavy. The creature resembled a man, had once been a man. Had she sinned? She dismissed the thought as irrelevant. It didn't matter. Her son was safe. She was safe. She starred down at the bloody body on the floor of her living room.

Now, her knees did give way, She collapsed on the sofa and wept.

4

July 4, Miami International Airport, Miami, Fl –

Noises filtered in from outside the tent, taunting Kyle for his lack of information. He caught a glimpse of suited military personnel peering in through the door and wondered at their presence. If the military was involved, things were getting serious. Something big was happening and he wanted to be a part of it. Inactivity was not his style. Over the next sixteen hours, twelve more of his fellow inmates disappeared through the rear doors, but the plastic cubicles in the tent remained full, as suited men brought in more patients. The disease was spreading rapidly.

The sounds of people running awoke him from one of his short naps. He came awake fully knowing something was wrong. Armed military personnel stood nervously at both entrances. White-suited CDC people scurried about, moving from cubicle to cubicle while jotting down notes on their clipboards. They released five of his fellow inmates, the only five besides himself who had endured their confinement with no apparent changes. These five raced through the double doors and disappeared. That gave him a rough estimate of the infection rate. Six non-infected out of seventy-five or eighty people was nearly a seventy percent infection rate. When his wardens ignored him and fled behind their freed patients, he began to grow concerned.

"Hey! What about me?" he yelled.

He began to pound uselessly on the plastic walls, but stopped when one of the armed guards shifted position and eyed him suspiciously. As if taking cue from his actions, the remaining inmates erupted into a frenzy of activity, screaming and tearing at the tough plastic walls with teeth and nails. One woman, her eyes focused on him, repeatedly slammed into the walls of her cubicle until her face was a bloody mess. Still, she did not relent. Slowly, her cubicle inched across the asphalt closer to his.

"Let me out of here," he screamed, but the soldiers ignored him.

One soldier, an officer, stuck his head into the tent and barked out an order. Kyle saw that it was dark outside. The guards abandoned their posts, leaving him alone with a tent full of fungus-infected people. His mind worked furiously. He had no doubts that given time, the infected could free themselves from their cubicles and just as easily get at him. Abandoned, he had no choice but free himself. His mind worked furiously. He had no tools, no weapons. His eyes fell upon the I-Pad. It was his only bit of luck so far. He noted the time and date, eight p.m., July 4 – Independence Day. He had been on ice for seventy-two hours.

"Happy Fourth of July," he muttered as he smashed the I-Pad with the heel of his foot.

The floor of his chamber was the same material as the walls and ceiling, but a heavy wrought iron metal frame around the perimeter anchored it in place. The welded bar could not be moved, but its rough surface provided the abrasion he needed to sharpen a shard of the I-Pad shell. He worked quickly knowing his life was at stake. It took much longer than he had hoped, but finally he was satisfied with the results. Using his newly sharpened cutting tool, he attacked the heavy plastic by the rear hatch through which he had passed his bodily wastes, deciding that it was less secure than the zippered door. He mused that escaping the same way as his shit was somehow fitting. As he worked, noises grew louder outside the tent. Bursts of gunfire erupted nearby. He redoubled his efforts. Making a tiny slit in the plastic, he wedged his fingers inside and pulled with all his strength until the hole was large enough to reach the outside zipper. He opened the hatch and crawled through to freedom.

He had not worked quickly enough. Undaunted by their injuries, several of his fellow patients had gnawed their way through their cubicle walls. One man, his eyes wild and his face muscles quivering with rage, attacked him. Kyle's first blow to the man's stomach, enough to double most men over, didn't faze him.

He lunged at Kyle and wrapped his hands around his throat. Kyle broke the man's grip and delivered a punch to his throat that sent the man reeling backwards, wheezing through a crushed windpipe. Still, he did not relent. Realizing that he didn't have time to waste, Kyle kicked the man's kneecap, shattering it. As he collapsed to the ground, Kyle stepped behind him and jabbed the sliver of sharpened plastic into the back of the man's skull until he stopped moving. Through the blood and bits of bone, a gelatinous mass emerged, oozing from the man's skull like a living creature – the fungus that had driven him insane.

Kyle gasped, "My God."

Just as he raced for the front entrance, another of the crazed fungus head creatures rushed in from outside. Barely breaking his stride, Kyle switched directions and exited through the rear double doors. He couldn't secure the doors, so he settled on tipping over a heavy metal rack and shoving it in front of the doors. He knew his makeshift barricade wouldn't hold long. He searched the room for a weapon, but it contained only an autoclave sterilizer, a rack of water pitchers and chamber pots, and a rack of disposable white hazmat suits. He grabbed a metal water pitcher and tested the weight of it in his hand. Only one other door offered escape. As he reached for the handle, the door swung open. He raised the pitcher over his head; then saw that it was Marli Henry.

"Detective Bane. I was coming for you."

He lowered the pitcher. "It's about time." He expended his pent up frustration at her like a weapon. "Your friends left me behind," he accused.

"I instructed them to."

"What?"

She eyed the pitcher as he shifted its weight in his hand. Seeing her nervousness, he dropped it to the floor.

"I was coming to get you myself," she continued. "One of the guards prevented me. When the shooting started, he left."

"What's happening?"

She ushered him through the door into an airlock, which she ignored, and into another tent. This smaller tent had windows. It was dark outside. Men and women hurriedly packed laptops and equipment into metal crates. No one looked up as he entered. A change of clothing, his cell phone, wallet, badge, and his gun, were stacked on a table beside a screen partition.

"You may change in there," she told him as she removed her mask.

"I could use a shower," he said.

"There's no time."

He stepped behind the screen and stripped off the one-piece jumpsuit, gladly dropping it into a garbage can. It had become a second skin and he was glad to shed it. He slipped into his boxers, socks, and a long-sleeved white shirt and examined the brown suit they had provided for him. The suit was several years old and a size too large. He had lost twelve pounds since he had last worn it. He shrugged and put it on. Beggars couldn't be choosers. It was better than the jumpsuit he had been living in. He slipped into the brown shoes they had provided; glad they had at least color-coordinated his outfit, but he jammed the garish tie someone had chosen into his pocket with the rest of his paraphernalia. Finally, he strapped on his shoulder holster, jammed his Glock G19 in place, and walked out feeling more like his old self. The two pounds of cold steel under his left armpit brought a spring back to his steps.

"What about the two officers I came in with?" he asked as soon as he stepped around the partition.

Marli's mouth tightened into a grimace. "I'm afraid they were infected."

He nodded. "Where are they?"

She glanced away. "They died."

He didn't bother asking how they died. He remembered how Roger Curry looked. He hoped their deaths had been painless, but he doubted it. He pulled his cell phone from his pocket. "I need to check in with headquarters."

She stopped him with a hand on his. "They know you're working with us. I requested your services for the duration."

He hesitated, not certain if he fully believed her, but placed the cell phone back in his pocket. If they were to work together, there had to be some semblance of trust. "I bet Chief Gilbert was glad to get rid of me."

She smiled. "He said you were a loaded gun."

"You smile like that's a good thing."

"The situation has worsened. Eleven cities in the U.S. are under quarantine, but the fungus is quickly spreading. The Miami authorities are overwhelmed. People are going mad and attacking anyone near them. The hospitals are over capacity. You saw what's happening. We have to relocate."

So that was the rush.

"I had to kill one man. He wouldn't stop attacking me."

"The fungus destroys the mind, turning people into raging beasts. Mobs of the infected are overwhelming the police barricades, killing people and destroying buildings. It's out of control."

"The police aren't equipped to deal with this. I saw military."

She nodded. "The military is moving into the city as we speak. They are going to place Miami under Martial Law soon. They're patrolling the streets to assure the populace that they'll be safe."

He frowned. "That's not good enough. They'll hesitate to shoot unarmed civilians."

"Would you?"

"After what I've seen? If this fungus, this Cordyceps Plague spreads, it'll wipe out entire cities. We have to stop them. If it means killing the infected before their heads burst open like a ripe melon and spew spores everywhere, then we have to do it. That's what we're here for, to protect citizens from threat. This time, it's a damn mushroom."

She stared at him as if assessing his mental stability. Finally, she nodded. "You're right. By the time the military can realize this, it may be too late."

He headed for the door. "I have to see things for myself. Do you want to come along?"

She glanced at her colleagues. "I should help them evacuate, but yes, I want to come." She pulled two cloth masks from a box on a table. "We'll need these. They won't guarantee we'll be safe from infection, but it will keep the spores from our lungs. The moisture there provides a perfect medium for their growth."

He slipped the mask over his mouth and nose feeling somewhat like a masked robber. "Do you have a car?"

"A Land Rover."

"Give me the keys. I'll drive."

She frowned at him. "I drive quite well, Detective."

"But you don't know the city. I'll drive."

She hesitated. He hoped she wasn't one of those women who resented men and considered any act of courtesy or chivalry as an affront to their individuality. He wasn't being chauvinistic; he was being practical. He had taken defensive driving classes, and a little rough and tumble driving might be necessary. To his relief, she handed him the keys without further argument.

"Thanks," he said.

As they stepped outside, he looked around in amazement. The tent city had grown. Now, six large tents and several trailers aligned in two neat rows separated by a wide boulevard had joined the original tent. Banks of portable LED light towers flooded the area with bright white light. Heavily armed military personnel patrolled the perimeter, but the Humvee parked in the middle of the boulevard with a 50-caliber machine gun mounted on its roof conveyed the true severity of the situation. The military was being deadly serious. The soldier manning the machine gun eyed them with curiosity as they passed near the Humvee, but dismissed them as he recognized Marli's security badge.

Gunfire erupted nearby. There was no mistaking the crack of an M16 for a Fourth of July firecracker, and the screams certainly were not squeals of delight. Given the situation, he doubted anyone in Miami was celebrating Independence Day this night. He shoved Marli behind him, drew his Glock, and faced the direction from which the shots had come. Marli tried to push past him, but he barred her way with his arm.

"They might need my help," she protested.

"That's a battle, not a cry for help. You stay here. Better yet, get in the Land Rover and lock the door."

"Look, I'm quite capable of ..."

"In the vehicle," he snapped, giving her a light shove. He didn't have time to be polite. If he was right, she was out of her league.

Just as he spoke, a mob of people dressed in white jumpsuits like the one he had recently worn, raced around the corner of one of the tents. The first thing he noticed about them was the look of intense hatred marring their faces. They resembled a herd of marauding beasts. The second thing he noticed was the blood covering their jumpsuits, their mouth, and their hands. They were mad with infection, and they were intent on killing, had in fact killed already.

"Halt!" the soldier in the Humvee called to the crowd. When no one paid attention to him, he repeated his order.

"Shoot them," Kyle yelled, but the soldier, unwilling to fire on civilians, hesitated. His eyes widened in fright and his hands trembled on the trigger. His hesitation cost him his life. He began firing just as the first of the no longer human creatures reached the Humvee and leaped onto the hood. The .50 caliber began chattering as it cut the man almost in half, but more of the creatures clambered onto the vehicle and dragged the young soldier screaming down into the interior of the Humvee. A spray of blood splattered the inside of the window as the former humans ripped the soldier apart.

Marli still stood beside the Land Rover, her mouth open and eyes wide with shock. This time, Kyle didn't bother talking. He grabbed her by the arm and shoved her into the passenger seat of the Land Rover, and then dived over her and into the driver's seat. By the time he had cranked the vehicle, a dozen people had already reached them. Marli had the presence of mind to shut the door. They surrounded the Land Rover and began beating at the windows and doors with their fists and rocking the vehicle violently. They were no longer human. They were a crazed mob. The fungus had erased all traces of their former humanity. Store clerks, schoolgirls, housewives, insurance salesmen – all were now a horde of marauding beasts intent on murder. Their face bore no traces of former intelligence. They were enraged killing machines. He knew that they could eventually overturn the vehicle. He pressed the accelerator and plowed through them. Two fell beneath the wheels of the Land Rover. He winced as it bounced over their crushed bodies, but didn't slow down. The others continued their frenzied assault, pounding on the passenger window until it cracked. Before it shattered completely, he pulled ahead of the pack, who continued to race after the vehicle as he sped for the commercial vehicle gate. The creatures disappeared in the darkness.

Noticing the direction they were going Marli protested. "We can't leave. My people are back there. They're in danger."

He ignored her protests. The Land Rover fishtailed as he avoided an abandoned luggage trolley. "We can't help them." He released the wheel with one hand long enough to wipe the sweat from his face and noticed that his hand was shaking. "Did you see them? How many infected were you holding?"

She averted her gaze. "Two hundred."

"Two hundred? My God! That's a freaking army."

"They were separated into four tents. The most severe cases were confined within a ten-foot chain link fence." Seeing his look of disdain, she added, "They were guarded."

He rolled his eyes.

"We had to observe … We didn't expect …" She gave up trying to explain and lowered her head into her hands.

To her credit, she didn't sob, but he knew she needed a healthy jolt of reality. "Pull yourself together, doctor," he barked at her.

She turned on him with a ferocity almost equaling that of the fungus heads. "Those were my friends back there. If they're dead, it's my fault."

Any sympathy he felt for her plight was mitigated by the dire circumstances they now faced. She saw the plague as a medical emergency. He knew it was an invasion; just like the zombie horror movies that he loved to watch as a child while cowering beneath the sheets with the lights on. His friends, too, were on the front line fighting off the invasion, unaware of the danger they were facing. He envisioned lines of frightened police standing shoulder to shoulder with shields and batons, not standing a chance against the enraged mob.

"This is no time for accountability or responsibility. I need to get out there with my men and fight this thing my way, but first, I need to get you to a safe place. You have to find a cure for this … this fungus head army."

She closed her eyes and slumped back in the seat. "We have an office downtown in the government building. That's where my colleagues will go." She opened her eyes and looked at him. "Can I use your phone to call Atlanta? I left mine back there."

He certainly wasn't going back for it. He fished his phone out of his pocket and handed it to her. She dialed a number and held the phone to her ear. After a few moments, she frowned. "That's odd. No answer."

"Maybe it's busy."

"No, I didn't even get a recorded message."

He turned to stare at her, a cold knot forming in his chest. "That doesn't sound good."

She didn't get a chance to respond. Kyle returned his eyes to the road and immediately slammed on the brakes, almost throwing Marli into the dash. Near the gate, a police car was on fire. Flames poured from the windows and from beneath the hood. Two badly mauled bodies lay nearby. It was difficult to be certain in the flickering light of the flames, but from the remains of their tattered and bloodstained clothing, he assumed they were the car's former occupants. One officer's head sat a few feet from his body, as if staring back at his dismembered corpse. Marli averted her eyes from the grotesque scene. No other bodies were present. The officers had not had time to retaliate against their attackers. The chain-link gate dangled from its hinges.

"It looks like things are getting pretty hairy," he commented.

She didn't reply, but he could tell that she was frightened. He didn't blame her. A good healthy dose of fear was a good thing to have. It kept you from getting too cocky, something he had been accused of a few times. He drove around the police cruiser and pulled onto Airport Parkway, driving south toward Dolphin Expressway. They met few cars. The army had blocked the roads to prevent the infection from spreading, but they couldn't stop the wind. To the east and to the south, smoke billowed from nearby neighborhoods. The destruction was spreading rapidly.

They didn't get far. A line of hastily abandoned automobiles blocked the entrance to the Airport Freeway. Just beyond the cars, an army patrol, eight men with automatic weapons, barred the way. He slowed to a stop and got out of the Land Rover, hands held high in case the men were jumpy.

"Who are you?" one of the soldiers, a corporal, challenged from behind a red and white sawhorse barricade.

"Detective Kyle Bane," he replied through his mask. He nodded toward Marli in the Land Rover. "She's with the CDC. We're on our way to the *Stephen P. Clark* Government Building. Let us through."

"I can't. It's too dangerous. Mobs east of I-95 are burning buildings and killing people. They dropped us off here to stop people from entering or leaving the city. We have orders to shoot to kill," he added. His expression of disbelief indicated his confusion. He glanced nervously at his fellow soldiers, and then back at Kyle. "Do you know what the hell's happening?"

"It's some kind of infection driving them insane. They're not people anymore."

"You mean zombies?" another soldier asked. He was tall and thin with a full black mustache beneath a prominent nose. One of his comrades giggled, but a stern look of disapproval from the corporal silenced him.

"Close enough, soldier," Kyle replied. "I've witnessed what they're capable of. Don't freeze up. Shoot to kill." He surveyed the eight men, too few for the task assigned to them. The military had not yet grasped the severity of the situation. "How did you guys get here?"

The corporal answered. "A truck dropped us off."

Kyle noticed the young corporal's nervousness. "What's your name, Corporal?"

"Ginson, Todd Ginson."

"Well, Corporal Ginson, my advice is to find one of these vehicles with the keys inside and get the hell out of here, and cover your mouth and nose with anything you can find. It might help."

Ginson nodded, but said, "We've been ordered to secure this exit."

"Forget your damned orders. If you see a horde of crazed killers coming at you, you run."

He turned and walked back to the Land Rover. Marli's eyes followed him all the way back to the vehicle, questioning him through the windshield. He wished he could see her mouth through her facemask, but he suspected that she was not smiling.

Sitting beside her on the driver's side, he said, "Looks like we'll have to find another way through."

5

July 4, Little Havana, Miami, FL –

Kyle drove south through East Little Havana. The city, normally so alive with its open markets, its buildings splashed with colorful mosaic paintings, and crowds of residents strolling the streets or playing games of dominoes in the parks, was eerily silent. They drove in darkness. The power was out in most of the city. He saw furtive movements in the shadows, but didn't know if they were infected people or simply cautious residents. No one attempted to flag them down. Driving parallel to the Miami River, it soon became apparent that large areas of downtown were ablaze. Even a few boats moored along the Miami River were burning. One thirty-foot sailing sloop's cabin and triangular sail were in flames as it slowly drifted down river. Rows of ubiquitous palm trees, already desiccated by the summer heat, flamed like tiki torches, raining down showers of sparks onto the roofs of nearby buildings, many catching fire in spite of their tiled roofs. Small brushfires broke out everywhere, spreading south as it was being pushed by a strong breeze.

They crossed the bridge onto Miami Avenue and into the heart of a raging war zone. Here, people raced around in small groups fighting the fires with water hoses and blankets, but it was a losing battle. They fought alone. The fire departments battled the larger blazes downtown, where the money was. A few blocks farther east, they encountered the first mobs of infected people. Scattered units of soldiers trapped in alleys and on roofs of buildings fought off frenzied attacks. Scores of bodies littered the streets and sidewalks. Two women, one with a shoe missing, lay crushed beneath an overturned dumpster. It was impossible to determine which corpses were victims of the plague carriers, and which ones were victims of army gunfire. In death, drenched in blood and gore, each looked alike. One thing he had noted in his career as a cop – victims of violent crime rarely had the serene composure depicted on television.

The mobs were unrelenting in their fury. Five soldiers trapped on the roof of one burning pharmacy continued their fight until the roof collapsed beneath them, sending them plummeting into the heart of the inferno and to their death. Marli threw her hand over her face to block out the horrifying sight, but their deaths drove an icicle into Kyle's heart. He suspected that very scene was being repeated dozens of times throughout the city. Crazed fungus heads, undaunted by the flames and intent on killing, ran into the building after the soldiers. One of the creatures exited with his clothing and hair on fire, stumbling blindly into others and spreading the flames. The sight of flaming humans did not move Kyle. He hoped they all burned.

Down the block, a second group of soldiers made a last ditch stand from the trailer of a parked flatbed semi. Kyle watched in dismay as the infected swept over them like army ants attacking a jungle insect. When the crowd parted moments later, the flatbed was empty, as if the soldiers had never existed.

He slammed on the brakes. "We can't get through," he told Marli.

"We have to," she insisted.

"The Clark Building is on fire. I can see it from here. Either they've evacuated, or they're dead. It looks as if the entire downtown is overrun with these things."

He didn't relish his role as silent witness to the death of Miami. By day, the Downtown Miami skyline is a white seawall separating the blue ocean from the rest of the city. At night, it's a world-renowned, picture postcard vista of glass towers thrusting into the night sky, a kaleidoscope of color offering refuge from the sweltering summer heat, and respite from the doldrums of the day. No longer. The upper ten floors of 50 Biscayne Tower was ablaze. Flames licked the sides of the building from shattered windows like a fire creature tasting its prey. A cloud of black smoke, pushed by the breeze, trailed away, obscuring other buildings from view. Flames likewise engulfed the Miami Tower, the Marquis, and the

Four Seasons, Florida's tallest structure. He pitied the hapless firefighters attempting to extinguish the raging infernos, while simultaneously under attack by crazed fungus heads. Not even the military could save downtown. He had often dined at *Brasileiros*, a downtown Brazilian steakhouse, when he could afford it, and at the *Hard Rock Cafe* when he was cruising for women. He doubted that either structure would survive the blaze.

Beyond the city, a fleet of small boats and yachts illuminated by flames of the dying city, spilled from the marinas into Biscayne Bay, intent on leaving the city in its death throes. Some headed for the imagined safety of Dodge Island or Fischer Island. Others, with no destination in mind, simply headed east into the Atlantic. How many, he wondered, carried the seeds of their destruction with them, mushroom spores lodged in their lungs. How many would spread that disease to new shores?

By now, a few of the rampaging fungus heads had begun to take notice of the Land Rover. Several began moving in their direction.

"We can't stay here," he said.

"We have to go back to the airport. I need to collect my team and return to Atlanta."

He didn't hold out much hope that any of her people had survived as he threw the vehicle in gear and made a U-turn in the street, knocking down a trashcan in the process. He retraced his route up NW 17th Avenue to the Expressway. Near the airport, he spotted four of the soldiers they had met earlier, including the corporal, racing madly down the Expressway exit ramp, followed by twice as many of the infected. He noticed that the soldiers had heeded his advice and had covered their face with handkerchiefs or ripped up t-shirts. He slid the Land Rover to a stop directly in their path and threw open the rear door.

"Get in!" he yelled.

Corporal Ginson stopped to fire his rifle at the nearest creature. The short burst from the M16 exploded its chest. It fell headfirst into the loose gravel beside the ramp and skidded almost to his feet. He ignored it as he directed his men into the back of the Land Rover. Kyle didn't wait for the door to close before speeding away just ahead of the remaining fungus heads. The corporal was out of breath as he spoke, his voice muffled by the handkerchief around his mouth and nose.

"They came out of nowhere and were on top of us before we could fire. Two of my men went searching for a car. They never came back. The others ..." He groaned and punched the back of the seat with his fist. "It was awful. Those things ripped them apart."

"The other squads we saw downtown didn't fare any better. They're gone, too."

"What are those things? They're like animals."

"Their minds are gone," Marli said. Her voice was cold and clinical as she explained. The shock of witnessing the deaths still lingered. "The infection eats away their minds, leaving only certain motor functions intact, and induces a blind killing rage. Each one of them will soon ripen and produce more spores. The infection is spreading like wildfire." She turned to Kyle. "In a few days, there could be tens of thousands of these things."

"We can't deal with this shit," Ginson cried. "They taught us how to kill the enemy, but we've never been in battle, certainly not against an enemy like this, not civilians."

"You're not alone, Corporal," Kyle told him, appreciating the soldier's frustration. "A lot of people are going to die because we weren't prepared for a situation like this." More quietly, he said, "How the hell do you prepare for something like this?"

At that moment, two Blackhawk helicopters zoomed overhead so low that they shook the Land Rover with the backwash of their rotors. The noise was deafening.

"Yeah!" Ginson shouted above the noise. "Somebody's doing something."

Kyle watched them for a moment; saw the direction the choppers were flying. "They're headed to the airport."

"There's four more," Ginson shouted, pointing to the north as more helicopters converged on Miami International.

* * *

Two armored Humvees blocked the airport's main entrance. A sergeant raised his hand to stop them. The two .50-caliber machine guns leveled in their direction tightened the annoying ache in Kyle's stomach into a writhing Gordian knot. The cloth masks the soldiers wore over their mouth and nose, indicated that someone knew what was happening.

"No one can enter," the sergeant, a slightly overweight older man warned. Then he noticed Ginson and his three men in the rear of the Land Rover. "What's your unit, Corporal?"

Ginson spoke up. "Third Infantry, C Company."

"Is this all of you?"

"It is now," Ginson growled. "What the fuck's going on?"

"Damned if I know." He gave Kyle and Marli a hard look, studying their faces. From the slight smile creasing his lips, Kyle surmised that the sergeant found Marli's appearance pleasing. However, he did not share the same of opinion of Kyle. "Who are they?" he posed to Ginson.

"Detective Bane and Doctor Henry," Ginson replied.

Marli cast the sergeant a broad smile and said, "I'm with the CDC, Sergeant. I was here until the infected patients escaped. We barely escaped with our lives."

"We took care of them," the sergeant said with a smirk. "We have a few of your people here, in the terminal. You can go in." He stared at Kyle for a long moment. Kyle returned the stare. Finally, the sergeant stood aside to allow them to pass.

"Where did you place the infected?" Marli asked him.

"Placed, ma'am? We didn't place them anywhere. We shot them."

Marli was aghast. "You killed them all?"

"Damn straight. Those things weren't human. You should've seen what they did to some of my men."

"But you ..."

The sergeant's expression quickly hardened. Kyle grasped Marli's arm tightly and shook his head. "Now's not the time."

She glared at him but said nothing more.

"Thank you, Sergeant," he said and put the Land Rover in gear.

While Marli silently fumed, Kyle took in his surroundings. Machine gun emplacements protected the entrances to the parking garages and to the terminal entrances. Soldiers patrolled the area and the roof. Two armored personnel carriers blocked the lower-level entrance. Having seen what the infected were capable of, this time the military was taking no chances. A corporal directed him to park the Land Rover beside a line of several jeeps. As they got out of the vehicle, Corporal Ginson offered Kyle his hand.

"Thanks for saving our bacon back there, Detective. I guess we'll report in now." He hesitated. "They might want to hear about what you saw, you know, about our troops downtown."

Kyle nodded. "I'll tell them." He grasped Ginson's hand tightly and shook it, hoping the corporal and his surviving men got a chance to rest before being flung back at the new enemy.

Entering the Central Terminal was an eerie sensation, quite unlike any previous visits when the terminal was like a small town, alive and noisy. Except for a few guards posted near the entrance and the occasional military personnel flittering about intent on some obscure errand, the place was deserted, silent, a far cry from the usual hubbub of one of the country's busiest airports.

"It's like a tomb in here," he noted aloud, and then winced as he remembered that many of Marli's colleagues had died there only hours earlier. He glanced at her and saw the pain of sorrow in her furrowed brow. "Sorry."

She nodded at his apology. A sentry directed them to the Miami Airport Hotel located in Concourse E. The 260-room, eight-story hotel had been evacuated with the airport. The meeting rooms now served as offices for military staff and its kitchens as commissary for personnel. The lobby's lighted barrel-vaulted glass ceiling with its colorful art deco murals and modern décor, normally conveyed an air of relaxation in an otherwise busy airport. Now, its size merely emphasized the complete absence of milling tourists, and its silence, the severity of the situation. A harried aide directed them to the office of the commander, General R. Lazenby Willows, whose offices had previously served as the manager's office. They waited outside for fifteen minutes, overhearing the general through the closed door bellowing orders into the telephone. Finally, an aide admitted them.

The general was a tall man, almost 6'4", with graying brown hair and piercing blue eyes. He was younger than Kyle expected – this side of his mid-fifties. By the dour expression in his eyes, the general resented taking time from his busy schedule to interview civilians. A disposable mask covered his mouth and nose. He wasted no time with formalities, nor did he offer them a seat.

"I was told you had information about the fiasco downtown."

"Fiasco is the proper word," Kyle replied. "Those men didn't have a chance. The fungus heads swept over them like a tide."

A slight smile cracked on Willows' face. He quickly suppressed it. "Fungus heads. Apt description." He glanced at Marli. "You're the CDC doctor?"

"Yes, sir."

He nodded. "I'm glad you managed to survive. Your colleagues, the six that are still alive, are upstairs on the third floor." His eyes narrowed. "How is it that you made it out alive?"

Kyle braced himself for the expected explosion, but if she resented the general's slightly veiled accusation that she had abandoned her colleagues, she had the good sense not to show it.

"Detective Bane saved my life. We were on our way to the Clark government building when we encountered your woefully unprepared troops," she said, throwing the accusation back in his court. She leaned forward and rested her palms on the desk. "General, you have no clue about what we're facing."

He cocked his head slightly and raised an eyebrow. "Clueless, am I? Perhaps you're right. This plague has erupted in ten cities, and I haven't found anyone capable of delivering a straight answer to me." He leaned forward until his face was inches from hers. "Just what the fuck is happening to these people?"

He leaned back, relaxed, and motioned to two chairs. They sat.

Marli took a deep breath and began. "A previously unknown species of *Orpicordyceps unilateralis* has recently come to light in Belize. The CDC became aware of the problem and monitored all flights into the U.S." She glanced sheepishly at Kyle. "We failed.

The source, a Roger Curry, slipped through MIA spreading the infection to everyone he encountered. The first symptoms develop within forty-eight hours. By day three, the infected go mad as the fungus destroys their brain, leaving them with the impulse to kill and destroy. When the fungus fully ripens, the infected seek a high place and become immobile. The growing fungus splits open their skulls and the spores spread on the wind. Unless we locate and confine every infected person, this plague will spread across the country." She paused. "We have no cure, no vaccine against infection."

He reached up and fingered his mask. "Do the masks help? They're a damned nuisance."

She shrugged. "I don't know. It certainly prevents spores from entering the lungs, but we just don't know enough about the mechanism of infection to determine exactly how effective it is. A biohazard suit is best, but …"

"But we can't suit up everyone," the general finished for her. He nodded. "I see. Thank you for your input."

"General, if you insist on using the airport as your HQ, you should at least filter all sources of air; make the building as airtight as possible. Thoroughly wash any fresh fruit or vegetables. Canned food is best."

"Cooking the food doesn't render the fungus inactive?"

"Some spores can survive intense heat and radiation. It would be best to take no chances."

"Doctor Henry, if you would please get with your colleagues and let me know what equipment you need, I would like you to set up a lab here to investigate this disease and find some way to stop it."

"I can't seem to reach the CDC by phone. If you could fly me to Atlanta, the CDC has…"

"The CDC is gone, doctor."

Marli's faced paled at the general's news. She slumped in her seat. Her lips trembled as she asked, "Gone? How?"

"Some fool made a mistake and allowed the fungus samples he was studying to escape. Another fool decided that simple quarantine was not effective enough. Bottom line – two 500-pound bombs were dropped on the CDC headquarters late this afternoon. The building and two square blocks surrounding it were obliterated."

"You … you bombed the CDC?"

"Not me, Doctor Henry. The colonel involved has been, er, replaced. It was a futile effort of course. The disease had already reached Atlanta by then. The southern suburbs near the Hartsfield-Jackson Airport is in chaos."

Kyle feared that the shock might prove too much for Marli to endure, but once again, she proved more capable than he had expected. If she continued surpassing his expectations in this manner, he would have to change his opinion of her.

"If it survived, most of the equipment we need is already here in the mobile lab we set up, but I want complete assurance from you that we will be protected."

"We'll move your equipment inside the building."

"No, General, we'll need someplace apart from the terminal. The risks of exposure are too great."

"Will a hangar or a nearby building do?"

She nodded.

"Excellent. I'll see to the arrangements." He turned to Kyle. "Do you wish to return to your unit, the Special Investigation Squad? I can have transportation for you within the hour."

It was a temptation to return to the job he knew, but he had made a promise to Marli. In reality, he could do very little as a cop in circumstances such as this. The situation had passed beyond the scope of local authority. The military now had control.

"No, I'll stay with Doctor Henry and help out any way I can."

She favored him with a smile. "Thank you."

"Doctor, if you need anything, contact Captain Lowery, my aide. He will be your liaison. If you have nothing else, I have a lot to get done and a short time in which to do it."

They both rose. The general's aide quickly ushered them out of the office. The enticing aroma of cooking food drifted down the corridor. A rumbling in his stomach reminded Kyle that he hadn't eaten in hours.

"I'm starving. Let's eat."

Marli looked at him as if he were joking. Her mind was already working on solutions to the problem. She was eager to get started. "Now?"

"Starving isn't going to help. Besides, I've been eating that swill you call food for the past four days. I could do with a cup of coffee and something with some flavor."

"All right."

Few people sat at the white-linen decorated tables. There was no wait staff. A burly private in camouflage fatigues greeted them as they entered. He spoke with a Brooklyn accent.

"Sit anywhere you like. The menu's limited. We've got vegetable soup, roasted chicken with basil mashed potatoes and steamed vegetables, baked pompano with rice pilaf, or a T-bone steak with mashed or baked potato. If I were you, I'd go for the T-bone. The cook treats chicken like it was his mother-in-law, and the fish don't look too healthy."

Kyle glanced at Marli. She nodded.

"A steak then, medium rare, and a baked potato with sour cream."

"I'll just have some soup, please."

"Lots of coffee," Kyle added. "Is the bar open?"

"You kiddin'? The first thing the general did was lock up the booze." He leaned closer, glanced around the room, and whispered in a conspiratorial tone, "There might be a bottle or two of cooking wine in the kitchen. I'll check."

They chose a table by the widow, looking out onto the runways with it silent rows of ghostly jets outlined by the moonlight. The horizon glowed from fires in the city, painting the underbelly of clouds with an orange tint. If not for the loss of life, it would have been a surreal, almost beautiful sight.

"I can't believe the CDC is gone," Marli said. "All my friends …." She stared out the window, but Kyle believed she saw something different from what he observed. She was reading the future, as one might divine omens from wisps of smoke or the entrails of a sacrifice. He wondered what future she saw. The one he imagined was bleak and filled with death.

"It won't be the first stupid blunder the military makes. Can you set up a lab capable of creating a vaccine or a cure?"

She nodded. "Maybe, if we have the right equipment. It depends on who survived. I should be there now with my team."

The corporal interrupted their conversation as he brought a plate draped with a large, thick-cut steak, a baked potato, and green beans, and set it in front of Kyle. The enticing aroma made Kyle's mouth water. He placed a large bowl of soup before Marli. The corporal then produced a bottle of Gnarly Head pinot noir from beneath a napkin.

"This red is mild with a hint of cherry and vanilla, but it can stand up to the robust flavor of the steak."

He poured a splash into Kyle's glass and stood back. Kyle, while no connoisseur, had observed others sample wines. He swirled the glass, sniffed the bouquet, and took a sip. The flavor was lighter than he had expected. He smiled and nodded his approval. The corporal filled their glasses.

"You seem to know a lot about wines," he said to the corporal.

"Nah, the cook told me what to say. I'm a beer man." He spun on his heels and left them to their meal.

"He has no clue about what's happening," Kyle said of the retreating corporal.

"I wish I didn't," Marli replied.

Kyle attacked his steak with gusto, his first real meal in days. After the tasteless food served in quarantine, it was a veritable feast. Marli didn't share his appetite. She toyed with her soup, plying her spoon around the bowl as if rowing. She performed an intricate dance but brought very few spoonfuls of soup to her mouth. He refrained from admonishing her. Her thoughts lay elsewhere. In the distance, an explosion briefly illuminated the city's skyline. The fires were growing larger. He watched her shudder and turn away from the window.

"Can you find a vaccine or a cure for this …" He waved his fork in the air as he struggled to find the proper word. "… this thing?"

"I don't know. Without the CDC …" She sighed. "We can try." She reached down and touched the mask dangling around her neck. "The simple act of removing these in order to eat might infect us. There aren't enough full bio suits for everyone, and people can't wear masks all the time. The spores can be anywhere – in the food, in the water, or simply on something we touch. Except in completely sealed environments, no one will be safe."

"We'll adjust."

She pushed her plate farther away from her. Some of the untouched soup sloshed from the bowl into the plate. "I can't eat." She rose from her seat. "I need to check on my colleagues."

Kyle pushed his chair back. "I'll come with you."

"No. You finish your meal. After I see who's still alive, I think I'll get some sleep. I'm very tired."

Her brush off stung, but he shrugged it off. It wasn't the first time he had been shut down. "Uh, yeah, whatever you say. I'll see you in the morning."

"Yes, all right, in the morning."

He watched her walk across the room, noticing the slight slump of her shoulders, her bowed head, and her plodding gait, as if the weight of the world were on her delicate shoulders, and then whispered to himself, "It just might be."

He finished his meal and drank another glass of wine. As the corporal had promised, the wine was tasty. He was a little uncertain about protocol, about whether he was expected to pay since the restaurant was now operated by the military. He decided that he wasn't. Satiated but not tired, he strolled around the concourse.

The moving sidewalks weren't operating; nor were the escalators. Whether this was a move by the military to save energy, or just an effort to avoid laziness in the troops, the walk from the Central Terminal to the South Terminal was a long one. He encountered more activity in the South Terminal. Concourse H had been converted into a barracks area with rows of two-tiered cots replacing rows of passenger seats that had been uprooted and stacked against a wall. Most of the soldiers appeared too young to wear a uniform, looking more like a high school baseball team than ruthless killers should look. They sat in groups and talked, smoking cigarettes despite the *No Smoking* placards on the walls, looking at complete ease in their new environment. Only five or six wore masks over their face. Kyle shook his head sadly at their lack of discipline. Every breath they took could be killing them. A few glanced at him, but otherwise, ignored his presence.

Halfway along the South terminal, a voice yelled at him from a stairwell. He turned to see Corporal Ginson and six men trotting up the stairs. They all wore full respirators.

"Settled in yet?" Ginson asked.

"Just looking for the emergency exits," he said.

"Too damned many, if you ask me." Ginson's scowl conveyed his opinion of the security arrangements. "I don't know how the TSA managed, but then they were just looking for terrorists, not fucking zombies."

Kyle noted the heavy weaponry the soldiers were carrying. Ginson had traded his sidearm for an M-1014 shotgun. Kyle had used the same Italian-made *Beneli* before, during a drug raid. It was lightweight and effective. This model was an HK American-made weapon with an extendable stock. It fired six 12-gauge shells, an excellent choice for close in fighting. The tall, wiry soldier with the black mustache carried an M-249 SAW, or Squad Automatic Weapon, capable of firing fifty 5.56 mm rounds per minute. He wore crossed belts of ammunition slung over his chest. With the bandoliers and his thick black mustache, he resembled a Mexican revolutionary. The others carried M4 carbines or M16s. This time, they were taking no chances.

"Where are you headed?" Kyle asked.

"We're clearing out a hangar for your girl friend."

The general works fast, he thought. "She's not my girlfriend."

A low whistle escaped Ginson's lips. "You need to make a move on that. She's a doll."

Though he agreed with Ginson's assessment of Marli's appearance, he redirected the conversation. "Where are you going?"

"A hangar north of Terminal D. It's just the right size and has its own generator."

"Can I tag along?"

"Sure, if you want." He nodded toward the bulge of Kyle's Glock beneath his left armpit. "You want something bigger than that?"

The Glock19 was an excellent weapon, but didn't have the punch he might need in a firefight. "I'll take one of those shotguns."

Ginson smiled. "Nice choice." He handed his weapon to Kyle and turned to one of his men. "Futterman, go fetch me another weapon. Meet us at the south parking garage."

Futterman dutifully trotted back down the stairs. Ginson dug a box of ammo from a belt pouch and handed it to Kyle. "You might need these."

They waited in the garage beside the Humvee until Futterman arrived with the extra weapon for Ginson, and then sped north across the runway toward the row of hangars. Kyle spotted the scars where the CDC tents had been, now piles of torn and burned fabric. He hoped some of the lab equipment Marli needed had survived intact. Nearby, a mound of bodies smoldered, small tongues of flames still licking the cremated corpses. The odor of burned flesh was strong, a cloying stench that permeated Kyle's clothing and passed easily through the thin cloth of his mask. He envied Ginson and the others their breathers. He was glad he hadn't had a view of the mound from the restaurant while he was eating. As it was, his stomach rebelled slightly at the gruesome site.

Two massive C-17 Globe Masters sat on the runway where they had been parked after delivering the troops. A row of Apache and Blackhawk helicopters sat beside them. As he watched, two Apaches took off and circled the field only a couple of hundred feet above the ground. Their backwash created swirls in smoke drifting over the field, remnants of the countless fires ravaging Miami. The air stank of burning oil and buildings. A few minutes later, a burst of gunfire erupted near the eastern edge of the field. Kyle hoped their target was fungus head zombies and not some poor schmuck trying to reach safety. From the air, all targets looked the same, and the military was taking no chances.

The Humvee pulled up in front of a 40,000-square foot metal building. The large sliding metal door was open and the cavernous interior was dark. The Humvee's headlights illuminated nothing, quickly swallowed by the inky blackness within. In spite of the plethora of armed men surrounding him, the hangar's interior spooked him. Entering a darkened building possibly full of hostiles was the most dangerous threat a cop faced.

Ginson, too, seemed perturbed by the lack of visibility. "Stay sharp, men," he called out. "Walters, find the light switch."

Walters disappeared into the building. A loud clang echoed from the opening, followed by, "Sorry, tripped over a stool." Two minutes passed with Ginson pacing nervously. "I can't find the damn thing." Walters bellowed.

"Damn," Ginson muttered. He motioned for the others to enter and fan out. Kyle stepped through the entrance and immediately hugged the wall just inside the door, listening for sounds. All he heard was the scuffle of booted feet on concrete and his own rapid heartbeat. The lights flashed on as Walters finally located the light switch. Kyle blinked until his pupils became accustomed to the sudden brightness. A white Gulfstream jet dominated the cavernous interior space. Kyle recognized it as a G-150 model, from a poster on the wall beside him depicting a series of Gulfstreams. The cowling was off the starboard engine and parts lay scattered around the floor. The same poster described the Honeywell TFE 731-40AR engine as one of the most reliable in the field. It didn't look too reliable now in pieces with a puddle of oil on the floor beneath it. One of Ginson's men climbed the retractable steps and entered the jet. He emerged a few minutes later and yelled, "Empty." He stopped at the puddle that Kyle had assumed to be oil, knelt beside it, and exclaimed, "Blood."

"Keep your eyes open," Ginson warned.

Two corner areas partitioned by opaque plastic drapes provided potential hiding places. Kyle picked one to check out and Ginson the other. Kyle's area was a small, but well-equipped machine shop with a heavy lathe, a milling machine, a drill press, and a long workbench. An overturned toolbox lying next to a pool of dried blood drew his attention. His nerves began to tingle as he scanned the spaces behind the machines. Drops of blood led away from the toolbox to an open rear door. A pool of light spilled from the door. Crates, dumpsters, and several vehicles offered several places for zombies to lurk. Moving carefully, wishing he had called for backup, he probed the area around the rear entrance. He found the body a dozen paces from the door beside one of the trucks. The man was obviously dead, his throat savaged and his green overalls drenched in blood. Flies buzzed around the corpse. Kyle could do nothing for him. He retraced his steps, locking the door behind him.

"A storage area," Ginson said, as he hitched his thumb at the area he had just investigated.

"I found a body outside," Kyle reported. "He might be the source of the blood. I locked the door." He nodded toward the one-story cinderblock building nestled inside the hangar against the front wall. "Shall we take a look?"

"Futterman, Riley!" Ginson called. "Guard the front entrance. The rest of you follow me."

Walters once again took point and opened the door. The door scraped a fluorescent light dangling from the ceiling and sent it swinging. One bulb was missing and the other flickered like a strobe light, casting eerie reflections from glass-covered photographs of jets hanging on the wall. Walters' boots crunched the shattered bulb into powder as he stepped on it. A bathroom with a shower just off the hallway was empty, as was a small break room. A pot of cold coffee rested on the counter beside a coffee maker, and a half-empty box of stale doughnuts sat on the table, along with three cups. These two rooms, plus two offices and a storage room took up most of the space of the building. So far, the building was clear. Double doors led to the front room.

Walters pushed through the doors into the darkened room and immediately stumbled backwards, as two crazed fungus heads fell upon him, pummeling him with their fists and snarling like wild animals. His first shots went wild, chipping concrete from the walls and punching holes through the acoustic-tiled drop ceiling. He fell with one of the creatures on top of him. His next burst caught the zombie in the side, but it ignored the savage wound, ripped off Walters' mask, and attacked the downed man's face and shoulder with its claws and teeth. Walters screamed in agony as the creature ripped a chunk of flesh from his shoulder.

Kyle fired his shotgun from the hip, cutting the remaining fungus head almost in half. It crashed backwards through the doorway and lay still. Ginson kicked the second zombie in the head, rolling it off Walters, who was bleeding profusely from cuts on his face and lip, and a bite to his shoulder. Walters and the creature were too entangled for Ginson to use his weapon. Instead, he took out his knife and stabbed the creature in the throat. It gurgled as blood spilled from its mouth, its arms spasmodically reaching toward Ginson until it bled to death and collapsed.

"See to Walters," Ginson said as he wiped his knife on his pants leg.

One of the soldiers helped the injured Walters to his feet and escorted him back into the hangar. Kyle and Ginson continued their exploration of the building. The large reception area contained an ornate desk, four leather chairs, a large-screen television, and an overturned water bottle. Spilled water soaked the carpet, making it squishy beneath Kyle's feet. The two fungus heads hadn't looked as if they were either customers or worked there, and had probably entered through the shattered glass front door.

"A little housekeeping and this place should do," he said.

"I'll find a tractor and move the jet outside," Ginson said. He turned and yelled down the hallway. "Get these two corpses out of here. There's another one out the rear door."

An hour later, with the bodies removed and the hallway mopped of blood, they rested. One of the men had located a wet vac and had vacuumed up the water from the carpet. The carpet was still damp, but it would dry quickly in the heat. The Gulfstream was gone, leaving an enormous space for the medical equipment. It was a suitable building for the lab. They could set up cots that would allow the technicians to remain in the hangar and not venture outside between the terminal and the hangar.

Walters' injuries had looked worse than they were, but you wouldn't know by his loud complaints. Finally, with a few bandages and a shot of morphine, he was resting comfortably in one of the leather chairs with his feet propped up on a second one. The broken front door, sealed with a double-stacked barrier of 5/8-inch plywood, would keep out even the most determined crazies. Kyle was amazed at how quickly Ginson and the others had adapted to the bizarre situation. Once the initial shock of what was happening had worn off, their months of training had kicked in. Whether facing a natural disaster, an invading army, or hordes of fungus driven zombies, the basics were the same – situational control, security, and safety. The how and whys didn't matter. You protected the helpless and eliminated the enemy. He hoped other units had as adaptable a leader as Ginson was.

"I'll leave two men here while the rest of us return to barracks. Walters needs a few stitches."

"Damn right I do," Walters moaned from his chair.

Kyle nodded to Ginson. "I'll go with you. I need to find a place to sleep."

"You can bunk with us." Ginson smiled. "Or had you rather take your chances with Doctor Henry?"

"I'll bed down alone, thank you," Kyle replied. "I have no desire for the company of a group of hot sweaty men, and now is definitely not the time for romance."

Ginson shrugged. "Whatever you say."

In spite of his flippant retort to Ginson, Marli was much on his mind, too much so. Was he staying with her because he thought she might provide a solution to the fungus plague, or did he just have the hots for her? In spite of the blessings of his boss, he should be with his squad killing fungus heads, saving Miami. Suddenly, a thought struck him, squeezing his heart with an icy fist until his breath refused to come. This was no battle. It was the start of a long and deadly war. He stumbled and grabbed the wall for support as the thought struck him in the stomach like a heavy fist.

"What's wrong?" Ginson asked. His face showed concern.

Kyle sucked down a ragged breath, shaking his head. "Nothing," he lied. "Just tired."

6

July 5, Miami Airport Hotel –

The Fourth of July was over, but Kyle awoke to sound of sporadic explosions inside the hotel somewhere below him. It was still dark outside. He switched on the lamp beside his bed, grabbed his Glock from beneath his pillow, and shoved it down the front of his boxer underwear. As he raced for the door, he snatched up the Beneli shotgun from beside the television. His room was on the fifth floor near the elevator. He slapped the down button and waited for the elevator. Just as he had decided to take the stairs, the door opened. He leaped inside and hit the lobby button. The sound of gunfire grew louder as he descended. On the ground floor, he emerged in the middle of a raging gun battle. A handful of fungus head zombies, all wearing army fatigues, were attacking a group of three armed soldiers. Two soldiers were down, as was the general's aide.

"Look out!" one of the soldiers yelled.

Kyle turned just as one of the zombies lunged at him from behind a stone column. He fired two rounds with the Glock into its head. Blood splattered Kyle's facemask and chest, but the zombie dropped. He quickly dispatched another with the Beneli, leaving a bloody smear on the mirrored wall. One soldier, too dazed by what was happening, dropped his weapon and tried to flee as two zombies zeroed in on him. He was too slow. Their combined weight carried him to the floor. He died in agony as the two creatures crushed his chest with pile driver blows. Blood spewed from his mouth as he gurgled out his last breath, but the creatures continued to pummel him in their blind fury. A sergeant placed a single round from his M4 in each one's head, and then stood staring at the corpses in shock disbelief, oblivious to the battle raging around him.

"There are more of them, Sergeant," Kyle yelled.

The sergeant shook off his distress and nodded. Kyle, the sergeant, and the remaining soldier stood shoulder-to-shoulder, firing their weapons at the last two zombies. A hail of bullets drove the creatures back, but they took an amazing amount of punishment before eventually succumbing to the murderous firepower. They were strong and fast, but they were composed of flesh and blood, and flesh fails where lead does not. Even after they fell, the three men continued pouring round after round into the creatures. The 12-gauge Beneli made an awful mess of one of the creatures. Its severed arm lay beside the flopping corpse. Kyle watched until it ceased moving. He glanced over at the sergeant and the soldier. The young soldier's face was ashen, his lips quivering. The sergeant, a grizzled old vet of Desert Storm, stared at the corpses with glazed eyes as he removed his empty clip. His hands shook as he attempted to replace it with a fresh one.

"My God, Sergeant," Kyle said. "You've got ten men lying here dead. What the hell happened?"

The sergeant glared at him, but as Kyle had hoped, his eyes cleared and he shoved the clip in with steady hands. "I don't know. I don't know. They just came at us as we left the dining room after drinking coffee." He repeated Kyle's question, "What the hell happened? I'll tell you what happened. I had to shoot my own men."

"They turned fungus head. Your men have to wear their masks at all times. Where's yours?"

"We're inside the building for Christ's sake. Besides, we were eating."

"Hell, Sergeant, I slept in mine. The air we're breathing in here is the same as the air out there." He jabbed his finger toward the window for emphasis. "Your mask is the only thing keeping you alive. Remember that, or you'll lose more men."

The sergeant looked as if had rather use his M4 on Kyle than the zombies, but he nodded. "I'll do that."

"Good." Kyle glanced around. "I heard the explosions. Where are the sentries? Didn't anybody come to investigate?"

The sergeant reached into his pocket and pulled out a cigar. He jammed it in his mouth and bit down on the end, but didn't light it. "One of the ... the things had a grenade. He pulled the pin and blew himself up. I don't know where the friggin' sentries are, but I'll soon find out if I have to kick some pups' asses to make my point. Come on Ignacio," he growled.

He stalked off down the corridor. Kyle felt sorry for any sentries he encountered.

The elevator door chimed. Kyle swung the Beneli around to face the door. When it opened, Marli and two others, a man and a woman, were inside. The man blanched when he saw the shotgun pointed at him. Kyle released his breath slowly and lowered the barrel. Marli wore only a t-shirt, shorts, and her mask. Kyle took a moment to admire her long, slender legs and her breasts beneath the thin t-shirt material for a moment before yelling, "What the hell are you doing walking into the middle of a firefight?"

She ignored his question, came over to him, and placed her hand on his chest. She stared directly into his eyes. "Are you hurt?"

He realized that she had mistaken the blood on his face and chest as his. He shook his head. "No." The woman carried a medical kit. She saw the bodies on the floor and took a step toward them. "Save your breath. They're all dead." He refocused his attention on Marli. "Next time you hear gunfire, lock your door and stay inside until someone comes for you."

"I'm a doctor. I thought I might be needed."

"The army has a medical unit." He pointed his finger at her. "Your job is to find a cure. We located a building for you. Tomorrow we can start transferring equipment. For now, all three of you go back to your rooms." He handed her his Glock. She stared at it but didn't take it. "Take it. Use it if you have to. It's ready to fire. Just aim and pull the trigger."

She shook her head. "I can't kill anyone."

He glared at her. "You'll kill if you have to. Every day you haven't found a cure, hundreds, maybe thousands will die. Remember that if you get squeamish about pulling the trigger. You're more important than the rest of us. You have to stay alive, you and your team."

Her face above the edge of her mask paled as his words sank in. She nodded and took the Glock, but she held it as if it were a living thing ready to bite her.

"Now, all of you go back to your rooms, and for God's sake, make the general realize how important it is for the soldiers to wear their masks at all times."

He didn't wait for a reply. He herded them back into the elevator and pressed the third floor button. As the door closed, Marli's eyes flashed him a brief smile.

Staring at the carnage marring the tiled floor of the hotel lobby, at the broken mirrors and shattered bodies, the blood and the spent shell casings, Kyle shook his head. If the soldiers started turning zombie, they were all doomed. They would fight the need to wear masks, as they would fight the need for condoms, as an affront to their manhood. They would need a clean area, like the one in which he had been quarantined, a place where the men could remove their masks for a while, a safe environment within the airport itself. Marli could work on that.

He looked down at the blood covering his chest, at his near naked body and felt a little vulnerable. He had only one shell left in the shotgun. Judging by the night so far, he might need more ammunition. Further sleep was out of the question, but he could at least shower and put on some clothes. He took the stairs rather than wait for an elevator. He hesitated on the third floor landing, wanting to check on Marli, but decided that she would need all the sleep she could get if sleep was possible after the night's events.

After his second shower of the night, he knew he should feel cleaner, but the sensation of the fungus head zombie's blood on his bare skin still lingered. He fought the impulse to scratch. He removed his mask just long enough to give it a thorough washing with soap and water to remove the blood. He was reluctant to put it back on, but it was his only mask. He would need to grab more to keep them handy. He hoped the fungus head's blood hadn't contaminated it. He had only the same brown suit Marli had provided after his quarantine, so he put it back on, minus the jacket and tie. He would need to locate some military fatigues soon. Returning to his apartment was out of the question, if it still existed. He had watched a large fire burning in that section of the city from his bedroom window. Smoke and ash filled the air outside to the point it was almost noxious. Combined with the Cordyceps spores, the air was doubly hazardous. It looked as if the entire city was in flames. The raging fires only increased the already oppressive summer heat. He felt sorry for any survivors trapped in the city's burning heart.

When he returned to the lobby, two heavily armed sentries stood nervously at their new posts outside the bank of elevators and the stairwell. Both wore masks. The sergeant he had chided, had taken his suggestions to heart. He nodded to them, but they were taking their tasks seriously. They ignored him and kept their eyes focused on the corridor. He felt somewhat unbalanced without the weight of the Glock under his left armpit. He would have to find another, perhaps smaller, weapon for Marli to use and retrieve his. He had reloaded the shotgun and shoved extra shells in his pocket just in case.

This time he explored the North Terminal, now known as Concourse D, American Airline's central hub. The Skytrain people mover, ran the length of the mile-long concourse and connected it with the car rental areas, but it was not operating. He walked the concourse, noting the numerous closed shops and restaurants. The 72-lane TSA inspection station was devoid of passengers, but Kyle swore he could hear the disembodied complaints of disgruntled spectral passengers wafting through the building on a ghost wind. With only the garish neon lighting operating, Terminal D was a spooky place.

He sat for a while and watched helicopters lift off, keeping no regular schedule as they rose into the night to survey the city and deliver their cargoes of death to rampaging hordes of zombies. He suspected no number of such forays could make a dent in the infected population of Miami. A third C-17 landed, the behemoth taxiing to a position beside the first two. The ramp dropped, dislodging fifty troops. They lined up, standing at attention as their officer delivered his words of wisdom, then hustled through a door on the first floor out of Kyle's sight. He was dismayed that none wore protective gear of any kind. As the first rays of dawn peeked through the haze of smoke above the city and spread its diffuse glow across the runways, he abandoned his perch.

Back in the Central Terminal, soldiers were lining up for a hearty meal in the hotel's restaurant. Most wore masks, but a few did not. The aroma of crispy bacon, fresh baked rolls, and coffee, drifted from the restaurant. Though someone had mopped up the blood from the tiled floor, the memory of the night's killings lingered. He didn't have much of an appetite and skipped breaking his night's fast. General Willows, an early riser, stepped from the elevator wearing battle fatigues. Kyle noted with satisfaction that he also wore a mask. The two sentries snapped a crisp salute in his direction. He spotted Kyle and headed in his direction.

"I understand you jumped down one of my sergeants' throats last night."

"I, er, cautioned him about the need for tighter security and about wearing protective gear."

"Good for you. They need their asses chewed out every now and then. It doesn't sound good coming from me. They get too defensive."

Relief flooded through Kyle. He had steeled himself for a nasty confrontation for overstepping his authority as a civilian. "Speaking of masks, where can I find replacements?"

The general reached into his pocket and pulled out several, handing them to Kyle. "Take these. I'm sure there will be a box waiting for me on my desk."

Kyle removed his old one, which was still damp, dropped it in the trash, and replaced it with one of the general's. "Thanks."

"I understand you located a site for the lab."

"Corporal Ginson did. I went along for the exercise. We ran into a little trouble, but Ginson handled it well. The hangar he chose should do nicely."

The general rubbed the square chin beneath the mask. "Ginson, huh? Maybe it's time I shoved a little more responsibility at him. I could use a few more sergeants with some initiative."

Kyle smiled, wishing he could be present when Ginson learned of his promotion. "He'll be pleased."

The general nodded toward the restaurant. "Have you had breakfast yet?"

Kyle shook his head. "Too early for me."

The general shrugged. "Well, suit yourself." He continued to the restaurant, passing the line of hungry soldiers, some of whom seemed a little awed to see their commander dining with them. Passing one man without mask, he remarked gently without breaking his stride, "Get a mask, soldier, or we might have to shoot you one fine morning." The soldier gulped and scrambled to pull a mask from his pocket.

Ginson had informed Kyle that Willows had come up through the ranks, distinguishing himself as a hands-on colonel during Desert Storm. This gave him a unique camaraderie with his troops. Given the bizarre situation in which they now found themselves, he applauded the general for his innovative style of discipline. Word would spread, and by midmorning, everyone on the base would be wearing masks. Kyle had worked under superiors in the police force more than once who made little effort to establish a bond with their men. That was the primary reason he had applied for transfer to the Special Investigation Squad. He felt a twinge of guilt as he thought of his comrades in SIS. He should be standing with them, fighting fungus heads, but he had committed to helping Marli.

He reached the loading dock in the South Terminal just as Ginson and his men completed loading crates and boxes marked 'Lab Equipment' into the back of two five-ton trucks. Walters was there with two of the scratches on his face covered with Band-Aids. Kyle was pleased to see that the soldier was recovering from his wounds.

"You're late," Ginson called out. His respirator muffled his words as he heaved a box into the back of a truck. "This is the last load. We've been at it since before dawn."

"I waited until I was sure all the grunt work was finished."

"Your girlfriend beat you up. She's there now directing the installation."

"She's not my ... oh, never mind." Kyle was annoyed that Marli had left for the hangar without him. How could he protect her if she refused to allow him? He pulled his shirt away from his skin. "Any chance of a fresh uniform and some clean skivvies?"

"I'll see what I can do. You coming with us or just seeing us off?"

"I'm assigned to Doctor Henry."

Ginson whistled softly. "Nice work when you can get it."

"The general had a word with me this morning."

Ginson snickered. "Oh, hobnobbing with the elite, are we?"

"He said you'd make a good sergeant."

Ginson stopped what he was doing and stared at Kyle. "You're kidding, right?"

Kyle shook his head and held up three fingers in a Boy Scout salute. "It's gospel."

Ginson swore softly, "Damn, now I'll have to work for a living."

"We'll still love you, Sarge," Walters quipped.

"For that remark, you drive."

He hitched a ride with Ginson in the Humvee rather than walk. By the light of day, the extent of the fire damage to the city wasn't as visible, but a pall of dark smoke hovered over Miami like a blanket of smothering smog, unperturbed by the morning's light offshore breeze, making the morning seem more like dusk. The sharp acrid smell of burned wood, melted metal, and the stench of scorched flesh, permeated the air. The runways were a hive of activity as Apache and Blackhawk helicopters lifted off, and heavily armed five-car convoys formed to spread out through the city.

"Any word from elsewhere in the country?" he asked Ginson.

Ginson scowled. "Information is sketchy, but Atlanta is a battle zone. The downtown area, Little Five Points, Buckhead, and Decatur, have been mostly evacuated, but the rest of the neighborhoods haven't. The Perimeter is the Kill Line. Anyone trying to pass beyond I-285 is shot."

Kyle nodded. Surrounding Atlanta like a ten-lane ribbon of asphalt, the Perimeter provided a clear field of fire. He felt sorry for anyone trapped within the arbitrary Kill Line, but even sorrier for anyone frightened enough or foolish enough to try crossing it.

"Omaha is as bad as Miami. So is Boston and Houston. I don't know about some of the other major cities. We're holding our own here along a line north of 36th Street and east of 27th Avenue south to Coconut Grove. Downtown … well, it's totaled. There are survivors trapped on the upper floors of some high rises, but it's going to be a bitch rescuing them. Right now, we're using the Blackhawks for ferrying troops and flying sorties."

"It's nice to see the military has its priorities straight."

"The plague is spreading damned fast. We're trying to stop it, but if we get a strong offshore wind …"

"Yeah, I know. The spores will spread all the way across Florida."

At the hangar, Marli stood outside directing men with carts as they unloaded the trucks. She wore a full mask and respirator like Ginson's. She glanced in his direction as he got out of the Humvee, but quickly turned and followed one of the carts into the hangar. Inside, the hangar didn't look the same. Four large white tents took up half the available space. Stacks of crates lined one wall. She directed the soldier pushing the cart to deposit his load beside the other crates. Men were spraying every corner of the building with expanding foam to make it spore proof. Kyle waited until she was finished before approaching her. She set her clipboard on one of the crates.

"I've only got a minute," she warned.

Kyle raised his hands in front of him. "Don't stop on my account. I'm here to help, but if I'm to be your bodyguard, don't run off and leave me."

She stared at him. "I don't need or want a bodyguard. If you want to help, you can assist Doctor Ozay in setting set up the office." She pointed to the smallest tent and turned back to her work.

"Where is the quarantine area?"

Her face revealed a mixture of regret and anger. "We won't be housing any infected here. We'll work with samples provided by the FEMA quarantine facility at Marlins Park."

After the earlier fiasco at the quarantine center at the airport in which he had almost died, he didn't blame her for not wanting a repeat.

"That might be best," he said hesitantly, not sure of her concerns.

She turned and marched across the room. Slighted but not offended by her brusque behavior, he entered the small tent and found Dr. Ozay, a short, pudgy, older man with thinning gray hair, assembling desks. Ozay might have been a fine doctor, but his skills with a power screwdriver were limited. He cursed as the screwdriver tip skidded across the table leg he was installing, gouging a long gash in the soft wood. Kyle gently took the screwdriver from him.

"Let me do this while you unpack the laptops."

Ozay looked grateful for the assistance. Kyle was familiar with tools. Almost all the furniture in his apartment had come disassembled from IKEA. He made short work of the desk assemblies. Within two hours, all six desks, chairs, a rack for computer equipment, and a table for the all-important coffee maker, were completed. Doctor Ozay and a technician named John Mavers, connected power cables, computer cables, and telephone cables to each desk. When they were finished, Mavers looked at him, smiling.

"You saved Doctor Henry's life. Thank you."

Kyle shrugged. "Right place, right time."

"She's very bright, you know, one of the top in her field. If anyone can solve this problem, she can."

"I hope so."

"Too bad about Ellis," Ozay said, shaking his head.

"Who's Ellis?" Kyle asked.

Mavers answered. "Doctor Ellis was a mycologist. He identified the species infecting everyone. He said it was an old species, not a mutation. The journal found with Roger Curry's luggage verifies this."

"Does that make a difference?"

"Oh, yes. Mutations are difficult to control because they can mutate again. An older, established species might be more resilient, but its very stability is a weakness. With the correct antifungal agent, we can stop it."

Kyle's spirits lifted. "That's great news."

"What Mavers is leaving out," Ozay interjected, "is that most antifungals are as deadly to humans as they are to the fungal parasite. Destroying the fungus *in sito* can be achieved. A cure for those infected ... that is another matter."

Mavers nodded.

A soft sigh escaped Kyle's lips. "So we're back to square one."

Ozay sighed. "We will try." He turned away and stared at the tent wall.

Kyle left Mavers and Ozay in the tent and set out in search of Marli. He found her outside instructing two army technicians in the installation of the tank of scrubbing chemical for the decontamination tent, a small, hemispherical dome just large enough to hold one person. The technicians placed the tank in the proper spot and ran a hose to the dome, which was secured to the frame of the door leading to the reception area with heavy bolts and more of the expanding foam.

"Why there?" he asked.

"We can use the front room as a staging area. Once the interior of the building is sealed and decontaminated, we can move about freely without suits or masks, except in the labs."

"I'm all for that," he said.

She stared at him for a moment. "It's amazing how much one relies on reading another's facial expressions. Masks make it difficult."

He returned her stare, feeling slightly uncomfortable by the heat her gaze generated. "There's still the eyes," he replied.

"Yes, the 'windows to the soul', the poets say."

"You'd better not look too deeply into my soul. You might not like what you see."

Her gaze quavered for just a moment, as if she already had an idea of what she might see; then she glanced at the technicians. The moment had passed. Realizing that he had blown his chance to become a little more intimate with Marli, he mentally kicked himself and then asked, "How can I help out?"

She, too, seemed relieved for the reprieve. In a business-like tone, she said, "Would you please help move equipment to the lab tent?"

He spent the remainder of the afternoon methodically moving crates and boxes to their designated destinations, unpacking them, and helping to set up equipment. He had no idea what function some of the equipment performed, but his task was simple enough – place it where one of the technicians pointed and move on to the next crate. It was back-breaking labor, but it served to take his mind from the turmoil surrounding them.

Miami was his home, and yet he felt no heartbreak at its ongoing demise. He hoped it was simply that the enormity of it all hadn't had time to sink in. He hated to think that his years spent dealing with the dregs of society had numbed his ability to empathize with others. People were dying by the thousands, his people, the people he had sworn to protect, but he could do nothing, not even weep. His skills, his weapon, served no purpose in this war, a war against a microscopic spore born on the wind.

Slowly, the stack of crates against the wall diminished and the tents filled with equipment. His back ached and his arms felt as if he had been doing handstands all day, but the exhaustion felt good. It was a clean feeling. A shower would wash away the sweat and the grime of labor, a marked difference from his usual days when even the hottest shower and the most vigorous scrubbing left the stink of the city on his skin and in his nostrils. He sat on the cold concrete floor with his back against the wall, drinking a bottle of lukewarm water, his eyes closed, and his mind foggy from labor. He opened his eyes when he heard footsteps approaching.

"Oh," Marli gasped, "I thought you were asleep."

He smiled at her. "Just resting."

She glanced at the tents. "Everything is almost ready. Tomorrow, we can begin work."

He nodded as he looked at her. This was the first time he had seen her without a biohazard suit, a respirator, or at least a mask covering her nose and mouth. He noticed the softness of her lips, which had a healthy red glow in spite of the lack of lipstick. Her nose was small and narrow, pert was the word that came to mind. Her face bore signs of the fatigue everyone felt, but he wouldn't trade it for most faces he had seen in his life. He thought her face almost cherubic in its innocence, not that he knew any of her darkest secrets, but her features remained untouched by the bleakness surrounding them, especially her eyes, which showed signs of defiance. If she harbored doubts about her ability to find a cure, her face revealed nothing.

"Are you staying here tonight?" he asked.

"Yes, it will take hours to calibrate the equipment. The shower isn't installed, but I suppose a sponge bath will suffice."

He briefly imagined himself administering the sponge bath. Then he made a show of raising his arms, sniffing his pits, and frowning. "Not for me. I'll head back to the hotel for a shower and a shave. Hopefully, Ginson can rustle me up a clean uniform to wear."

"Are you coming back tonight?"

Did her voice sound hopeful? "Sure. You've got me for the duration or until Captain Gilbert reassigns me."

A brief smile flickered on her lips. "That's good. We can use your assistance."

He decided to push. "We?"

She blushed. "Okay, Detective, *I* can use your assistance. I ... trust you."

Not the answer he was hoping for, but it was a start. "Call me Kyle." He patted his Glock. "This is the only thing I'm good at. I don't have much to offer as a lab assistant."

She hesitated. She had something else to say, and he was too tired for word games or dancing around the subject.

"Spill it, Marli," he urged.

"The military has its agenda and I have mine. At some point, those agendas may clash. I hope I can count on you if that happens."

"This is my city. I'll fight for it. If you're trying to save lives, I'll be right there beside you." He nodded his head at the military personnel still moving around the hangar. "These guys might decide to write the city off. I can't let that happen. Will you?"

"I'll do my best not to."

He spread his hands. "That's all I ask. I'll run errands and keep you safe. If … if things go to hell in a hurry, I'll get you safely away from the city, but then I'll have to come back. I won't give up Miami. I'm a cop and this city's my beat."

Her smile warmed his heart. If he hadn't been so tired, and afraid of what she might do, he would have leaped to his feet and kissed her. Instead, Ginson walked up. He glanced at the two of them, guessed he had arrived at an inopportune time, and cleared his throat to announce his presence.

"We're headed back to the terminal for more supplies. Need a lift?"

Kyle cast one last lingering look at Marli before answering, "Yeah. I'd better head back." *Before I do something stupid, like make a play for the good doctor.*

7

July 5, Little Havana, Miami, FL –

At dawn, Rita dragged the dead body to the alley; then scrubbed the floor and walls on her hands and knees with soapy water until her back ached. She didn't stop until every sign of the creature's foul blood was gone. She tossed the bloody baseball bat in the garbage can out back.   Afterwards, she showered with Tomas lying on the floor outside the shower where she could watch him. The water was frigid, but she endured it as the freezing spray washed away the blood and the stink of the creature from her body.

During the night something inside her had snapped. The killing of the *demonio* had awakened some primal instinct for survival that had lain dormant within all her life. She now felt some small portion of what her father must have felt, to endure six long years in Castro's prisons, resisting the often brutal ministrations of Castro's 're-educators.' Ricardo had not returned. She had to face the possibility that her husband may be dead. The thought, once it took root in her mind, spread to her heart, chilling her more than the cold shower. She didn't have time to mourn. Her son depended on her. She could not be weak. She had to survive if her son was to grow up and experience the freedom for which her father had fought so hard.

Daylight did little to reduce the pall of fear hanging over the neighborhood. The sky was gray, overcast, and filled with smoke. Occasional explosions and gunshots still broke the deathly silence, but the sounds were distant and meant nothing to her. Help was not coming, of this, she was certain. She would have to seek it out. She wrote a hurried note to Ricardo just in case, and placed it on the refrigerator door with a magnet in the hopes that he would yet return. Then she bundled up her baby and set out toward Flagler

Street. If she found any help, it would be there, a main thoroughfare. At the last moment, she picked up a photo of Ricardo, removed it from its frame, and shoved it in her pocket.

She moved cautiously through alleys and backyards. Neighbors peered furtively from dark windows, but no one offered her help. Twice, more of the creatures that had once been men appeared on the street, but they didn't see or smell her and passed her by. They were skulkers of the night and their numbers seemed fewer in the daylight hours.

On Flagler, armed men, not military, patrolled the street as a line of people entered a small market. She took her place in line. When a man spotted her child, he allowed her to move forward several positions. Another man wearing a dirty business suit began to complain loudly, the guard stopped and stared at him.

"You were here yesterday. No more food until tomorrow."

"You can't do that. I'm hungry."

The man's pathetic whining got on Rita's nerves. What did he think the others were doing – dining out?

"We're all hungry," the guard said. "We have to share to survive. Move along."

The man was still protesting as she entered the store.

She was shocked to see the store's shelves were almost empty. People were allowed only a few items each. She chose two jars of baby food and two of canned milk for her child and a box of animal crackers for herself. She offered money to an elderly man behind the counter, but he shook his head.

"We aren't charging. We're trying to help."

"Thank you."

On the way out, the store owner's wife, a tall, thin woman wearing a flowered scarf over her nose and mouth, called her back. She handed Rita a bag filled with sandwiches and bottled water.

"Take this honey. You look hungry."

Rita was too overcome by the woman's generosity to speak. She nodded.

"You shouldn't be out on the streets. It's dangerous. And cover your face. I heard it's some kind of disease driving people insane." The woman reached beneath the counter and pulled out two bandanas. "One for the baby, too."

Rita took the bandanas and hugged the woman. "Thank you."

"You had better find a safe place to stay, especially at night." She glanced outside and scowled. "They prefer the night."

Rita wrapped the bandana around her mouth and nose and placed the other over her sleeping child. Hoping against hope, she pulled out the photo of Ricardo.

"Have you seen him?"

The woman looked at the photo, and then shook her head. "Sorry, honey, I haven't."

Disappointed, Rita went back outside. The guard was still arguing with the man in the suit. The man was becoming more agitated, shaking his fist in the guard's face and screaming at the top of his voice. The guard warned him to be quiet. Suddenly, the man pushed past the guard and ahead of those waiting patiently in line and ran toward the store.

"Get back," the guard warned.

The man ignored him. The guard raised his rifle and fired. The man spun, stared at the guard bewildered, and fell dead with a bullet through his back. Two other men dragged his body to the curb. The guard turned to the crowd.

"Stealing, hoarding, or ..." he glanced at the dead man's body, "just being a rude asshole won't be tolerated. We either work together, or you're on your own."

She wondered if the dead man had been someone's husband or father. It no longer mattered. All that mattered was her child who had not awakened from the shot. She didn't want to eat in front of hungry people, but it was too far back to her home. She had no reason to return there anyway. She took shelter a few blocks away in an abandoned electronics store. Its contents had been looted and the front window broken, but the office door locked. Once safely inside, she devoured one of the bologna sandwiches and drank a full bottle of water. She was still hungry but decided to make her small stash of food last as long as possible. She didn't know how long the meager food in the store would last.

The office had a working toilet, for which she was grateful, but now she was afraid of the water for drinking. What if it was contaminated? From now on, both she and Tomas would drink only bottled water. A two-day-old copy of the *El Nuevo Herald*, a Spanish-language newspaper, did little to explain what was happening. The headlines decried *'Los Ultimas Dias'*, the Last Days. One article devoted two paragraphs to quotes from the Public Health Service stating that an 'unknown' disease was spreading through the city and that officials were concerned. A quick scan of the articles revealed that people all over the country were going insane with Miami being at the center of it all. The police could not stop the crazy ones, so the army had arrived and declared Martial Law. There was a six p.m. curfew and people were advised to stay indoors. There was no mention of where to go or when help might arrive.

Twice she heard more gunfire and occasionally a passing vehicle. She napped, fed and changed Tomas with one of the few remaining diapers, and waited. The light slowly faded from the tiny barred window high on the office wall and the room darkened. She found a flashlight but sat in the dark, alternately crying and praying. A noise from inside the store startled her. Was it one of the creatures or someone seeking shelter as she had? The person stopped outside the office door as she held her breath. From the sniffing and loud, gasping breathing, she assumed it was one of the creatures. After a few moments, it moved on. Breaking glass and overturned shelves marked the creature's path through the store and back outside.

Several times people or creatures passed down the alley beyond the office but didn't stop. Once, deep into the night, she heard a woman screaming nearby. The scream ended abruptly. This, more than anything else, brought the reality of the situation home to her. People were dying, maybe thousands of people. Things would not get better any time soon. In fact, they could become much worse. She could not depend on the kindness of others or wait for her husband's return. Her child's safety was her responsibility. If she and Tomas were to survive, she would have to find a means to defend herself.

She searched the office and found the storeowner's revolver and a box of .25 caliber ammunition hidden in the bottom of a drawer. She had never fired a gun, but if the same rage she had felt while killing the creature with the baseball bat overcame her, she knew she could use one. The small pistol felt heavy in her hand as she held it out experimentally, closing one eye to sight down the barrel as she had seen in the movies. The pistol had a safety catch on the side. She removed the bullets for safety and tested it, to determine which position locked the pistol and which allowed her to shoot. Then she reloaded it and laid it on the desk in front of her.

Now, she was ready.

8

July 5, MIA, Miami, FL –

Freshly showered, shaved, and dressed in a set of new skivvies and borrowed army fatigues slightly too large for his lean frame, Kyle felt like a new man. He hand-washed his shirt, underwear, socks and pants in the sink, and hung them over the shower curtain bar to dry. He appreciated the use of the uniform, but he had been a cop too long to be mistaken for military. Ginson had informed him that the hotel gift shop might have clothing to fit him. If not, he could check out one of the duty free shops in the airport.

Chow was served buffet style with a long row of chafing dishes brimming with fried chicken, baked fish in a lemon butter sauce, two kinds of potatoes, steamed vegetables, a roast beef carving station, and trays of deserts. He was amused to see soldiers pulling down their masks just long enough to shovel food into their mouths, and then replace them. The general's warning had quickly spread throughout the ranks. Kyle was hungry, but eager to return to the hangar. Ginson had advised him that he was leaving at 1900 hours sharp. He checked his watch – 6:30, 1830 hours in Military time. He didn't have time for a sit-down meal. Picking up two slices of rye from a stack of bread, he had the chef carve off a thick piece of medium rare beef. He spread a combination of horseradish and mayonnaise on the bread, added lettuce, slices of tomato, and wrapped it to go.

He arrived at the dock, but instead of loading the Humvee for the return trip, Ginson and his men were performing a weapons check.

"What's up?"

"Trouble," Ginson growled. "A mob broke through the perimeter headed for the parking garage."

"How many?"

Ginson shrugged. "Thirty or forty. Enough to be a problem."

Kyle didn't want any part of a gun battle with fungus heads. He wanted to return to the hangar and Marli, but Ginson needed help. He sighed; unslung the shotgun he had been carrying around, and pumped it to load a shell in the chamber. "I'll help."

"It's your funeral. A squad from Fox Company is supposed to meet us there."

"Bunch of pansy-assed slackers," Walters growled.

Ginson spun on his heel and snapped, "Can that shit."

"Sorry," Walters answered, and then shrugged. "Must be my medication."

Ginson scowled at Walters, and then turned back to Kyle. "Glad to have you along."

Kyle nodded.

They double-timed it across the sky bridge to the Skytrain station. The morning was overcast and gloomy, setting the mood for the coming battle. The thirty or forty people Ginson had mentioned looked more like a hundred to Kyle, as he caught sight of the crowd rushing down 21st Street through the underpass of Perimeter Road, filling it from side to side, and surging forward like a wall of angry human flesh. Bursts of gunfire rang out from behind the crowd, indicating that some survivors from the forward guard posts were still active, but their fire did little to slow the mob. The men from Fox Company crossed the short term parking area beneath the Skytrain station moving directly along the tracks toward the oncoming crowd. They were far too few to be effective in a frontal assault, but seemed oblivious to the danger they faced.

"There're barely a dozen of them," Kyle said, "they'll be slaughtered."

"Not if we get those things in a cross fire," Ginson replied. "Come on."

They raced down the length of the North Parking garage, better known as Dolphin Parking, and took up positions along the third level southern wall facing the long term parking area. The crowd spread out as it poured through the underpass, but the majority, noticing the soldiers, aimed directly for the terminal. An

Apache gunship thundered overhead, flying just above rooftop level. Its guns raked the crowd with a hail of 30 mm bullets, but it couldn't maneuver in the narrow space between parking garages, or fire into the leading edge of the crowd for fear of hitting the men of Fox Company. Several zombies fell to the withering fire, but most made it through unscathed.

"Open fire!" Ginson yelled.

Immediately, a barrage of M4s, M16s, and the M-249 SAW Walters carried, tattered the leading edges of the crowd, as C Company joined in, pouring a lethal wall of lead into the fungus heads. Walters held the heavy SAW in one hand, sweeping it back and forth across the crowd. The recoil must have played hell with Walters injured shoulder, but he fired it with a grim determination and deadly accuracy. Creatures fell by the dozen, but the crowd didn't slow as their lust for killing drove them to leap the bodies of the fallen. Grenades from Fox Company exploded, tossing broken bodies like chaff in the wind, but still the crowd surged forward, diminished in size but not in rage. An M113 armored personnel carrier rolled up behind the crowd and got in its licks with its .50 caliber machine gun. A dozen or so creatures pounded uselessly on its metal sides, but fell beneath its tracks as the APC lumbered after a small breakaway group continuing to spew death around it.

As Kyle had direly predicted, the squad from Fox Company, though it fought valiantly, was no match for the superior numbers or the fungus-driven rage of the unheeding mob of the infected. They vanished beneath a sea of corrupted flesh.

"They're going to reach the terminal," one of Ginson's men shouted.

"We've got our own problem," Riley said, pointing to a dozen or so fungus heads racing up the ramp toward them.

Kyle quickly reloaded the shotgun and pointed it at the zombies. One of the infected men looked as if he were wearing a mask. As the creature got closer, Kyle realized with a sickening feeling that it was not a mask. Ropes of slimy growth draped over the man's face, covering his eyes and ears. Smaller tendrils sprouted from open wounds on his arms and chest. The fungus was literally eating him alive from the inside out. With mounting disgust, he fired. The man's chest opened up. Blood and globs of fungus poured out as he fell to the pavement. His moment of satisfaction passed quickly as more creatures followed the dead man.

The first five creatures fell quickly, but the remainder became wary and spread out. The battle soon disintegrated into a hand-to-hand melee. Three of the creatures slammed one of the soldiers to the concrete and ripped at him with claws and teeth. His screams echoed through the garage. Ginson slammed his rifle butt into one of the creature's head until it collapsed, but then he was forced to fend off his own attacker. Kyle fired until the shotgun was empty, and then took out his Glock. When the infected zombies got too close for his Glock, he used his knife and hacked at anything that moved – arms, torsos, and faces. His hand and face were soon covered in blood and gore, making seeing difficult and maintaining his grip on the knife hazardous. He struck blindly, fending off the creatures with his free hand and kicking at them with his legs. One creature got through his flurry of blows and shoved him backwards. He slipped in a pool of blood and tottered over the edge of the garage wall, staring backwards at the ground three floors below. As he struggled to right himself, the zombie tumbled over after him, almost taking him with it, its head a ragged wound. He felt a hand gripping his shoulder, pulling him up, and he looked into Ginson's smiling face.

"Don't leave yet. The party's not over."

Two of Ginson's men were down now, Futterman and another whose name he didn't know. The two remaining creatures stood a few yards away, snarling their anger but wary. Walters lifted his SAW and made short work of them, grinning as he held down the trigger.

Ginson looked at his two casualties. "God damn it! This is getting us nowhere. We can't kill them all and we can't keep losing men."

"Marli and her group will come up with something."

As he spoke, he worried that Marli might be in danger, though the hangar was sealed tight and Ginson had left two of his men on guard. He didn't have time to dwell on her safety. They still had to stop the zombies.

The Apache helicopter made another pass as the zombies rushed across the short term parking area, risking crashing into one of the sky bridges. Bodies piled up. Less than twenty zombies remained, but they smashed down the glass doors and poured into the terminal. Isolated, sporadic gunfire from inside the building did little to impede them. The military had been caught off guard by the large number of fungus head zombies and had failed to mount a proper defense.

"We've got to go help," Ginson said. He took one last glance at his two fallen men, swore under his breath, and led his remaining men back to the terminal.

The zombies had left a wake of destruction as they spread out through the terminal, overpowering the few scattered defenders, overturning tables and chairs, smashing mirrors and reflective surfaces, as if images of themselves were abhorrent to them. And there were bodies. Kyle counted over a dozen bodies, most of them unarmed soldiers.

"Where is everyone?" Walters complained as he peered down the empty corridor.

As Kyle wondered the same thing, shots rang out somewhere ahead of them.

"At least someone's fighting," Ginson commented. "Let's go get in on the action."

As they headed deeper into the terminal, Kyle spotted movement within the shadows of an opened door. The figure disappeared so quickly he thought he might have imagined it. He mentioned it to Ginson.

"Mmm. Riley, go with Bane and check it out. We don't want any bad guys sneaking up on us."

The door led into a darkened service corridor paralleling the terminal concourse. Kyle searched for a light switch, found it, but the lights did not function.

"The power's off," he groaned. Hunting for bad guys in the dark was a worst-case scenario.

"That's the army for you," Riley groaned, "trying to save a buck. Like they're paying the friggin' power bill."

Kyle switched on his flashlight and swept the darkened corridor with its feeble beam. Doors lined the corridor, several of them yawning open and uninviting in the gloom. The entire scenario reminded him of a video game he had once played with the twelve-year-old son of a woman he had dated – *Doom*. He had sucked at *Doom*. The kid had kicked his ass. He hoped there were no mutants. He and Riley didn't bother with the closed doors. As far as Kyle knew, fungus heads hadn't yet learned to open doors. However, each opened doorway would have to be checked out. The first was a supply closet. Riley, in his nervousness, almost shot a rack of mops when he brushed into them and they fell over him. His sharp chuckle didn't fool Kyle. Riley was as frightened as he was.

The second room was a break room. It too was empty. Kyle was beginning to think he had imagined seeing a figure in the darkness, but he didn't let down his guard. His instincts were kicking into full gear, telling him to watch his ass. As they approached a third open doorway, Kyle motioned Riley to be quiet and take the point. He leveled his shotgun at the open doorway to cover him, as Riley took a deep breath and stepped inside, hugging the right side wall. Kyle followed quickly, taking the left side. Riley's flashlight revealed three zombies, a male and two females at the far end of an office. The male wore a policeman's uniform covered in blood. One overweight female, about forty years old, wore gray sweat pants and a too mall t-shirt. The second woman, a young girl, wore white panties and no bra. Her young breasts were full and pert, but any carnal thoughts he might have had at her state of undress were quickly dispelled by the look of pure animal rage on her face and the splotches of blood on her chest. While Riley stared at the bare-breasted teen, the older woman snarled and raced across the room at him. Riley ripped his gaze from the girl and fired his M4, almost cutting her in half as a stream of bullets ripped across her midsection. Kyle shot the policeman, feeling a little guilty about killing a fellow officer.

Using the cop for cover, the young girl nimbly leaped upon a desk and sprung at Riley, before either of them could fire. Riley's punch to her face bloodied her nose but otherwise didn't faze her. The two fell to the floor struggling. The flashlight rolled across the floor, adding a surreal light to the fight as Riley used his rifle to push her away from his face. She was too close to Riley for Kyle to use the shotgun. He laid it on a desk, grabbed the girl by the arm, and swung her off Riley. She spun across the floor, but recovered quickly and now focused her attention on him, and she was between him and the shotgun. He pulled his Glock, pointed it between her eyes, and pulled the trigger. It clicked empty.

"Shit," he moaned.

The girl lunged at him before he could reach his knife. He outweighed her, but she was strong, agile, and propelled by her fungus-born rage. She forced him backwards into the hallway, growling as her mouth sought his neck. Forgetting nicety, he grabbed her by the throat and smashed her head against the wall. It took several blows before her skull split open and she finally stopped moving. He released her and she slid to the floor, leaving a smear of blood and brains on the wall. Reflected in the light of the flashlight, her lifeless eyes continued to stare at him hungrily.

He had no time to rest. From the darkness of the hallway, another zombie rushed at him. Like the one in the garage, this one had no discernible face, just a mass of purplish growth sprouting from his eyes, nose, and ears. *Can he even see me?* Kyle thought. See him or not, the creature sensed that he was there and came unwavering in Kyle's direction. Kyle pulled his knife and braced himself to face it. When it was almost upon him, the creature's head was suddenly backlit by a flashlight beam; then exploded. Its lifeless body fell to the tiled floor and slid several feet before coming to a rest beside the girl's body. Ginson stood twenty yards down the hallway, his rifle pointed toward Kyle.

"Thanks," Kyle said.

"Don't mention it," Ginson said, lowering his rifle. "I was following him. Ugly bastard."

Kyle had to agree.

Riley stuck his head out the door and stared at the young girl, blood pooling around her battered head. "Hey, Sarge. This naked chick threw herself at me. It was great. Almost like sex."

"I'm not a sergeant yet," Ginson reminded him. "She must have been really brain dead to go for you."

"She is now," he snorted.

Kyle nodded his head at the fallen zombie. "Is this the last of them?" Kyle asked.

Ginson shook his head. "I don't think so."

* * *

Two hours later, the remaining zombies were finally eliminated. Ginson's squad suffered no more deaths, but others had not been so lucky. The zombies had poured into the dining room, catching unarmed soldiers unaware. A total of thirty-one men had died during the attack. Such a fiasco lowered morale. Delays in communication and a lack of preparedness had cost lives. Kyle imagined the general would have a few words to say about that. The infected bodies were unceremoniously dragged into a pile in the long term parking area, doused with aviation fuel, and burned. The dead soldiers were treated with a little more respect. They were placed in body bags and loaded onto one of the Globemasters, their final destination a mystery.

It was after midnight before Kyle finally reached the hangar, exhausted and hungry. His sandwich had disappeared during the melee. He was pleased to see two of Ginson's men patrolling the building. He entered the decontamination tent, stripped naked, and dropped his clothes in a hopper. A suited technician sprayed him with foam, and then water. He suffered the indignity of the process in silence. He yanked off his blood-soaked mask and tossed it into a sealed container. It felt good to remove it. The acrid odor of disinfectant assaulted his nose. The technician provided him with a towel to dry off and a one-piece jumper like the one he had worn in quarantine. He eyed the nondescript clothing with disgust. If he was going to go through this every time, he would need more clothes.

Marli met him on the other side of the decontamination tent, her face showing her concern.

"We heard the shooting. What happened?"

"Fungus heads broke through the main gate. They're dead, along with thirty-one soldiers. It was a God damned disaster."

"You look exhausted."

He nodded. "I am. I could use some shut eye. Have you slept?"

"I wanted to …" She glanced away. "I waited to see if everyone was all right."

"Ginson lost two men. He's placing more guards outside now."

Kyle was surprised to see that everyone was still awake. In spite of the late hour, technicians sat behind microscopes or poured over laptops. Machinery hummed as it sought answers to the fungus problem. They were taking their job seriously. He liked that.

"We killed two fungus heads whose faces were covered with growth. They couldn't see. How the hell do they function?"

"We've heard of several like that. It's the Tertiary stage, just before they become immobile during sporogenesis. They seem to develop a higher sense of smell and hearing to compensate for lack of vision. Have you eaten?" She pointed to a table laden with sandwiches and an urn of hot coffee.

He shook his head. In spite of his hunger, the sight of food revolted him after seeing the tertiary fungus heads. "I'm too tired to eat."

"Take any bed," she said. "We'll be up all night."

As much as would have liked to remain and talk with her, he could see that her mind was on her work, and his was too muddled to think clearly.

"In the morning then," he replied.

She smiled; then walked away to join her crew. He chose the first cot he came to and collapsed onto it. Sleep came quickly.

9

July 6, East Little Havana, Miami, FL –

Dawn came silently, creeping up on the city as if ashamed of what the new day would bring to the frightened people it shone upon. The first fingers of smoke-filtered sunlight speared through the tiny window of the office in which Rita had sought haven, scrolling invisible words on the wall. She awoke with a start and looked around. Baby Tomas was sleeping soundly, oblivious to the new world in which he would grow up, a world of broken promises and unattainable dreams; a world touched by the fungus threat of Cordyceps, a world of mankind falling and Cordyceps Rising.

During the night, Rita had come to a momentous decision. She had to save her child. The only way she could accomplish that was by leaving the city. Her cousin ran a small charter fishing boat out of Campeone's Marina on 7th Street. If she could reach the marina, located on a canal just across the Miami River, she was certain that she could persuade Elian to take her north to Jacksonville and to her Aunt Marisa. Marisa would welcome seeing Tomas. She doted on him. She could get word to Ricardo later and have him join them.

Rita's stomach grumbled and she realized she was starving. She dug into the bag the store owner's wife had given her and devoured one of the Bologna sandwiches and some crackers. She drank most of a bottle of water and used the remainder to thin down the canned milk for Tomas, who awoke hungry, but sat quietly cooing and playing with a staple remover she had given him. After giving him his bottle, she washed her face with water from the sink, quickly washed and rinsed two soiled diapers, and prepared to leave. She listened with her ear pressed to the door for several minutes but heard nothing – no traffic on the street, no gunshots, and no helicopters. She bundled Tomas into a blanket slung from her shoulder and across her chest, shoved the pistol she had found inside the blanket, and ventured out onto the street.

The sky was dark with the threat of rain, but with none of the usual sticky humidity that preceded a storm. There were no people in front of the store she had visited yesterday. In fact, there were no people anywhere. Except for several bodies that had not been there the previous day, the streets were deserted. The air was still and hot despite the early hour and filled with a haze of smoke that brought tears to her eyes. Rita wrapped the bandana tighter over Tomas' face to protect his young lungs. As she walked east, she checked out several stores, but they had already been looted of any food or water. She even entered one home whose front door was open wide. She announced herself first, but no one answered her call. A smear of dried blood on the Saltillo tile of the kitchen floor and a broken glass patio door spoke of an ill end for the home owner. She searched the pantry but found nothing edible. A moldy orange sat on the counter beside the open refrigerator. She peeled it and ate what she could of it. In a hall closet, she found a gallon of distilled water used for ironing, and added it to her small larder.

To a stranger, at five-feet-six inches tall and as thin as a ballerina, Rita would appear overburdened carrying her child and a large bag as she hurried down the street, but she was no stranger to hard work. Her muscles were firm and her resolve even more so. The weight she carried was nothing in comparison to the heavy burden of her heart. All around her, her city was dying, its people turned into crazed creatures, vanished, or in hiding. No aroma of cooking food or soft Latin beats came from the stores or the shuttered windows. Miami was used to storms. Hurricanes came as frequently as elections, but this storm was not one thrown at them by nature. It was a spawn of the devil, an army of demons who looked like men and women but possessed no souls. Miami was a wicked city, but surely all its people weren't evil. She attended mass and prayed to the saints and to the Virgin Mary, just as almost everyone in her neighborhood did. Why had they not been spared? Must the innocent suffer the same fate as the sinner?

As the day wore on, the city awakened. An automobile passed one block over, but she could not see it or flag it down. Shots rang out several times. Each time her heart raced as she sought cover, but each time no one appeared. She felt eyes on her, watching, but saw no one in the windows she passed. It was an eerie feeling, walking down a deserted street in a neighborhood that had once been so vibrant, so alive. She feared it would never become so again.

She saw the first police officers in over a week at an intersection which they had blocked with their patrol cars. She was overjoyed as she rushed up to them. Her joy, however, proved short lived.

"Oh, thank God," she cried. "I need help."

One of the officers was wary and kept his hand on his weapon as she approached. All four wore masks over their nose and mouth, but she could see distrust in their eyes.

"Who are you?" he asked. His voice did not sound friendly.

"Rita Hernandez." She held out her son. "This is my son, Tomas. I live near Riverside Park. Can you help me?"

The cop lifted his cap and scratched his head. "We've been ordered to guard this intersection and send anyone who comes by to Marlins Park. We're a collection point for refugees." He pointed to a nearby building.

She bridled at the word 'refugee' and the connotation it evoked, but she supposed that was exactly what she had become, a refugee in her own city. She could see figures behind a broken window in the building staring at her.

"I don't want to go to Marlins Park. I need to cross the river. My cousin has a boat."

The cop shook his head. "No one is allowed to cross the river. It's too dangerous. Hell, it's bad enough here." He pointed to six bodies lying in a row in an empty lot. "We killed this lot just today."

She pointed to one of the patrol cars. "Take me to the bridge at least. I'll walk from there."

"Look, lady. We can't leave our post. You're welcome to stay here until an army truck comes by to pick up the refugees for transport."

She bit back a curse. "Do you have any food?"

"We don't have any food, but I do have some water." He nodded to one of the other officers who walked to his car.

"I can't stay."

"It's your choice. I can't force you to, but for the sake of your child, you should stay here."

"For the sake of my child, I must continue."

He pointed toward the river. "Not that way. We have our orders."

The second officer returned with a two-liter bottle of water. She placed it in her bag.

"Thank you for the water."

"I wish we could do more, but the city's a disaster area. Marlins Park is just one of six quarantine camps. The military's calling all the shots now. If we left, they might shoot us."

She nodded. She didn't want to get them into trouble. If she could not pass through the checkpoint, she would go around it. "I can't stay here," she repeated. She showed him Ricardo's photo. "Have you seen my husband?"

"He's not here, lady."

She cast one last glance at the people in the building, wondering if her decision to continue was foolhardy, and left. She walked two blocks south until she was out of sight of the police before turning east again. Here there was no checkpoint, but the officer had been right about one thing – it was dangerous. Her danger came not from the crazed creatures, but from her own kind, a young Latino barely out of his teens. In his hand, he held a knife. To her, it looked like the longest knife she had ever seen. His eyes roved up and down her body as his tongue caressed his smiling lips. He wore brand new sneakers looted from some store and had three packs of cigarettes stuffed into his shirt pocket.

He waved the knife in the air, motioning toward the alley. "Come with me, bitch. I need some loving."

She summoned her courage. "Leave me alone, *pendejo*. Put your stupid knife away. Don't we have enough trouble?"

He glared at her. "You do."

He took a step toward her. She took a step away and pulled out the pistol, making sure the safety was off. The boy stopped in surprise, but when he saw how badly her hand shook, he laughed at her.

"Don't hurt yourself with that thing."

His smile vanished when she cocked the pistol. "Leave!" she yelled. "Leave now!"

He hesitated, glancing toward the alley. She wondered if he had friends nearby.

"Look, we can talk this over," he said.

He didn't look as nervous as he should be while facing a loaded gun. Lowering his knife, he took another step forward and stopped. She caught a blur of motion out of the corner of her eye. He wasn't alone and had been trying to distract her. When she foolishly turned her head to glance at the other person, the boy lunged at her. She fired. She put no thought into the action, did not remember pulling the trigger. There was a loud report, and then he fell against her, his eyes wide with fright and pain. His hand went to his chest where blood stained his shirt. He pulled his hand away and stared at the blood on it.

"Help me," he moaned as he slowly slid down her body.

She knew he was dead the moment he hit the ground. His dead eyes stared up at her. The boy's companion had stopped moving and now gaped at his dead friend. She whirled and pointed the pistol at him.

"Leave," she demanded.

He didn't hesitate. With a whimper that was almost a cry, he turned and ran. As he disappeared into the alley, her body shook so badly she had to sit on the sidewalk. She dropped the pistol from her limp hand. It landed in a pool of spreading blood. She kicked it away in disgust with her foot and began weeping. She had killed someone, a boy. It didn't matter that he was scum, preying on the helpless. He was a human being, someone's son. She had committed a grave sin. She quickly crossed herself but felt no absolution. Only the sound of her crying child brought her back to reality. She gently rocked Tomas in her arms.

"Hush, Tomas, my baby. Mother is here. You'll be all right."

Eventually, her son quieted. She hated the gun and what it stood for, but now she knew she needed it, if not for her protection, then for Tomas. She wiped the blood from the handle and stuck it back in the blanket. She left the boy's body behind. There was nothing she could do for him. She turned north back toward Flagler Street hoping to find more people. Twice more she saw *demonios* with sightless eyes shuffling around buildings, but they did not scent her and moved away. As she neared Flagler, she spotted what she at first thought were people standing on roofs watching her. She waved to them but they did not respond. As she drew nearer, she gasped when she saw their immobile bodies draped with thin filaments like hair waving in the breeze. Their misshapen heads sprouted purple growths. As she watched, one man's head exploded, popping open like a ripe melon. A cloud of dust shot from the open wound and rode the wind.

It's like flowers pollinating. That's how the disease spreads, she thought. She was relieved that the people were not demon possessed, but still as confused as before about what was happening. She was thankful for the bandana covering her mouth. The sound of several large vehicles in the distance lent speed to her legs as she raced for Flagler Street. She reached it just as a convoy of army vehicles approached. She realized that even if they forced her to go to Marlins Park, she and her child would be safer there, than out on the streets.

She waved her arms to flag them down.

10

July 6, Miami Airport, Miami, FL –

Kyle awoke with Ginson shaking his shoulder. He sat up suddenly, fully awake.

"What is it?"

"Relax. Nothing's wrong. You've been out about eight hours. Thought you might like some breakfast. You missed dinner."

Kyle rubbed the sleep from his eyes and yawned. "Eight hours. That's a record for me." He noticed the new sergeant's stripes on Ginson's uniform. "I see its official now."

Ginson smiled. "Yeah, now I can afford that second vacation home in the Bahamas."

Kyle doubted the extra three hundred bucks a month would purchase a good weekend in the Bahamas, but he was glad to see the promotion had come through. The aroma of cooked bacon, sausage, and hot coffee reignited his appetite. He followed Ginson to the breakfast area, heaped his plate with scrambled eggs, hash browns, sausage, and toast, and poured a cup of strong black coffee. Most of the others had already eaten, or judging by the amount of food remaining in the stainless steel chafing dishes, had not stopped working long enough to eat. He looked around but didn't see Marli anywhere. Ginson took a seat beside him with only a cup of coffee.

"You're not eating," Kyle noted.

He snorted derisively. "I ate two hours ago. The army gets up early."

Kyle wondered just how much sleep Ginson had gotten. He looked pretty tired too. "How did you manage to keep your uniform? They took mine."

"Some of us think ahead. I had the men bring extra uniforms sealed in plastic bags. No white coverall for me."

Kyle was upset with himself for not thinking of that little trick. "Next time, I'll remember."

"I'm not sure of your taste in clothing, but I guessed at your size and brought along a few pairs of pants, shirts, and all the extras I found in a gift shop. All I could find in your size were sports shoes. I left a note in your name on the counter. I'm sure they'll bill you later."

"Thanks. White isn't my color either."

After his self-imposed fast, the meal hit the spot. The coffee, strong and black the way he liked it, drove the lingering cobwebs from his mind. Ginson sipped his coffee slowly, watching Kyle eat his meal. Finally, Kyle pushed his empty plate away and downed the last of his coffee. He considered a second cup, but Ginson seemed eager to show him something.

"What's on your mind?" he asked.

"Captain Isaacson is leading a convoy to a couple of checkpoints to pick up evacuees and deliver them to Marlins Park. I'm taking Riley, Walters, and some of the new men they assigned me and going with him. Want to tag along?"

He hated to turn Ginson down, but he had promises to keep. "I told Marli I would help her out around here."

"Too late. I told her I was going to ask you. I don't think she liked my suggesting you accompany us." Ginson suddenly became very serious. "Look, you know Miami. I don't. You're good in a fire fight, and most of these new recruits haven't fired a weapon except on the range. I could use your help."

It was difficult to refuse a man who had so recently saved his life. He nodded. "Okay. Where are those clothes you mentioned?"

Dressed in the beige slacks and canary yellow polo shirt Ginson had chosen for him, he thought he could pass for a mannequin in the window of Rafaelo's Department Store, but beggars couldn't be choosers. Next time, he would do his own shopping. When he found Marli, she looked as if she had been awake all night. Her hair was mussed and her lab smock was wrinkled and stained. Even so, she greeted him with a wide smile.

"Sleep well?" she asked.

"Too long. I almost missed my bus."

Her smile morphed into a frown. "Yes, I spoke to Sergeant Ginson earlier."

Did he detect a touch of regret in her voice? "I can't schlep boxes and sweep floors. My skill set is rather limited." He raised his arms over his head to show her his new outfit. "Like the new clothes." Her eyes came to rest on the Glock snuggled under his left armpit. "Ginson picked them out," he continued. "At least I'll be the best dressed guy at the party."

Their eyes locked for only a second, a brief moment in time, but days of familiarity flashed between them in that instant. She was as far above him, as the Queen from a commoner, but she intrigued him. It was more than the fact that she was beautiful – Miami overflowed with beautiful women. Marli was a woman who knew what she wanted from life. He was used to vacuous beauties that lived for the moment and clung to whichever man could provide the most immediate comfort, the widest spectrum of drugs, or threw the most lavish party. Women such as Marli were rare, at least in the circles in which he usually traveled.

"Please be careful," she said. To his surprise and delight, she reached out, grabbed his hand, and gave it a strong squeeze. Not quite the parting he would have preferred, but her concern lifted his spirits. He hadn't really expected her to break character and kiss him, as much as he would have enjoyed it. "Please come back safe," she added.

He spotted Ginson by the door looking eager to get going but not interfering in their parting. He returned her squeeze. "I will," he promised, meaning it.

He left before she could say anything else that might make him regret leaving. This time he donned a full respirator instead of a simple mask. It was more uncomfortable, but if he was going to spend hours outside, he wanted to take every precaution against the fungus. He readjusted the straps around the back of his head for a tighter fit. Outside, there was a promise of rain in the clouds.

"Maybe rain will knock down the spores," he said to Ginson. The sound of his voice through the respirator annoyed him but there was little he could do about it.

Ginson glanced up. "Last weather report I heard, didn't say anything about rain."

"Maybe we'll get lucky."

Ginson snorted. "Yeah. Like luck's been a close companion lately."

Kyle had to agree. The convoy consisted of three armed Humvees, five trucks, an APC, and sixty men. Two Blackhawks accompanied them for air support. Miami had been under siege for only three days, but those three days had taken their toll on the city. Dolphin Expressway was blocked. The convoy headed south on 37th Avenue, and then took Flagler Street east. Kyle looked out on block after block of rubble and smoldering buildings. Entire neighborhoods of West Little Havana were in ruins. The *Shops at Flagler and Douglas* was gone, vanished as if a bomb had been dropped. Of the entire block, not a single wall remained standing. A few people emerged from the ruins along the way to stare at the convoy, but made no attempt to flag them down. One of the Humvees opened fire on a small group of fungus heads trashing a storefront as the convoy crossed Beacom Street.

East Little Havana fared slightly better. Fewer gutted or ransacked buildings lined the street. A few small groups of armed men patrolled the streets. Two bodies hanging from lampposts with placards reading 'Looters', spoke to a type of vigilante justice he would have abhorred a few days earlier, but turned a blind eye to now. With a breakdown of civil authority, neighborhood watches were all that stood between chaos and survival. The convoy stopped at one building with an American flag flying on an antenna above the roof and a police patrol car parked out front. Two police officers walked out of the building with eight men and women trailing behind them. None of the people, including the officers wore masks. The people silently climbed into one of the trucks. Their subdued behavior worried Kyle. They acted more like prisoners than people seeking shelter and safety.

A few blocks later, the captain called a second halt at an intersection manned by two patrol cars. Four heavily armed cops eyed the convoy warily, but cleared the intersection to allow the convoy to pass through. This time five people, including a woman towing two small children, marched to the waiting trucks. As before, no one wore masks. He turned to Ginson as the convoy started up.

"No one's wearing masks. Word's not getting out to these people."

Ginson shrugged. "No electricity, no television, no radio. How could they know?"

"Maybe we should drop leaflets from helicopters explaining the situation. They need to reach a quarantine center. We passed more people on the streets than we're picking up."

"We can't force them to go. If we start rounding up people at gunpoint, they'll start shooting back."

Kyle sat back in his seat. "You may be right, but at this rate, we'll never win."

Suddenly, a slim young Hispanic woman carrying a child raced from an alley. She wore a red bandana over her face. At first, Kyle didn't think the convoy would stop for her, but the captain raised his hand and the trucks slowed. Captain Isaacson exited his Humvee and helped the woman and child into the vehicle. When he took the child from her to help her in, she threw her arms around him and hugged him. He looked embarrassed by her intimacy.

Downtown, once so beautiful, a tropical paradise, now resembled a war zone. Burned shells of buildings, wrecked autos, bodies littering the sidewalks and streets – he could have been in Damascus, Syria, rather than Miami. Individual zombies rushed at the convoy, only to be shot down by the soldiers in the Humvees. A fire truck, its hoses still strung from hydrants and snaking into one building, was curiously unmanned. Had the firefighters fled or had they died at their posts?

They passed the Miami Art Museum. Smoke billowed from the eaves of the tiled roof and the front door was shattered. Paintings and sculptures, some priceless, lay smashed on the mosaic tiled courtyard, discarded by looters. Kyle wondered what type of human being would ransack a museum during a plague, and then recalled some of the heartless characters he had dealt with who wouldn't think twice about allowing such an opportunity to slip past. He had once attended a fund raising event at the MAM as a guest of one of the artists. Her work, a very vibrant oil painting of highly stylized people dancing around a blazing bon fire, had not been to his taste, but the artist, a buxom blonde, had been. Try as he might, he just couldn't grasp the underlying theme of the 20th and 21st Century American art displayed at the MAM. To him, most of it looked gaudy and hastily contrived, but then he was a cop and made no boast of possessing a discriminating mind. Still, he hated to see such a building dedicated to the arts damaged or destroyed. A lot of beautiful things were going to be lost forever before the city could recover. *If Miami ever recovers.*

The Miami-Dade County Courthouse was their final stop. The building looked antiquated compared to Miami's newer skyscrapers, but its Neo-Classical design radiated an aura of quiet dignity befitting a building dedicated to justice and housing the county's historic records. The eighty-six-year-old building was a museum, a visual reminder that Miami may appear fresh and new, but its history and its people had deep roots. Rising twenty-eight stories, the building's base was clad in Stone Mountain granite, while the upper floors were terra cotta tiles stained to match the granite. Massive fluted Doric columns guarded entrances. Topping it was a three-story pyramid.

In a bizarre picture of incongruity, zombies patrolled the slate-paved terrace and the wide steps. The convoy parked in a semi-circle on the North entrance of the building. The Humvees' machineguns fired hundreds of rounds into the creatures, chipping slate and gouging the granite façade in a blatant disregard of the structure's historic significance. History, it seemed, took a backseat to present-day circumstances. The machine guns quickly cleared the grounds of zombies.

"Twenty of you remain outside," the captain called out as he exited his Humvee, and then motioned for the others to follow him.

Kyle was surprised to see the woman with the baby get out of the Humvee as well. Concerned for her safety, he walked over to her. She was pretty with petite features and long black hair. She clasped her child inside the blanket sling with delicate but strong hands.

"Wouldn't it be safer to remain in the Humvee?" he asked.

She stared at him. He expected to see fear and confusion in her dark eyes. Instead, he saw anger, but in spite of her hardships, she looked determined.

She shook her head. "No. I will not stay out here." She waved her free arm around to indicate the dead zombies. "I will go inside with the soldiers."

She reached into the blanket in which she carried her baby and produced a pistol. Kyle could tell by the way in which she held it that she was not familiar with firearms. He was afraid she might be a bigger danger than the zombies.

"Why don't you put that thing away and let me do the shooting. I'm a cop."

"Really? Where were you two days ago?" she asked.

Her remark stung. He didn't blame her for not trusting cops. He had run into the problem many times in the past, especially among the Cuban population.

"Trying to stay alive. I won't let anything happen to you or your child."

She stared at him for several seconds before putting away the pistol. "My name is Rita Hernandez, and this is my son, Tomas."

"I'm Kyle Bane. Pleased to meet you. Stay close."

With Rita dogging his heels, he caught up to Ginson waiting outside the entrance. Three soldiers entered first with weapons ready, checked for zombies, and then motioned for the others to follow. The group entered the building carefully through a shattered revolving door, aware that zombies could be anywhere. Kyle spotted a camera set high on the wall tracking their progress.

"Someone's alive," he said, pointing to the camera.

The camera wiggled from side to side in answer. A few minutes later, two uniformed officers appeared, walking down the hall toward them. They stopped in front of Captain Isaacson.

"I'm Harris, head of security. We sealed off the security center and holed up there." Harris was a burly man with a deep cut over his right eye. A large bruise, barely visible through the beard stubble of his dark skin, marred his right cheek. Kyle suspected the blood on his shirt didn't come from his cut. Harris eyed the armed men with obvious relief. "The fourth through tenth floors are sealed as well, but the rest of the building isn't. These … things are everywhere." He shuddered. "They're like animals. They don't feel pain. They killed two of my men."

"Take me to security. I need to see the building plans."

The guard looked puzzled. "Didn't you come for us?"

"We came for everyone," the captain told him. "We need to round up everyone and get them out of here and to a quarantine center."

"Are there any prisoners in lock up?" Kyle asked. The building's upper nine floors housed a jail facility and a lock up for prisoners during their court trials.

The guard shook his head. "I don't know. No one's been that high in the building and came back."

"What about the security cameras?"

The guard shook his head. "We're on battery power, this level only."

"We'll deal with prisoners later," the captain replied, "first, we evacuate the personnel."

"There may be armed officers up there," Kyle argued, miffed at the captain's quick dismissal of the prisoners and guards. "We need all the trained people we can get."

Kyle could almost see the captain's mind working as he considered the percentages in risking his men in a dangerous rescue that might yield nothing.

"Okay, but only you, Sergeant Ginson, and five of his men. I'll need the others for the evacuation." He turned to Ginson. "Go with this man but don't take unnecessary chances."

Ginson snapped a salute. "Yes, sir."

After the captain had left, Ginson stood in front of Kyle and shook his head. "You're determined to get me killed."

"You invited me along, remember?"

"I'm coming too," Rita challenged.

"Absolutely not," Ginson and Kyle replied simultaneously.

Kyle added, "It's too dangerous, especially for a baby. Wait for us in the security office."

Rita was not to be denied. "You promised to keep me safe."

"You're not making it easy."

"I'll feel safer with you than in the truck, and I won't be trapped in another room. If anything happens, I want to be able to leave."

He couldn't argue with her reasoning. "Okay, but for God's sake try to keep out of the way."

A smile flicked on her lips. "For God's sake, I'll try."

They waited while the captain familiarized himself with the building plans. The guards had sealed the building's other four entrances with furniture piled in front of the doors to keep the zombies out, and had locked the stairwell doors, keeping the creatures inside confined to the upper floors. Without power, the building's eight elevators didn't work. Kyle wasn't looking forward to a twenty-eight story climb up the steps, but there was no avoiding it. After the captain returned from looking at the building blueprints, the entire group went up the stairwell. They encountered a few zombies that were quickly dispatched, but Kyle knew more would be drawn to the sound of the shots.

"We'll take it two floors at a time," the captain said. "Check each room and make sure you don't shoot anyone that isn't obviously infected. We'll take the survivors down to the trucks in groups. If you encounter an infected individual, shoot them. Ginson, you and the detective check the jail. Bring anyone you can back down, prisoners in handcuffs. If prisoners are infected, shoot them. We can't allow them to gestate."

With Ginson and Walters leading and Kyle staying close to Rita, the small group bypassed the first levels and climbed to the first level of the jail. By the time they reached the 17th floor, his legs were aching. The others took the effort in stride, so he refused to complain. The stairwell door was locked. Walters solved the problem with a fire ax he removed from the wall. Beyond the door, the corridor was dimly lit by patches of sunlight entering through open doors and the windows beyond.

"Spread out," Ginson said.

By the time they reached the far end of the corridor without finding anyone, Kyle was beginning to believe the trip was a wasted effort. The cell doors were all open. Either no prisoners had been inside, or the jailers had released them to fend for themselves. The last room was a cloak room. A whimpering sound came from behind a closet door. Ginson raised his hand for silence. With two men aiming their weapons at the door, Ginson stood along the wall and reached for the doorknob. Kyle shielded Rita and her child. Ginson yanked the door open. A woman sitting on the floor saw the masked men with guns and screamed. Ginson motioned them to lower their weapons.

"It's all right, ma'am. We're here to evacuate you."

She stopped screaming and stared at them for a moment before standing slowly on shaky legs. Ginson offered her his shoulder for support. She blinked back the sunlight.

"How long have you been in that closet?" Ginson asked.

"I'm not sure. Two or three days," she croaked. "I ran out of food and water yesterday."

Rita offered her a bottle of water. She drank half the bottle, sputtering as she almost choked on it.

"Are there any others upstairs?" Ginson asked.

She shook her head. "I don't know. After ... after people started going crazy, I hid. I heard shots from upstairs." She looked at the masks everyone but Rita wore. "What's happening?"

"It's some kind of plague," Kyle told her. "It drives people crazy." He didn't add that they turned into fungus heads. He figured the woman had enough to comprehend for now.

She covered her mouth with her hand. "Can I catch it?"

Ginson pulled a disposable mask from his utility belt and handed it to her. "Put this on. If you haven't caught it by now, you probably won't."

Whether she believed Ginson's reassurances or not, she donned the mask.

"We're going to check the other floors. You need to remain with us until we can get you downstairs."

She nodded. The next two floors were empty, but blood-stained carpet and smears of blood on walls proved its occupants had not gone untouched by the Cordyceps plague. On the fourth floor of the jail, two policemen met them at the door with weapons drawn. They eyed the group warily, but holstered their weapons.

"We're glad to see you," one of the officers said. "Joe and I are the only ones left. I had to shoot two of the guys. They went insane and tried to kill us."

Kyle stepped forward. "I'm detective Kyle Bane, SIS. What about the floors above? Any prisoners?"

The two officers looked at one another. One closed his eyes and turned away.

"Speak up," Kyle demanded of the first officer.

"One prisoner went crazy and killed two others. I shot him. I didn't have a choice. I released the other prisoners. I don't know what happened to them."

The officer jumped nervously at the sound of machine gun fire outside the building. Ginson went to the window and looked down. Zombies were attacking troops left with the trucks, but the .50 calibers in the Humvees were keeping them back for now. "Are we done here? We don't have much time."

With the three survivors in tow, the group descended the stairs. They didn't get far before they ran into trouble.

"Damn!" Ginson called out from one level below. "We've got visitors."

Zombies from one of the unsecured floors had been attracted to the noise and filled the stairwell. Now, they surged up the stairs, a mass of once-human flesh covered with fungus cilia. Many of them no longer had eyes with which to see, but their sense of smell and hearing remained undiminished. The guttural sounds they emitted raised goose bumps on Kyle's arms. These creatures were no longer human, merely vessels for the Cordyceps fungus' convenience. Driven mad by the plague, they sought release through violence and rage.

The first wave fell beneath a salvo of bullets from Ginson's men, but death meant nothing to the creatures. They surged over the bodies of their comrades, crushing them beneath their feet as they advanced. Ginson waved his men to fall back, retracing their steps up the stairs. After ascending several floors, Kyle heard more feet on the stairs above them. They were trapped.

"They're above us, Ginson," he yelled down.

"Son of a ... Back to the 16th floor," Ginson said.

One of Ginson's green recruits became overly excited and rushed forward to lob a grenade into the midst of the creatures, unaware of the consequences of such an explosion in a confined space.

"No!" Ginson shouted too late.

The young soldier didn't have a chance to toss the grenade. He fell under an onslaught of creatures and vanished beneath them. A few seconds later, the grenade exploded. The blast scattered the creatures. Bits and pieces of flesh, bone, and concrete showered down on the soldiers, along with metal shrapnel from the grenade. Ginson took a piece of hot metal in his side and staggered in pain. A second soldier standing beside him was hit in the throat, dying instantly. The concussion shook the stairs and knocked everyone down. At first, Kyle thought the entire stairwell would collapse beneath them, but it soon steadied. The air quickly filled with smoke and the stench of scorched flesh. Walters fired a burst from his M-249 SAW; then grabbed the injured Ginson around the waist, helping him up the stairs. Kyle picked himself up and helped Rita and her child to her feet.

"Are you okay?" he asked.

She coughed and nodded. Her child wiggled beneath the blanket but made no sound.

They reached the 16th floor just ahead of the zombies below them, but the creatures rushing down toward them were waiting for them. Kyle began firing his Beneli into them as he cleared the landing. The heavy 12-gauge slugs ripped chunks of flesh from their bodies and severed limbs. Several of them were so ripe with the fungus, they almost disintegrated when hit. He didn't stop moving, plowing his way through them by brute force using the shotgun held crosswise as a ram. One creature grabbed his arm with surprising strength, almost wrenching free the shotgun. To his astonishment, Rita pulled out her .25 caliber revolver and shot the creature in the head at point blank range. Its head exploded, showering them both with blood and gore. He kicked its body away. He didn't have time to thank her. He shoved her through the door ahead of him and stood in front of it fending off zombies.

Walters crested the stairs and opened up with the SAW, sewing a 5.56 mm swath of destruction through the creatures, providing an opening for Ginson and the others. Ginson staggered through the door under his own power, but collapsed to the floor as soon as he was inside. The others followed with Walters entering last. He closed and locked the door behind him.

Kyle knelt beside Ginson. "Are you hurt badly?"

Ginson grunted and removed his hand from the wound. Blood gushed from beneath his hand. "Bleeding like stuck pig. Hurts like hell, but no artery."

Kyle removed Ginson's med kit from his belt, took out a compression bandage, and wrapped the wound. When Ginson saw the morphine hypo in Kyle's hand, he shook his head.

"Not now. We may have to move quickly. Nobody carries me out."

Kyle understood the sergeant's reluctance, but Ginson was in obvious pain. "You need this," he insisted.

"No. I'm not dead yet. I can make it back down under my own power."

"Fungus heads are outside. We may be stuck here for awhile."

"Captain Isaacson knows where we are. He'll come for us."

Walters sat with his back against the door as zombies pounded on the door. The distant reports of gunfire outside the building and the muted sound of some firing within the building, revealed that they were not the only ones under attack

"We could try the other stairwell," Kyle suggested.

"It takes us too far from the North entrance. Captain Isaacson will look for us here."

Kyle sat down on the floor beside the bleeding Ginson, listening to the fungus heads pounding on the door and hoped the captain arrived soon.

11

July 6, Miami-Dade County Courthouse, Miami, FL –

Rita sat cross-legged on the floor and fed the last of the baby food in her bag to Tomas. During the entire fight, he had not cried. He stared at her and cooed, making smiley faces between spoonfuls.

"He's a good baby," Kyle said.

She looked over at him. He had bandaged the injured sergeant earlier and had sat talking to him until the sergeant had dozed off. Now, he seemed as restless as she was. "Yes, he is. He hardly ever cries. He's less afraid than I am."

"You seem to have your shit together pretty well."

She laughed. "Ha! On the outside, maybe. Inside, I'm scared to death."

"We'll be out of here soon."

"To where? To a FEMA camp, herded up like an illegal alien? I was on my way to my cousin's boat, a way out of Miami."

"I saw a lot of boats leaving two days ago. He may be gone already."

That had been the fear nagging at Rita's mind. That Elian would leave without her, was unthinkable, but without word from her or Ricardo, he might have assumed the worst. That was why she had flagged down the army convoy.

"No," she insisted with a conviction that somehow felt hollow, "he has to be there."

"It's too risky. You've seen what it's like downtown. The fungus heads are everywhere."

Fearing he might be right and wanting to hear no more, she began singing softly to Tomas until the detective walked away.

An hour later, the sounds of gunfire in the stairwell heralded the other soldiers' approach. Ginson awoke with a start, but then relaxed. Ten minutes after that, someone knocked on the door and yelled, "It's clear out here."

The big man with the even bigger machine gun, Walters, stood, opened the door, and grinned. "Anyone bring a pizza?"

The captain saw sergeant Ginson lying on the floor and walked over to him. He glanced at Rita and smiled at her. "How bad is it, Sergeant?" he asked.

Kyle helped Ginson to his feet. He was unsteady and pale from loss of blood, but he shook off Kyle's grip and stood on his own.

"I'll live, sir. I lost two men."

Isaacson frowned. "I lost eight men, Sergeant. It's been a bad day all around, but we recovered twenty-five people. We need to get you to the medics and the others to the FEMA facility ASAP."

Rita sighed. She had no choice but to allow them to take her to Marlins Park. She should have known that her quest to reach the marina had been a pipedream born of desperation. Elian would be gone. Ricardo was gone, perhaps dead. She was alone with her child in a city overrun with *demonios*.

They stepped over scores of dead bodies and bits of bodies strewn across the stairs. Most were zombies, but several were soldiers. The blood underfoot was sticky, grabbing at her shoes as if trying to keep her there. She fought down a wave of nausea from the intense smell and sense of foreboding and took the steps downward more quickly. The soldiers stationed outside the building had killed their share of the 'fungus heads' as Detective Bane called them. A ring of *demonio* zombies littered the terrace and the street beyond the vehicles, but the number of zombies was growing, as more poured into the area from downtown and along the river drawn by the sounds.

The captain quickly loaded the civilians into the trucks with armed soldiers accompanying each truck. Before she joined the other evacuees, Detective Bane came up to her and handed her a business card.

"It has my cell number. If you need anything, call me. I don't know if I can do anything, but sometimes it's just good to talk."

She smiled at him. "Thank you."

"Take care of little Tomas," he said.

"I will."

The detective looked embarrassed, but he smiled when she stood on her tiptoes and kissed him on the cheek.

"Stay safe," she said.

No one on the truck took notice of her. Each person was enveloped in their own private cocoon of fear. Their faces, slack-jawed and lifeless, made her wonder if her own features betrayed her fear. The policewoman they had rescued was on the verge of shock, her hands trembling and her eyes staring blindly into space. With the help of a helicopter firing into the midst of the zombies, the convoy broke through the mass of creatures as if they were barricades to be swept aside instead of once living humans. Many fell beneath the massive wheels of the five-ton trucks. Any of the creatures that attempted to board the trucks received a face full of bullets. Rita kept her grip on the pistol secreted beneath the blanket just in case.

As they crossed the bridge over the Miami River, she had a good view of the area around the marina where her cousin kept his boat. Her heart sank. It was just as well she had not gone there. Many buildings and boats were smoking piles of ash. The river was filled with the debris of a dying city and corpses floating to the ocean. She didn't know if Elian had escaped unharmed, but he and his boat were not there. She said a quick prayer that he was safe.

Riding back through her neighborhood, she saw just how badly it had fared. From street level, it had appeared undamaged except for a few buildings. Now, she realized how lucky she had been that the extensive fires had not swept through her block. Many of the creatures stood immobile on the roofs more dead than alive. According to Detective Bane, they were gestating, hollow vessels ready to spew out more of the fungus spores and infect more 'fungus heads.' His apt description of the creatures made them seem less menacing than *demonios*, but she suspected names meant very little. The fast ones were deadly and the immobile ones deadlier still.

Marlins Park loomed before them, a massive white stucco and glass structure. She had visited Marlins Park only once after it had first opened. She and Ricardo had sat beneath the new retractable roof with programs over their heads to keep dry from the leaks. She recalled the scandals that came with the stadium – rising costs, unpopular bonds to pay for it, the recall of a mayor and a county commissioner. The final cost, over 600 million dollars, would become two-and-a-half billion before it was repaid.

Marlins Park had been built to blend in with its Little Havana neighborhood. No fence separated it from the nearby homes. Now, however, a sturdy chain link fence surrounded the structure. They passed through a guarded double gate in the fence and parked on the west main entrance between the two giant pillars that held the retracted roof. The roof was now in place over the stadium. Guards escorted them inside. She didn't know if they were there for protection or to keep anyone from attempting to escape. She paid little attention to the art work or the stadium's beautiful architecture. Her eyes remained fixed on the neat rows of tents covering the field, and the high fence surrounding each one like a mini-prison.

"It looks like a prison," one man wearing a dirty shirt and jeans commented as if reading her thoughts.

Men in white suits with hoods asked them to undress, men in one area and women in another. Their manner was polite but businesslike. The guards with guns lent power to their request. They took her meager belongings and disposed of them. She stripped and allowed them to scrub her naked body, trying to cover her embarrassing nudity with her hands. They had allowed her to keep Tomas with her. He, too, received a scrubbing. His screams of outrage kept her silent ones in check. After drying off, they were all handed white coveralls, cloth shoes, and masks, and pointed to one of the tents. She donned the too-large coveralls, sans underwear, and joined the long line of evacuees. Before entering the fenced compound, each person's eyes and ears were examined. Her group of forty-five joined another dozen men, women, and children, most of who sat in silent dismay on cots as their children ran wild around the small open area surrounding the tent.

"Food will be served in a few hours," one man in uniform informed her as he slammed shut the gate. "Don't miss out," he added as he padlocked the gate.

She was hungry but too upset by the impersonal treatment she had just endured to think about food. They had stripped her of her few possessions, her clothing, and her dignity. Now they wanted to regiment her time like a prisoner. She lashed out at the man.

"I want food for my child. I want it now!"

He stared at her. Her verbal eruption had caught him by surprise. At first, she thought he might consider her a troublemaker and try to separate her from Tomas. *Let him try*, she thought. Instead, he nodded. "I'll see what I can do."

She was suddenly ashamed at her outburst, but a bit of her lost dignity returned. She surveyed her new home. A quick count revealed over twenty separate enclosures on the one-time baseball field. A few of the enclosures were empty, but almost a thousand people resided in the makeshift FEMA camp. She had overheard talk of half a dozen other camps throughout the outlying areas, but even if they each held a thousand people, it was a small pittance compared to the number of dead or the thousands of people still hiding in their homes afraid to venture out. Was her Ricardo among those dead?

The man she had accosted returned a short time later with a sealed bag containing jars of baby food, formula, disposable diapers, a few extra masks, and two pair of latex gloves.

"It's all I could find for now. I'll see that more supplies are brought for the children. You know – toys and stuff."

"Thank you," she said, wishing she could think of a word more encompassing for how he made her feel. Even a small act of kindness in a world gone mad seemed monumental. The soldier was simply performing a task he might have personally found repugnant the best way he could. She looked again at the languid parents and bored children around her. Many of the children, even some of the adults, were not wearing the masks they had been issued, a perfect scenario for a potential disaster. The children were not frightened, just confused and filled with excited energy. They needed a creative outlet.

Rita thought for a moment, removed one of the latex gloves and blew it up. She tied the end to keep the air inside, like a balloon.

"Children," she called loudly, "let's play a game."

At first only a few of the younger children came to her, but as she tossed the makeshift balloon in the air, more became curious and joined them. When she had a crowd surrounding her, she said, "We're going to play a ball game."

"We don't have a ball," one ten-year-old boy said.

"We have a balloon. We'll form two teams. Each team will have the same number of older kids and younger children to make it fair. The object of the game is to keep the balloon in the air, but without holding on to it. You must pass it back and forth, like in soccer, but with your hands. Remember if the balloon touches the ground before you reach the goal line, the other team gets the balloon at that point and gets to try for their goal line. Another rule is that everyone must wear their masks."

"Oh, they hurt my nose," the same boy said rubbing the bridge of his nose.

"No mask, no game."

He hesitated, and then said, "Aw, all right." He pulled his mask up over his nose and mouth. The others followed. "What do we use for goals?"

She looked around for something to serve as goals. "Each end of the tent."

She sat on the ground and watched the children play. They didn't need a referee. The team with the balloon tossed it back and forth while their opponents stood on the sidelines cheering for them to drop it. The game continued back and forth with neither team able to score a goal, but they didn't seem to mind. It was the running, the yelling, and the burning of energy that mattered. They were in an unfamiliar environment, unsure of what was happening around them, and the game was familiar, something to focus on. Watching the children at play took her mind from the conditions around them as well. Even some of the parents took an interest in the game, cheering the children on. After half an hour, the white-suited men and women arrived with carts of food – burgers, hot dogs, and chips for the children; baked chicken, rice and vegetables for the adults. The children received bottles of water and juice, the adults, coffee and water. Once again, each person was examined as he or she was handed food – their eyes, ears, and mouths.

The food was lackluster in taste but filling. At least it was more wholesome than what she had been eating for the past few days. After the meal, she encouraged the younger children to go around collecting empty food containers and place them in the trash bins behind the tent. They made a game of even this chore, seeing who could discard the most used containers. Though it was only early evening, after the rigors of the game, many of the children napped. This allowed her to speak with some of the parents around her.

"Does anyone know exactly what is going on?" she asked.

One gray-haired man cleared his throat before replying. He wore his coveralls like a suit, the zipper fastened all the way to the top. He toyed with the zipper as if straightening an imaginary tie.

"My name is Simon Benoit. Most everyone calls me Benoit. I'm a high school biology teacher. From what I've pieced together, a few days ago someone entered our country at Miami International who was infected with a heretofore unknown type of fungus. It is a species of the Cordyceps mushroom, the so-called 'zombie' fungus. The fungus drives people insane before consuming their organs and using their bodies to reproduce spores for more fungi. It is airborne and highly contagious, thus the masks." He reached up and touched his mask. "It has spread to other cities and is one-hundred-percent fatal."

One woman gasped at this. "We're all going to die!" she screamed.

Benoit turned to her. "No, madam, not all. Most of us are either somehow immune or not infected."

"Most of us?" another man asked.

"We are under observation. I have no doubts that if any of us began to exhibit signs of bizarre behavior, they will quickly remove us. You noticed the examinations of the eyes and ears?" A few heads nodded. "They're looking for signs of infection."

"What about the children?" the first woman asked.

"The same parameters apply to the children. They are either immune or not. They must keep their masks on at all times. We all must."

"Even when eating?" one man asked.

"That would be difficult, but replace it as soon as possible."

The mood of the crowd swung from desperation to despair. An undercurrent of gloom descended on them like a dark cloud, smothering all hope. Rita was certain the biology teacher's explanation had been meant to be informative, but he could have couched it in less pessimistic terms.

"Mr. Benoit," she said, "how long does it take for the first symptoms to appear?"

She was as concerned for her own condition as that of the others. Was she safe? Was Tomas safe?

"Apparently less than twenty-four hours. The first symptoms are irritability, coughing, and then sudden rage."

Relief flooded over her. It was possible that she and Tomas were safe. "I've seen men with no eyes."

A few people stared at her in disbelief, but Benoit nodded. "Yes. Eventually the fungus growth covers the eyes, ears, mouth, and, er, other orifices while it eats away at the brain. These blind creatures hunt by sense of smell, but mostly by hearing. By the later stages, they are nearly dead, mere flesh repositories for the maturing fungi. They instinctively seek out a high place and become immobile. The mature fungi burst from their bodies and spew spores that travel on the wind."

One woman bouncing a young child who refused to nap on her knee asked, "How long will they keep us here, if we're not infected I mean?"

Benoit looked at her. Sympathy flooded his features as he answered, "They won't let us leave until the Cordyceps Plague is over. As yet, there is no cure and no vaccine. Without our masks or a sealed environment, we will invariably become infected."

His statement silenced everyone. Like Rita, most thought their stay only temporary. At worst, she imagined they might be transferred somewhere free of the fungus threat. If, as Benoit had said, the plague was in many cities, where could they go? She glanced down at Tomas, sleeping in her lap. Would he be forced to wear a mask for the rest of his life? What kind of life could he lead as a perpetual prisoner? Her heart became so heavy that she had difficulty breathing. She imagined each breath she took teeming with millions of tiny spores, finding moisture and growing in her body.

She shook her head. *No! I will survive. So will my son. They will find a cure.*

Conversation died. Slowly, the adults drifted off to their assigned cots to join their children, either in sleep or in quiet talk. Rita wasn't sleepy. She strolled to the edge of the fence and stared out the sixty-feet-tall glass wall. The light of the setting sun reflected from the glass through a smoky haze, casting a red aura over the city outside. The quiet was peppered by sporadic gunfire, as infected people approached too close to the fenced perimeter of the stadium. One more convoy arrived delivering a handful of people to the refugee camp. She watched them as they lined up to enter one of the enclosures. Two people failed to pass the inspection. They struggled hopelessly as armed guards forced them out of the line. They disappeared into one of the openings beneath the outfield.

She wished she could look up at the stars in the night sky, but knew they couldn't open the roof. She and Ricardo had often sat in the bleachers in Riverside Park at night and studied the night sky. She found the multitude of colors of stars and their infinite numbers amazing, a gift from God. Staring at the stars had been peaceful; a reminder that man was just a speck in God's universe but chosen by him as special creatures worthy of his love. She dropped her gaze from the closed roof back to her surroundings. The pervasive smoke and haze would have blocked her view of the night sky anyway. She sat that way for several hours, afraid to go to her cot, knowing that when she did she would be committing herself and her child into the care of others. If it were she alone, she would try to escape, make her way far from Miami, but it wasn't. She was a mother with a child, and the world had suddenly become a very dangerous place.

12

July 6, MIA converted Gulfstream Hangar, Miami, FL –

After evacuating the Miami-Dade County Courthouse, Kyle, Ginson and his men left the convoy and returned directly to the airport. Rita had said her goodbyes to him before joining the other exhausted evacuees in the trucks. He hated to see her swept up with the others. She had saved his life and he was grateful, but in all reality, he could do nothing for her in return. She was safer at the FEMA camp than at the airport. The zombie attack the previous day had proven that. He had given her his card, but doubted that she would ever use it. He tried to erase her plight, multiplied by countless tens of thousands of other people in the same position, from his mind. He couldn't save them one at a time. Marli and her people had to find a cure. Nothing else would stop the spread of the Cordyceps Plague.

Ginson had lost two men at the courthouse, both raw recruits, and the loss had hit him harder than his own injury. He had brooded in silence during the entire return trip. Of his original squad from the night Kyle had first met him at the roadblock, only two remained. Kyle understood Ginson's dilemma. Kyle didn't know if any of his fellow SIS officers remained alive or if he was on his own. He had worked alone before while undercover, but this was different. Then, he knew that his squad had his back. Now, he had only Ginson. Ginson had shown his mettle numerous times, but he was still an unknown factor and Kyle hated unknowns.

Ginson roused from his lethargy long enough to say his goodbyes at the decontamination tent.

"We've got to resupply." He winced as he held out his hand for Kyle to shake. He glanced down at his bandaged wound, still seeping blood. "I guess I had better go see a medic about this. I have to see if I can pick up some replacements and give these new guys some additional training." He made a fist and slammed it against the dash of the Humvee. "Damn it! I can't keep losing men."

"It's inevitable," Kyle said. "It's dangerous work."

Ginson shook his head. "That's no excuse. When I was a corporal, I just followed orders. Now, as a sergeant, I have to lead. So far, I haven't been doing such a great job in the leadership department."

"Look, beating yourself up doesn't solve anything. It's a new situation, one that's not in the manuals. It's a slow learning curve. You just have to get through it as best you can. Train your men, but stop selling yourself short. They can sense your doubt."

Ginson looked up at him. "You seem cool and collected."

"Believe me, I'm not. Inside, I'm shitting bricks."

Ginson's short, sharp laugh forced a grin to his face. "You and me both, brother." He waved his hand at the driver. "I'll be back as soon as the doc fixes me up. Give your girlfriend my love." The Humvee took off before Kyle could respond. He watched the vehicle speed across the silent runway toward the terminal.

Once more, he subjected himself to the indignity of the decontamination procedure at the hangar. He was beginning to hate it. At least this time he had fresh clothes waiting for him. He donned another of the outfits Ginson had picked out for him, garish plaid shorts and a *Bahama Mama* t-shirt. His blood-soaked sports shoes had to be discarded with the rest of his clothes. The new ones were black and white checkered. He swore silently that Ginson chose his wardrobe to embarrass him. If he wanted anything nearer his own taste, he would have to find it himself.

The laboratory had taken shape during his absence. Most of the crates were unpacked and the remaining ones had been stored on a platform on top of the office structure. The extra space was now a sitting area with tables and chairs that appeared more comfortable than the folding metal ones they had been using. A vase with artificial flowers sat on one table. Real flowers would not have survived the decontamination procedure. Slowly, the hangar was becoming homier but not home.

Marli was in the office making notes at her laptop. She stopped working when he entered and jumped up to greet him with a hug.

"You're safe," she said.

Surprised but pleased by this unexpected show of emotion, he returned her hug. She felt good in his arms. "I said I'd be back."

"I'm glad." She glanced around and realized some of the others were staring at them. She pulled away. "What's it like out there?"

"It's bad. We killed a lot of fungus heads, but we rescued some people from the courthouse and picked up a few more along the way. Most are staying in their homes afraid to venture out. The convoy transported them to Marlins Park."

Marli's eyes went cold. "Marlins Park," she spat. "Sometimes I think the military are complete fools."

"Why?"

"They're keeping everyone together, using a useless visual scan for the infected. They're not enforcing the mask rule or using any sterile procedures other than scrubbing everyone down with a topical fungicide. The only thing they did to secure the stadium was to close the roof. It's no better at the other facilities. Fools!"

"Did you warn them?"

"Of course I did. They ignored me. They said it would require allocating too many valuable resources. They might as well have left them where they found them."

He worried for Rita and her child. "Doesn't FEMA know better?"

She sighed. "FEMA might, but they're spread too thin. Most of the FEMA facilities are under military authority. They run them like a prison."

Sensing her frustration, he changed the subject. "Any progress on a cure?"

She sighed and lifted her arms. "Maybe. Some tissue samples arrived earlier. We're studying them now, but this fungus is so unique, so virulent … It's going to be extremely difficult to control."

He had hoped for better news. "Is it impossible?"

She hesitated before answering. "It's too early to tell." Sensing that her answer was not the one he was hoping for, she quickly added, "We're hoping for a breakthrough. We're not the only ones working on the problem."

"You have Roger Curry's body. He's what you call 'Patient Zero' isn't he? Have you learned anything from him?"

"We now know that even the Primary stage of infection is contagious, though not as contagious as the last stage, the Tertiary stage, when the spores mature. They are the real problem, the immobile ones, spreading millions of spores into the air. The military needs to concentrate on them, not the crazies on the streets. People who don't look infected or even know they're infected can spread the plague. It will be impossible to quarantine entire cities. We don't have the facilities or the manpower." She lowered her voice so no one else could overhear. "I'm afraid the military might do something drastic."

He understood her fear. "Like nuking a city?"

She widened her eyes and nodded. "It's possible. They think that way."

"Would it work?"

She stared at him. "I don't know. They would have to sterilize the entire infection zone, millions of people, dozens of cities, but with the radiation, it could be as disastrous as the plague itself. It might be too late anyway."

"Then we can't let them, can we? We need a cure or a vaccine."

Her shoulders slumped. "We're trying."

"Tell me what to do."

She smiled. "You're used to reading reports, sifting through data. I could use another pair of eyes."

"I don't understand technical jargon."

"You're a detective. You understand patterns, follow threads and investigate leads. Use your skills for me. See if we've missed anything. All our projections have proven useless. The spread is chaotic. We're missing something. Maybe you can see a pattern we're missing."

He didn't see how he could spot something that a trained professional couldn't, but he had nothing better to do. "I'll try."

"Thank you. I'll find you a computer and a desk."

Kyle was familiar with paperwork. Catching crooks and getting shot at were just part of being a cop. After all the fun and games, there were the reports, hundreds of them. He didn't enjoy it, but it was part of the game, and he put as much effort into the desk work as the rest of the job. As he sat staring at the computer screen hour after hour, the graphs and charts seemed to swirl on the screen, different colors for each city, different lines for each series of incidents. Most of the numbers meant nothing to him, but he was searching for patterns, not specifics.

Marli and her group had already determined that they could place the infected into three groups – Primary, Secondary, and Tertiary. The Primary cases exhibited initial signs of infection within twenty-four hours. They became irritable and angry, but with no outward indications of infection. Most didn't know they were infected. Though not as infectious as Tertiary cases, they could still spread the infection. Roger Curry had passed through the airport as a Primary. He, like a significant number of people, had taken longer than the usual forty-eight hours to reach the Secondary stage. Kyle assumed that was why Marli had kept him on ice for so long, to be certain he was clear of infection. Secondary cases were those he had witnessed at the airport quarantine and on the streets, people driven insane by the fungus growing inside their bodies, their minds consumed by blind rage. Eventually they became what she had designated as Tertiary cases, immobile as Roger Curry had finally become. These people were ripe with mature fruiting bodies, seeking high places to spread their burden of spores. Even with the Tertiaries, times varied. Some remained Secondaries for days, slowly becoming covered by the fungi cilia, while others became immobile within seventy-two hours of initial infection. These time anomalies made quarantine difficult. Quarantine facilities such as Marlins Park were not sterile environments and still required people to wear masks. Any lapse of these protocols by individuals could result in more infection spreading. He didn't envy the military or FEMA their positions of authority.

The screen began to blur. He rubbed his eyes but they kept burning. He realized that he had been working for hours. His muscles ached and his mind was Jell-O.

"I need some rest," he said to himself.

He left his desk, picked a bunk at random, and collapsed on it. The sheets felt warm and inviting, and the pillow was a woman's soft thighs. His eyes had barely closed before he was asleep.

13

July 7, Marlins Park, Miami, FL –

Rita managed only a few hours sleep. The banks of portable lights dimmed for the night but were not extinguished. The perpetual near dusk bothered her, keeping her awake. From the sounds of heated conversations and quiet sobbing from the others, she wasn't the only one having trouble adjusting to their new environment. The children rose early, eager to play. To them, each day was a recess. At least their guards had brought toys. Children played ball, spun hula-hoops, played jacks, or had their face buried in video games. To all outward appearances, they were normal, healthy children.

Not so the adults. A shroud of despondency had descended over the camp. Arguments broke out even before breakfast was served. One fistfight erupted between two men, quickly broken up by those around them. It only highlighted the sense of helplessness most were feeling. Breakfast didn't help. The unseasoned scrambled eggs were cold, the toast soggy, and the hash browns both cold and overcooked. Rita took just a few bites before deciding that coffee would do.

Tomas slept peacefully on the blanket beside her cot. Rather than face the others, or become infected by their melancholy, she remained with Tomas. She tried reading a paperback romance novel delivered with the toys, but the words would not penetrate her awareness. Reading about unrequited love among the magnolias during the Civil War seemed to incongruous to present reality. Mostly, she considered her failures. She had failed in her attempt to leave Miami. Her husband was missing, perhaps dead. She had failed to protect her son. Now, they were at the mercy of the military in a FEMA camp with a thousand other refugees. If it had been a natural disaster – a flood or a hurricane – waters eventually receded and storms passed, but this plague continued to grow in strength. In the end, would she still have a home?

The hours of the day passed slowly. To take her mind from her problems, she joined the children in their games. The other parents seemed grateful for her help. She could see in their eyes that some had already given up hope. Many looked like images she had seen of war refugees in Third World countries, only this was a war with an invisible enemy who converted friends and family into rampaging creatures in an unstoppable army.

By lunchtime, her growing hunger overcame her reluctance to eat. The offering of roast beef or turkey on rye or white bread, Cole slaw, potato salad, and fruit reminded her of picnic outings with Ricardo when they had first married. The memories of such times were bittersweet. She ate with only half her mind on the food. Logic dictated that Ricardo was dead, but her heart told her otherwise. There was an empty place in her heart for him, but no dark gaping hole as she imagined she would feel if he were dead. Her faith and her love offered hope, though all around her was chaos. Watching her fellow detainees eat, she could see the lack of faith, the acceptance of their fate in their eyes. She resolved to avoid that trap.

After lunch, several of the people gathered in front of the tent. Talk about the plague dominated conversation. As before, Benoit was looked upon as an authority.

"How long will we be here?" one woman asked. She had decorated her white coveralls with flowers hand drawn with a children's blue crayon. Her disheveled hair was held in place using a plastic fork as a hairpin.

"I can't answer that," Benoit said.

Clearly, it was not the answer she wanted to hear.

"They can't keep us here forever," she cried. She attempted to regain her composure. She sat up straight and lowered the tenor of her voice. "My brother is on the city council."

"Tell him I need some cigarettes the next time he drops by for a visit," one blond-haired young man said. His wiseacre remark produced a sharp intake of breath from the woman, but Rita noticed several smiles and repressed chuckles in the crowd. He rolled his eyes at her. "Hey, I like to smoke. Maybe I'll vote for him next time, provided we ever have a government again."

Benoit decided to steer the conversation away from personals and back onto the plague. "I'm sure the CDC is working on this. They will find a cure. It's going to take time. We just have to stick together and not give up hope."

"I feel like a prisoner," the woman said. She held out the fabric of her coverall punched between two fingers. "Look at this. I can only do so much with crayons."

"*Haute couture* is the least of our problems," the blond answered. "We can't all ..."

Benoit held up his hand to stop him. "This petty bickering serves no purpose. Whatever we were in our former lives," he paused and looked pointedly around the group, "we are all in the same boat."

Rita snickered. All eyes turned to her.

"My father came to Florida during the Mariel Boatlift. He said much the same thing."

"A wise man," Benoit said. "Too many of us are looking at this situation as an inconvenience. It's much more than that. This plague could become a world changing event."

"How?" Rita asked.

"If cities fall, if too many people die, the country might be too weakened to recover. Some cities might even be abandoned."

"Surely not Miami," Rita said, alarmed at his statement.

"No, maybe not. We have a good climate and nearby farmland. The northern cities might become too decimated to supply with food and too difficult to heat in the winter. Their surviving populations might have to move south."

"That's all we need," the young blond said, "millions of illegal aliens." Benoit shot him a withering look.

"You're talking about forced relocation, aren't you?" Rita asked.

Benoit nodded. "It could happen. Granted, that's a worst case scenario, but thinking everything will return to normal in a few days or even weeks is delusional. We're in this for the long haul."

Conversation slowed to a standstill as everyone tried to come to terms with Benoit's pronouncement. There was a chance he was wrong. After all, he was only a high school science teacher, but to Rita, his words had the ring of prophecy. The world had changed and would never be the same again.

Tomas, as if he sensed the fear floating around the group, began to cry. Rita picked him up and checked his diaper. It needed changing. Perhaps his innocence was still intact after all. She knew hers wasn't. She left the others sitting and staring off into space and returned to the tent. She changed Tomas' diaper and fed him mashed apricots, his favorite. Afterwards, she sang him softly to sleep. Footsteps behind her startled her.

"It's just me," Benoit said as she turned around quickly. "Fine child," he said, looking at Tomas.

"He's precious. I wish he didn't have to wear a mask. Every time I feed him, I fear for his life."

"Same here. I'm almost afraid to eat." He patted his stomach and smiled. "Almost. Given time, they might seal the stadium or move us to better quarters. Then we could move around more freely."

"I think you frightened them," she said, referring to their fellow refugees.

"Yes. Sometimes I speak without thinking. I must watch that."

"You make sense."

He shrugged. "In ancient times, the bearer of bad tidings has often paid the price with his life. I should learn from their examples and remain quiet."

"Do you have family?"

His jaw tightened as he glanced away. She immediately regretted her question. "I did," he finally replied. "My wife became infected. The military carried her away. I don't know where she is, but I suspect she's dead."

"I'm sorry."

"All of us have lost loved ones. Many more of us will." He looked at her. "I sometimes wonder if this is a judgment from God."

"No, God would not do this."

"No? He's been pretty heavy handed in the past – Sodom and Gomorrah, the Tower of Babel, Noah's Flood, the destruction of Israel."

As they were talking, Rita noticed a commotion outside the tent. Dismissing it as simply the children engaged in some raucous game, she ignored it. She shook her head to refocus her thoughts. She could not allow Benoit's doubt to confuse her. "No. God did not cause this. He is watching over us. I have faith."

"I once did. Now, I'm not as certain." His voice became more strident. "Keep your faith. Hold on to it like you do your child. I'm an old man. Most of my life is behind me. You and your child will have a future."

A woman's shrill scream pierced the growing din. It was a cry of pain and anguish and of heartbreak.

"Stay here," Benoit cautioned. He strode to the edge of the tent to peek out and was almost knocked down by the blond young man rushing in. His ashen face matched his hair. His eyes darted around the tent as if he were seeking escape.

"It's here!" he screamed.

Benoit tried to grab him to question him further, but he broke free and raced out the opposite end of the tent. By this time, Rita was worried. Deep down she knew what was happening – infection. She picked up Tomas, wrapped him in his blanket, and secured it around her neck and shoulder like a sling carry. She joined Benoit by the opening.

It was one of the older children. The young boy stood in a circle of other alarmed children who, too frightened to run, stared dumbfounded at their stricken companion. The boy snarled as his eyes searched the crowd for a target. His chest heaved and his hands twitched uncontrollably. Rita spotted the boy's alarmed mother, the woman in the blue-flowered coveralls, racing toward him. The boy's eyes darted to his mother at the same time, but there was no sign of recognition in them. His target selected, he intercepted her. Uncomprehending of the danger, his mother opened her arms to him. He slammed into her, knocking her sprawling backwards to the ground. He sat atop her and began beating savagely at her face with both fists. Her futile efforts to block his enraged blows quickly grew weaker. Within a matter of seconds, she lay still. He continued to pummel her lifeless body. No one moved or offered to aid her. It was as if time had frozen, but for the boy, his mother, and Rita, observing them. Finally, the boy ceased his pounding and stood, his face and arms covered in his mother's blood, searching for his next victim.

"Run!" Rita shouted, but most ignored her. People continued to stand frozen in horror, unsure of what was happening.

Almost as if the boy's attack had been a catalyst, several more people in the compounds on the verge of changing erupted into a frenzy of activity, catching the guards by surprise. Then, as realization hit them, panic swept through the crowd like a disease itself. Those that screamed drew the infected toward them. The confusion masked the attacks. In the chaos, the guards were unable to fire. People swarmed in all directions, but most rushed toward the closed gates. The guards faced them through the wire but made no move to open it.

In the background above the screams, a siren began to wail, but to Rita it sounded distant, unimportant. The blood rushing to her ears was more deafening. Her chest pounded so hard that she was afraid she would wake up Tomas. She glanced down at her son, who was awake staring up at her, but he made no sound. She had nowhere to run, and the guards had taken her pistol. She knew that the guards were not going to let them out. If anything, she feared they might shoot them all.

"Come with me," Benoit said.

His voice sliced through the confusion in her mind. She focused on it until her heart calmed.

"We can't go to the gate," he said. "The infected will follow the crowd. The guards won't open the gate."

While she had been watching, he must have ripped apart one of the cots, for in his hand he held a piece of wood. She followed him out the rear of the tent to the row of trash bins. They found the young fair-haired man hunkering down behind them. He stared at them in terror.

"This is my spot," he yelled.

"Shut up," Rita said, "you'll bring them here."

His eyes scanned the area before leaning his back against one of the bins. "What do we do? The army," he said suddenly, "they'll come, right?"

"Don't count on it," Benoit answered. "They're here to prevent the disease from spreading."

As he began to understand Benoit's meaning, the blond's eyes rolled, and he shoved a hand in his mouth to bite back a scream.

Rita risked a peek around one of the bins. A man, his face a mask of rage, stood less than ten feet away. His eyes searched the area. A ring of blood circled his mouth, and more blood stained his coverall crimson. She pulled her head back and motioned her companions to silence. She eyed the ten-feet-tall chain link fence behind them. It had been constructed more as a means to separate people into smaller groups than as a serious barrier. It was sturdy, but there was no razor wire across the top as there was on the fence surrounding the stadium. Other than its height, it should present no real obstacle. A row of six portable toilets near the corner of the fence that faced the visitor's dugout along the first base line would provide cover. She was certain she could scramble up the fence. In the back of her mind, she wondered if the *demonios* could climb. She pointed to the fence. Benoit guessed her intention and nodded, but the blond shook his head.

"No. We have to stay here." His voice cracked as he spoke and his hands trembled. Rita sensed that he was on the verge of hysteria.

"We can't stay," she said, "it's too dangerous."

The fence began to rattle as people piled against it near the gate trying to escape. The noise startled the blond. Only Benoit's firm grip on his shoulder kept him from jumping up and running. The first shots came moments later. She didn't bother checking to see if the guards were killing only the attackers or firing indiscriminately into the enclosures. They had no choice but to attempt the fence.

"I'm going," she whispered.

She rose to her knees and peeked out again. The infected man had wandered away, but at least four others were inside the tent, trashing the beds and attacking the people who cowered there. She knew they couldn't wait any longer. She stood and sprinted for the portable toilets with Benoit keeping pace beside her. The blond boy remained where he was. She put him out of her mind. He had made his choice. She kicked off her cloth shoes and climbed the fence. Tomas kept slipping from side to side threatening to throw her off balance, but she clung to the wire with all her strength. Benoit, agile for his age, reached the top first and offered her his hand. He pulled her on top of the fence. Her heart stopped for a moment as one of the guards looked up at them, but to her relief, he waved them down.

Two of the infected inside noticed them at the same time as the blond belatedly decided to join them. The guard brought one creature down with a shot to the head, but the other was too quick. It grabbed the young man's legs as he climbed the fence and yanked him back down. He fell onto one of the toilets, knocking it over. Benoit started to go back down for him, but Rita stopped him.

"You can't help him."

Benoit threw his wooden cudgel at the zombie, but it bounced uselessly off its back. The guard finally killed the second creature, but the blond boy lay still. She didn't know if he was alive or dead, but there was nothing they could do for him. The guard urged them away from the fence, past the two aquariums filled with dead fish, and into the Diamond Club seats above home plate. From their vantage point, it looked as if a war had erupted on the field. All the enclosures were in turmoil. The guard stared down at the scene with tears in his eyes as he watched his fellow guards kill anyone trying to escape.

"I don't understand," he said, "they just all went crazy at once. Usually, they show some sign of turning – dilated pupils, nervous twitching, or something. It was like, like spontaneous combustion."

Benoit placed his hand on the stricken guard's shoulder. "What do we do now?"

He shook his head. "I don't know. I have to go back, keep them from killing everybody if I can. Get out of here. Use a service tunnel."

The soldier walked calmly back to the killing floor. Rita hoped he could stop the slaughter. Fear on both sides of the fence fed the frenzy. If order couldn't be restored, it might mean the end of quarantine centers.

Benoit pushed her toward the visitors' dugout. "Let's go."

The power, like in most of the city, was off throughout the stadium. Portable generators powered the light towers in the field and smaller strings of lights in the below ground corridors. They passed beneath the stands and through the visiting team's locker room, meeting no one. The screams of the dying and the sounds of gunfire continued behind them, growing fainter as they progressed deeper into the bowels of the stadium. Once, they heard the footsteps of more soldiers rushing toward the field and hid in a supply closet. They waited in the darkness until the soldiers passed. The service corridor was lined with boxes of supplies but empty of soldiers. They stopped long enough to fill a bag with MRE's, bottled water, flashlights, and batteries. Benoit spotted an exit sign above a door. He placed his ear against the door and listened before opening it a crack.

"It's clear," he whispered.

They emerged into a small parking area outside the building. Several jeeps, canvas-covered trucks, and two Humvees sat in the lot.

"Can you drive?" Benoit asked.

Rita didn't have time to answer. A Humvee came around the corner moving fast. As soon as the soldier behind the .50 caliber machine gun spotted them, be began firing. Bullets stitched holes in the side of the jeep and ripped through the canvas of a truck.

"They're shooting at us," Rita gasped.

"Back inside!" Benoit yelled.

They rushed back inside the stadium, but before Benoit could close the door, a bullet hit him in the shoulder, spinning him around. He fumbled with the door, but got it shut. Blood rolled down his arm and dripped onto the floor. The bullet had only grazed him. A direct hit would have shattered the bones in his shoulder. As it was, his right arm was now useless. Tomas, until now lying quietly in his sling, began to wail. Rita tried to quiet her baby while helping Benoit. She knew they didn't have much time before the soldiers entered. The trail of blood Benoit was leaving marked their path. She ushered Benoit into a linen room and sat him on a box. Grabbing a towel from a stack of linen on a shelf, she made a bandage and pressed it against the wound to staunch the bleeding. Benoit gritted his teeth against the pain as she tightened the bandage.

"There. That will help."

"At least I'm not leaving a trail of blood."

The sudden attack on them confused her. "Why did they shoot at us?"

He shook his head. "I don't know. Frightened maybe, or else they thought we were zombies."

"But we were ..."

She didn't finish her thought. Whatever the soldiers' reasons, attempting further contact would be useless. They couldn't escape, but they couldn't remain where they were. The soldiers would quickly find them. Returning to the enclosures was equally out of the question. Between the zombies and the soldiers, they wouldn't survive long.

"We need a place to hide," she said.

"We must go up."

"Up?" she questioned.

"They will search the lower levels first. We must stay ahead of them."

Rita looked at Benoit concerned about his condition. He was not a young man and he had lost a considerable amount of blood. His already pale skin was now ashen. She was afraid he might go into shock.

"Can you make it?"

He rose unsteadily to his feet. "I have no choice."

They could hear shouts and booted feet behind them. They located a stairwell and went up several levels before emerging on the Founders and Legends Suites concourse behind home plate. Choosing one of the suites at random, they slipped inside. Benoit immediately collapsed on one of the seats, while Rita edged closer to the glass to peer onto the field below.

Chaos reigned. Several of the fences were now lying on the ground. Bodies littered the field. In death, it was impossible to distinguish between the infected and the innocent. The body of the young blond-haired boy still lay atop the crushed portable toilet where he had fallen in his escape attempt. She realized that she didn't know his name. People in white hazmat suits and armed soldiers were everywhere. She watched in shock as one soldier shot two children as they climbed into the seats behind the Marlins dugout. A few moments later, in what she considered an act of karma, one of the infected attacked and killed the soldier. She felt a moment of guilt at his death, but it quickly passed as she stared at the corpses on the ground around him.

More soldiers poured inside through the main entrance, forcing everyone seeking to escape back onto the field and into the horde of rampaging zombies. A few detainees had picked up weapons from fallen soldiers and fought back, but it was a one-sided battle. Some managed to make it off the field and into the tunnels chased by zombies, but most, meekly accepting their fate, sat on the ground and waited for death. This submission saved them. Now able to distinguish between crazed infected zombies and the non-infected sitting on the ground, the soldiers concentrated their fire on the zombies. They spread out and encircled the field, working their way inward. Many soldiers and many civilians died, but slowly they began to make headway. Within half an hour, all the zombies on the field were dead, as were several hundred other people. She had no doubt that those who had escaped into the stadium would soon be captured or killed, making her and Benoit's position questionable.

When she turned away from the window, Benoit was already asleep. The run through the building had exhausted him. With no medication for his pain, sleep was the best thing for him. Searching the suite, Rita found water, soda, and beer in a small refrigerator. They were warm, but she drank a soda for the sugar content. Tomas whimpered a bit as she laid him on one of the seats and piled whatever she could find against the door. When she was finished, she admired her handiwork. Her makeshift barricade wouldn't keep out the soldiers, but it might prevent zombies from breaking in.

She had no baby food or bottle. She opened one of the MREs and laid out its contents – a beef ravioli dinner, a side of beans, a package of wheat bread, grape jelly, a fudge brownie, lemon-flavored drink mix, trail mix, matches, toilet paper, seasonings, and a flameless heater. She mixed the lemon powder with water and dipped the bread in it, allowing Tomas to suck the liquid from the bread. She read the instructions and added water to the flameless heater. It just warmed the beef ravioli, but it sufficed. She mashed the raviolis with the plastic spoon and fed it to Tomas, taking bites from it between his bites. When he was full, she finished the ravioli, the brownie, and the trail mix.

She stiffened in fear when she heard someone passing by outside, but whoever it was didn't stop. Throughout the afternoon, the soldiers removed the bodies from the field. They had herded the survivors, numbering less than six hundred, into the three remaining undamaged compounds. She searched the crowd for familiar faces but didn't see anyone she recognized. From the way they huddled in small groups, she knew they were expecting to be killed. When the soldiers completed the grisly task of removing the dead and brought food and water to the survivors, some semblance of normalcy returned to the camp.

By the time Benoit awoke, it was almost dusk. Several of the light stands were out, damaged in the melee, leaving large areas of the field in darkness. People huddled in the pitifully small pools of light cast by the remaining light stands. Benoit groaned in pain. She checked on him. He was responsive but groggy from loss of blood. She forced him to drink a soda while she prepared another of the MREs for him, this time chicken with noodles. It reminded her of the chicken noodle soup her father used to prepare for her when she was sick.

"How's your shoulder?" she asked.

He moved it experimentally and groaned again. "It's very stiff. Is there anything for pain in there?" He nodded toward the MREs.

She shook her head. "I'm afraid not. I think I saw a first-aid kit on the wall in one of the restaurants on the concourse. I wanted to wait until you were awake before going to check it out."

"Absolutely not. It's too dangerous."

She smiled at Benoit's adamancy, but his male-inspired chivalry didn't sway her. "I have no choice. You can't make it. You need something for pain and a decent bandage."

He nodded his agreement, but he was clearly upset with her decision and by his inability to go in her stead. She checked on Tomas before leaving, and then removed the barricade from the door as quietly as she could. The concourse beyond was dark. She was glad for the flashlight, but to remain as invisible as possible, she kept it off and used her hand on the wall to guide her. When she neared the spot where she remembered seeing the first aid kit, she switched on the flashlight and searched for the restaurant. Unfortunately, in the dark, all the food kiosks looked the same. In a moment of panic, she raced up and down the concourse trying to remember in which restaurant she had seen the kit. She was at the point of giving up when her light flashed across the first aid kit. She climbed over the counter and yanked the entire box from the wall. After tucking it under her arm, she switched off the flashlight. In her panic, she had relied on it too much, risking attracting soldiers or worse.

On the return trip, she stumbled over something in the floor. She fell and dropped the flashlight and the kit. The metal kit clanged as it hit the floor and bounced, echoing down the concourse. The darkness seemed to amplify the sound. She groped along the floor searching for the flashlight. Her hand fell upon it at the same time as her shoulder encountered something soft and yielding. When she picked up the flashlight, it was wet and sticky. She switched the flashlight back on. The beam outlined the ghostly face of a dead soldier. One side of his face was crushed, and one of his eyes dangled from the socket. She stifled a scream. As she recovered the first aid kit, she noticed the soldier's rifle beside him and picked it up, cursing when she found that it was empty of bullets. Then she noticed the dead soldier's cell phone protruding halfway out of his shirt pocket. She replaced the rifle and took the cell phone.

Finding the corpse fed the flames of a growing panic. She kept the flashlight on and hurried her steps. At a low snarl and the soft sound of footsteps running in the darkness behind her, she broke into a run. Soldiers wore boots. Only the detainees and zombies wore cloth shoes.

Back in the Legend's Suite, she paused only long enough to catch her breath, and then began rebuilding the barricade as Benoit watched on in silence. Finally, satisfied that the barricade would hold, she forced her racing heart to calm.

"What did you see?" Benoit asked.

She shook her head. "We need to expose your wound."

She realized immediately that lowering the top of his coverall would be a problem. He could barely move his injured arm as he tried to help her. The thin material stuck to the edges of the wound, causing him considerable pain as the fresh scab broke free. The bleeding had stopped, but began to bleed anew. The wound was deep, but the bullet had missed the bone. His eyes searched her face as she examined the wound.

"How bad is it?"

"You'll have a nice scar to show your students."

"Ha! I teach the tenth grade. They're not easily impressed."

"I'm going to clean it now," she warned.

She ignored his facial contortions and suppressed moans as she gently poured cold water into the wound and wiped away the blood, but when she poured a liberal amount of disinfectant onto the tender flesh, he pulled his arm away. She grabbed his arm and held it tightly.

"That was the worst of it," she promised him.

He bore her continued ministrations stoically, but he sucked in his breath when she pressed a wadded gauze pad against the open wound and taped it in place. He swallowed two pain killers without protest and lay back down, exhausted by the ordeal. Then she told him about the cell phone.

"Do I dare call anyone?" she asked.

"Is there any coverage?"

She checked the phone. "Two bars."

"Better than I expected with so many cell towers down. I don't know anyone who might help. Dial 911."

She did as he said and got only a recorded message. She shook her head.

"Figures. Any family you can call?"

His innocent question bit deeply into her heart as it evoked memories of Ricardo. "No."

Before he could comment, turmoil erupted on the field below. This time the trouble came not from inside the stadium, but from without. Soldiers ran to the entrances as gunfire and explosions outside ripped into the stillness of the night.

"It was the siren."

She looked at Benoit. "What about the siren."

"The noise of the siren and the gunfire attracted more of the zombies from all around the stadium."

A lump formed in Rita's throat. "Can they get in?"

"If they are determined enough. The creatures show no fear."

She glanced at Tomas, who had begun to cry as more explosions lit up the night outside the stadium. She held him in her arms as the sound of gunfire drew closer. One large explosion shattered the glass wall. Shards of glass fell into the stadium, followed by a mass of human figures pouring through the opening – zombies. The lights flickered and went dark, leaving the field pitch black except for the muzzle flashes of the soldiers' gun, which grew fewer and fewer as the screams of the dying rent the darkness. The stadium was quickly overrun. She and Benoit no longer had to fear the soldiers, but they were even more trapped than before.

She remembered the cell phone in her hand. Who could she call? Detective Bane. He had promised to help. She no longer had his card, but she remembered his number. It was only one digit different from the local pizza place whose number she knew so well. She held her breath as she punched in the number. The phone rang several times. She was losing faith that he would answer when a voice said, "Detective Bane here."

She was almost too choked up to speak. She cleared her throat and said, "Detective Bane, this is Rita. We need your help."

14

July 7, MIA, Miami, FL –

Kyle awoke dreaming of Marli. He awoke slowly, imagining her shaking him awake after a night of passionate lovemaking. When he saw that he was still fully clothed, his fantasy dream faded. He was still half asleep sitting on the edge of his cot trying to recall the dream when she walked into the tent.

"You should eat," she said.

"What time is it?" he asked, rubbing his eyes.

"Almost ten a.m. You worked throughout most of the night."

"I thought I was on to something." He shrugged. "It slipped away."

"Eating will help," she said.

He stumbled to his feet and followed her to the dining area. Breakfast was over for the others. They were already hard at work. He glanced at the cold leftovers on the table and dismissed them. Searching the refrigerator, he found a box of microwavable sausage and biscuits. He removed one and popped it in the microwave to cook while he poured a cup of coffee. The coffee was strong and felt warm going down, kick-starting his heart and slapping him awake. When the microwave chimed, he removed his food. The sausage and biscuit was hot, but all semblances to real food ended there. The sausage was a wafer-thin poker chip of tasteless meat, and the biscuit was chewy. Still, beggars couldn't be choosers. He downed it quickly. Marli joined him for coffee.

"What did you find?"

During the night as he slept, something had clicked inside his exhausted brain. The colored spaghetti lines of the graphs began to make sense as they danced through his dreams like a scene from a Disney cartoon. He noted hidden cycles in the pulsing lines, day-night cycles and peak activity cycles where they intersected. He remembered that like most fungi, the Cordyceps fungus preferred darkness for growth. This was when the infected were more active. He hadn't seen it at first because attacks had occurred at all times of the day and night. Then, it had hit him. The constant haze of smoke and the heavy gray clouds blocking the sun had created an artificial dusk over the city, allowing the creatures to remain active day and night. He also knew why they had seen so few of the Tertiary cases. Seeking darkness, the creatures would not all choose rooftops for their perches. Any high place – an upper level apartment, a parking garage, a skyscraper – sufficiently dark could become a location from which they poured forth their lethal load of spores to the air.

"We need infrared equipment," he said.

Marli looked at him questioningly.

"The fungus heads are more active at night. I didn't see it at first because the clouds are blocking the sun. When the sun comes back out, they'll go to ground. We'll need infrared gear to spot them. We have to comb the upper floors of buildings, not just rooftops."

"Are you certain? They've attacked during daylight hours."

He shrugged. "As certain as I can be. There's a pattern to their activity. The fungus is driving them. The anomalies match maximum smoke or cloud cover."

Her mouth made an open 'O'. "Yes, I see."

"The more infected ones are anyway. The others ... well, we need to deal with the Tertiaries first."

"I suppose you're right. Are you going to alert General Willows?"

He smiled. "I'll let Ginson. He could use the brownie points."

He thought of Ginson and realized he hadn't checked to see how the new sergeant was recovering from his injury. That would have to wait. He leaned back in his seat and crossed his arms over his head, satisfied that her faith in him had not been misplaced. It got them no closer to a cure, but it might help locate and eliminate the source. It would not be an easy job locating the Tertiaries. He hoped he could convince General Willows that the time and effort would be worth it. The only other option would render a lot of prime real estate uninhabitable for a very long time.

Ginson saved Kyle a trip. He showed up mid-afternoon with an ear-to-ear grin on his face.

"Why the wide smile?" Kyle asked.

"The general called me in his office to offer a well done for the mission to the courthouse."

"No Silver Star or promotion to colonel?"

"That comes later." He sat down opposite Kyle.

"How's the wound?"

Ginson rubbed his belly. "Six stitches and a penny-sized chunk of metal as a memento. Now I've got two belly buttons about four inches apart."

"That just makes you a freak, not a hero."

"You're just jealous." He glanced around. "I saw the doctor when I came in. You two doing the horizontal two-step yet?"

"You've got a sick, demented mind. I like that in a friend. No, we haven't advanced past the languid looks stage."

"You move too slowly. If you don't pick up the pace, I might cut in."

"Be my guest, but I warn you, she doesn't like men with twin belly buttons."

He waited on Ginson to broach the subject he had been dancing around with small talk. After a slight pause, Ginson said, "There's been trouble at the FEMA site at Marlins Park."

Kyle sat up in his seat. He had sent Rita and her child to Marlins Park. "What kind of trouble?"

"It seems there was a rash of spontaneous infections."

Ginson's news stunned him. His stomach tightened. "What?"

"Several people who showed no previous signs of infection turned violent at the same time. It was chaos. A lot of people died." Before Kyle could ask about Rita, Ginson continued, "It's under control now, but there's talk of scrapping the whole quarantine idea. If people can turn zombie with no notice, what good is quarantine?"

"Marli said it was a shambles over there. The army didn't quarantine anyone. They just stuck them all together to keep an eye on them, like prisoners of war. What a cluster-you-know-what."

If Kyle's disdain of the military bothered Ginson, he ignored it. "Look, I agree. I just thought I should give Doctor Henry a heads up on how things are going."

"Yeah, you're right. She should know about this."

She walked up as they were speaking.

"I should know about what?" she asked, looking back and forth at the two of them.

"Let's go to your office," Kyle suggested.

Inside with the door closed, he let Ginson explain. The news upset Marli more than he had expected. She ranted and paced her office looking as if she wanted to strike out at someone or something. Both he and Ginson remained safely out of harm's way. After a few minutes of venting her anger, she turned to them.

"I warned them. Without a proper quarantine procedure and constant observation, detention is useless."

"In all fairness, you can't watch thousands of people constantly," Ginson said.

Kyle waited on Marli's backlash, but she surprised him. She took her seat and stared at them.

"You're right, Sergeant. We've been so busy trying to develop a vaccine that we completely ignored a proper test for infection. If the report is correct and people suddenly became Primaries with no visible precursor signs, quarantining everyone won't work." She nodded her head as if confirming her decision. "They must feed off each other's rage, remaining on the edge of sanity until one small spark sets them off. I'll get some of my people working on a test right away. This couldn't have come at a worse time. We're so close to a vaccine."

Before she could elaborate further, she abruptly left the two of them in her office.

Ginson looked at Kyle. "That went better than I expected. You need to marry that woman."

Kyle ignored him. His mind was busy focusing on the possibility of vaccine.

While Marli busied herself with her staff, Kyle explained his discovery about the nocturnal preference of the fungus heads to Ginson. Ginson thought it excellent news and left to report it to the general, while Kyle considered his options. He had promised Rita that he would help her, but he didn't even know if she was in danger. *Or still alive*, he thought bitterly. He didn't have the authority to remove her from quarantine. Maybe Marli did. He would ask her when she came up for air. She had submerged herself in the depths of her work, almost becoming a blur as she raced from tent to tent keeping abreast of the results of testing of the vaccine on animals. Kyle could offer no assistance and knew he would only be in the way. He sat on the sidelines and watched, preparing fresh coffee when someone emerged from a lab for a refill. Like cops, technicians and epidemiologists ran on coffee.

Ginson returned a few hours later carrying two pairs of night vision gear. He handed a pair of goggles to Kyle.

"What's this for?" he asked as he examined the goggles.

"This is the PNVG-PVS 7 night vision goggle," Ginson recited as if he were reciting the training manual to a raw recruit. "The PVS 7 has a single ocular lens and can be used as a hand-held unit, worn strapped around the head, or mounted to the helmet."

"I don't have a helmet," Kyle said.

Ginson glared at him. "Don't interrupt when I'm in training mode. Now, we can't wear these with full respirators, so we'll have to wear masks."

"We? What's this 'We' shit?"

"It's your theory, so it's only fitting that you get to test it. The general and I agreed that you would be pleased to accompany my team for a little night excursion."

"Thanks for volunteering me. I'll try to repay the favor someday."

A loud yell from the lab caught both of them by surprise. Kyle expected the worst when Marli emerged from the tent, but she was smiling broadly. Applause and more cheers erupted behind her.

Kyle's hopes rose a notch. "What's all the celebration?" he asked.

Marli did a graceful pirouette as she danced across the hangar floor toward him. Her face was all smiles. "Gentlemen, we might have a vaccine. Mind you, it's too early to tell. We'll need to test it thoroughly, but it looks extremely promising."

"That's great news," he said. It was, in fact, the best news he had heard in a long while.

"Yes it is, but don't get too optimistic. Doctor Ozay said its effects might be limited to fifty or sixty percent of the population."

Kyle's hopes diminished slightly, but he refused to be dismayed. He wouldn't up the ante in a poker game for fifty-fifty odds, but against a killer fungus it was better than no odds at all. "That's a start."

"This calls for a celebration," she said. "We deserve to drink a toast. I have a bottle of *Glenlivet* twelve-year-old scotch in my office. Would you two gentlemen care for a glass?"

Ginson perked up at her offer. "Single malt?"

"Yes."

"You're on," he said.

When she closed the door of her office behind them, she noticed Kyle's look of curiosity.

"I don't want everyone to know I have scotch," she explained.

"Wise move," Kyle said.

She produced three glasses from a shelf, took the scotch from a drawer, and poured three fingers in each glass. "Would either of you gentlemen like ice?"

Kyle shook his head and reached for the glass. "No. I like my scotch neat." He took a tentative sip and smiled. "Very smooth." He took a larger sip and let the scotch burn its way down his throat until it warmed his stomach.

"Ah! This is good stuff," Ginson commented. "I haven't had good scotch in a while."

Marli sipped hers slowly. "I prefer vodka, but I'll drink scotch if I have to."

"Vodka and rum is for belting down and for parties. Scotch is for sipping and conversation."

"Well then, what should we talk about?"

"You," Kyle suggested. Marli was in a good mood. He thought it might be the perfect time to learn more about her.

She frowned. "Me? I'm not very exciting."

"Don't kid yourself. You're smart, you're pretty, and you've got guts. That's a start."

Her face flushed. "Not so smart. I can't find a cure."

"You found a vaccine. That's a start. I have confidence in you."

She stared at the top of her desk as she swirled the scotch in her glass. Her desk was untidy and disorganized for someone whose job required structure and organization. It was littered with file folders and stacks of paper. It reminded Kyle of his own desk, outwardly messy, but he could quickly lay his hands on anything he needed. He had his own system of filing that often clashed with proper police procedure.

"You just don't realize how difficult this is going to be," she said. "Killing the fungus isn't the problem. We can sterilize surfaces, filter the air, but once it begins to grow in a human host ..." She shook her head. "We've tried Azoles, Polyenes, Allylamines, Echinocandens ... Hell!" She slammed her glass down on the desktop, sloshing some of the liquor onto the wooden surface. She quickly wiped it off with the edge of her hand. "We've even tried oregano, garlic, citronella oil, and Neem Seed oil – anything strong enough to kill this Cordyceps species damages the host."

"But you can create a fungicide that will kill the fungus."

"Yes, but as I said, it kills the host."

He didn't broach the subject with her and doubted she would agree with him, but it could become necessary to fumigate the entire city, regardless of the consequences. It certainly would be less destructive to property and with less environmental risks than a nuclear bomb. One thing he had learned while undercover with drug lords. Sometimes you just had to cut your losses and move on.

"How effective is the vaccine?"

"That's unknown. We worked with a derivative of *Ciclopirox*, a respiratory antifungal. Since the fungus attacks the lungs first, it might prove effective, but the amount needed for a large population would be enormous. It would tax all pharmaceutical production facilities. No one is ready to call the shot on that one until all of our tests are completed."

"How long?"

She hesitated. "A full-scale test would take weeks, maybe months."

Kyle shook his head. "It might be too late by then."

Marli stared at her glass, and then downed its remaining contents. Kyle lifted his glass to his lips and emptied it as well. Marli yawned.

"When was the last time you slept?" he asked her.

"I'm not sure. I sometimes nap at my desk."

"I'm a cop with a small brain. I can survive on no sleep. Ginson here is a soldier. They never sleep. Your brain is bigger. You need sleep."

She smiled at him. "Our brains are relatively the same size."

"Yours has more folds or whatever. Mine's as smooth as a baby's butt."

She pointed her empty glass at him. "You would make a poor biologist."

"Some say I make a poor cop, but I try."

Their eyes locked for a moment. Kyle considered himself a good judge of people, but he couldn't read her. At times, she exhibited all the signs of being attracted to him. He liked that. At other times, she seemed repelled by him. That, he didn't like. He thought he knew the problem. Her job was saving people, while his sometimes entailed killing people, bad people but people nonetheless. It was the dichotomy of police work – protecting some people sometimes meant killing others. Soon, her job would reach that point. Maybe that was what he was reading in her eyes – fear of the future.

They broke eye contact at the sound of his cell phone ringing. He hadn't used it in a week, wasn't even aware it was still charged. The sudden sound startled him. Figuring it was his superior, Chief Gilbert, he took it out of his pocket and stared at the screen but did not recognize the number. "Who the hell?" he directed at no one in particular. He placed it near his mouth. "Detective Bane here," he said.

The voice on the other end was tense and frightened. "Detective, this is Rita. We need your help."

15

July 7, Little Havana, Miami, FL –

With Ginson's chilling account of the trouble at Marlin's Park fresh on his mind, Kyle felt an air of urgency as he listened to Rita's description of the outbreak and the army's deadly response. *At least she's still alive.*

"Tomas and I are trapped in one of the Legend's Suites. There are more of those creatures outside. Benoit is injured. A soldier shot him. He needs medical attention."

Shot! Who was Benoit? "I'll be there as soon as I can. Don't leave for any reason."

Her "I'm not going anywhere", produced a chuckle from someone in the background. He assumed it was Benoit.

The signal died. He tried redial but got nothing. He cursed and turned to Ginson.

"I heard," Ginson said, "I'll round up my men."

To Marli he asked, "Do you have any vaccine available?"

She crossed her arms over her chest. "But it hasn't been tested," she said as she slowly shook her head.

Marli was disturbed by what Kyle was suggesting, but he had no choice. The vaccine had to be tested sometime. "We'll be your guinea pigs. I hate that damn mask anyway."

"If it doesn't work …" Her voice trailed off.

"Yeah, I know. No night out on the town for us."

She surprised him by smiling. "Detective Bane, are you asking me for a date?"

"It's Kyle, and yes, if I manage to prove that your vaccine works, I'd like to go out with you."

Ginson finished his scotch and slammed the tumbler down on the desk. "It's about time. I thought I was going to have to play match maker."

Kyle turned on him. "Don't sit there. Go get your men. We can start killing zombies in Marlins Park."

Ginson left the room, leaving Kyle and Marli alone. Kyle thought it might be a good time to lay his cards on the table.

"Look, I know I sometimes come off as cold and hard, but that's my job. I deal with some real bastards, the lowest spectrum of humanity. You're something different for me and I'm not sure how to deal with it. I'm very attracted to you." He took a deep breath and blurted, "Hell! You're smart and hot. I wouldn't mind the chance to get to know you better."

Marli walked from behind her desk. "I would like that, Kyle."

Their lips met like two thunder clouds exchanging charges. Lightning flashed between them. The hair on the back of Kyle's neck stood at attention, as did another part of his anatomy. He broke away just long enough to whisper, "If it wasn't for this emergency ..."

She drew him back. As their kiss deepened, his hands explored her body. She responded to his probing touch. He released her with great reluctance when she slowly pushed him away.

"You have to go."

He nodded. "You're right. Rita needs me."

"Who is this Rita? Is she pretty?"

"She's just a woman with a child that I promised to help."

"Then keep your word. I'll be here when you get back. I'll go get what vaccine we have available. I hope it works." When she removed her hand from his chest, it felt as if he was losing a part of his body.

"You and me both," he said as she disappeared through the door.

* * *

The overburdened sky had finally reached its breaking point. Rain, not a sudden summer shower, but a heavy monsoon downpour began falling as they loaded into the Humvee. The rain brought with it bits of ash and dust, staining their clothes. Kyle rubbed his arm where Marli had administered the vaccine with the admonition that it might take time to strengthen his body's defenses. He didn't have time to wait. It felt good to be shed of the mask and the respirator, but playing guinea pig had its risks. He just hoped he lived to enjoy the benefits.

Ginson took only six of his men. "If eight men aren't enough for the job," he said, "we've stepped in some deep shit." Kyle would have felt better with the entire army at his back, but Walters had his trusty M-249 SAW. He also sported brand new E-4 corporal's chevrons on his sleeve.

"I see you finally got a promotion," Kyle said.

"Yeah, I'm a real brown-noser. I keep my face so far up sarge's butt that when he farts, I know what he had for lunch."

"Don't believe him," Ginson said. "I practically had to order him to take the promotion."

Walters shrugged. "I'm not good at taking orders. Hell, I'm barely housebroken."

Walters deserved the promotion. He was a good man and very good with the SAW. Kyle rolled up the sleeves on his uniform. He would have preferred his civilian clothes, but he didn't want anyone to mistake him for a fungus head and put a bullet in his brain. For armament, he carried both his Glock and his Beneli shotgun. He also had a heavy metal flashlight and his knife stuck through his belt. He refused a helmet, but the night vision goggles rested firmly atop his head. Judging by the dark night, he would have the opportunity to use them. The moonless night brought out the fungus heads by the droves. The rain didn't seem to bother them. The Humvee plowed them down if they got in the way. Otherwise, the soldiers ignored them. They had no time for pot shots.

When they neared the stadium, it was apparent that something was terribly amiss. Only a few lights flickered in the otherwise dark building. Entire sections of outer perimeter fence were down. Through the darkness, figures moved – too numerous to count. The main entrance was surrounded by a dark mass of zombies and more poured through the enormous opening where the window wall had stood.

Ginson motioned the driver to stop the vehicle, and then let out a soft whistle. "It looks like all hell has broken loose."

While they were taking in the horrific scene, a large shard of glass fell from the top of the window wall frame, slicing a zombie neatly in half. The upper portion of the torso still managed to crawl across the threshold before dying. Shots rang out from inside the building.

"We can't fight our way through this. Head around back," Ginson told the driver.

They skirted the crowd. A few noticed them and gave chase but couldn't catch the Humvee. They did not fire at the creatures for fear of attracting more. When they reached the eastern side of the stadium, only a few zombies prowled the outside entrance. Walters cut them down with the SAW. The heavy slugs passed completely through their bodies and tore a neat row of holes in the side of the building and the door.

"Take it easy with that thing," Ginson warned, "we don't want to kill any good guys inside." He turned to the others in the vehicle, most of them looking like nervous boys before the prom. "Have a clear target before you shoot, and don't forget, not all civilians are zombies."

They left the Humvee's headlights on pointed at the door. One of the recruits threw open the door while Walters covered him with his SAW. Beyond the small pool of light cast by the Humvee, the corridor was dark and eerily silent.

"Switch on your IR," Ginson ordered after they had passed beyond range of the headlights.

Kyle had difficulty with his depth perception as he scanned the corridor through the goggles. Everything was flat and two dimensional. He reached out his hand to the wall and missed it by two inches. Everything around him had a ghostly greenish hue, as if bathed by the light of an Aurora Borealis. Ginson had no problem. He produced a map from his pocket and stared at it through his goggles. After a few moments, he pointed down the corridor.

"This way."

Walters took the point. Crates of supplies lined the walls of the corridor, blocking some of the doors. As Walters passed one open doorway, he stopped and took a deep whiff of air with his massive nose. He stuck his head inside the door for only a few seconds; then, standing against the outside wall, motioned the others up to his position. The slightly metallic smell of blood tickled Kyle's nostrils. His grip on the Beneli tightened as he peered into the room. Inside what proved to be a small break room, three bodies, a female in white coveralls and two soldiers, lay sprawled on the floor. The woman's body was riddled with bullet holes. The soldiers had been savagely beaten to death. A pool of sticky, but not yet dried blood covered the floor around them. Several sets of footprints led from the room, disappearing into the darkness down the corridor.

"Stay alert," Ginson whispered.

Kyle pumped his shotgun to load a shell into the chamber, wincing at the sudden loud click. Walters sent a frown his way. The corridor was eerily quiet, but that didn't mean there were no fungus heads prowling around. The bodies in the break room proved that thought. The bloody footprints continued down the corridor and beyond a series of rooms. Ginson referenced his map.

"The field is this way," he said.

They ignored the footprints, which led away from the field, and continued to the FEMA enclosures. Ginson, eager to come to the aid of his comrades fighting off the zombie horde, kept the pace quick. His haste almost cost him his own life. Appearing almost magically in their midst from a small broom closet, a white-clad zombie lunged at him too quickly to avoid. The zombie's weight and large size carried the smaller Ginson to the ground. The enraged creature landed a couple of blows to Ginson's already injured side before Walters managed to kick the creature in the head with his size-thirteen boots, rolling it off Ginson's chest. It recovered quickly and focused its attention on Walters. Unable to bring his weapon to bear in the crowded corridor, he met the creature head on, enclosing its body in a bear hug with his massive arms. Like two sumo wrestlers trying to throw each other from the ring, they circled the floor. The creature pounded on Walters' back with its fists, but Walters ignored the pain and concentrated on keeping the gnashing teeth away from his neck.

As Kyle helped Ginson from the floor, he noticed a damp spot on Ginson's side, blood seeping through his uniform where the stitches had ripped loose. Ginson leaned against the wall to catch his breath. Kyle drew his knife to go to Walters' aid; however, the pair was spinning so rapidly he was afraid of injuring Walters by mistake. A snap loud enough to make Kyle wince came from the zombie's chest, as Walters broke several of the creature's ribs with his bear hug. The injury would have been sufficient to incapacitate a normal human being, but the zombie ignored the pain and continued raining blows to Walters' back. Walters noticed Kyle holding his knife in his hand and backed the zombie toward him. At the last moment, he released his grip on the creature and shoved it backwards. Kyle drove the blade through the creature's back and upward toward its heart. His first thrust missed its mark. He spun the creature around by its shoulder and jammed the knife through the bottom of its chin into the brain. Death did not come instantly, but the creature's moves became less frenzied as blood from a severed artery filled its skull. It emitted one last snarl, stumbled backwards and slid down the wall. Only then did Kyle turn his attention to Ginson.

Ginson waved him off. "I'll live," he said.

As they exited onto the field level, the din of fighting grew louder. The sound of a thousand snarling creatures filled the structure. A damp breeze blew in through the destroyed window wall, but the scent of death and cordite still lingered, cloying in its intensity. Kyle quickly counted less than a dozen weapons still firing. The field was almost in total darkness. Without the night vision goggles, he would have been totally blind. Through the shambles of shattered fences and demolished tents, he saw the flashes of gun muzzles and bright spears of flashlights pinpointed the remaining soldiers gathered in a small group in the visitor dugout. The pile of zombie corpses in front of the dugout spoke of their resolve, but the zombies, fearless and enraged, used the stack of bodies as springboards to leap into the dugout. Time was running out for the soldiers.

Of the nearly one thousand evacuees housed in the facility, less than fifty remained alive. They had taken refuge inside the visitor's bullpen. Sections of chain link fence placed over the top of the bullpen kept zombies from leaping into the bullpen from the stands, but the makeshift fence barricade was near the collapsing point under the combined weight of dozens of zombies atop it.

Ginson faced a dilemma. He had two choices – they could concentrate on freeing the survivors or go to the aid of the soldiers. They didn't have time to do both, and splitting the small group would place all of them in danger. Kyle could read the hesitation in Ginson's eyes, even through the Infrared goggles. Walters sized up the situation succinctly.

"What do we do, Sarge? Civilians or soldiers?"

The sound of gunfire was growing weaker. Ginson, to his credit, did not allow the enormity of the situation to slow him. "The civilians."

No one questioned him. They all knew how much the decision to abandon his fellow soldiers must have cost him. It was like battlefield triage – harsh but necessary. They withheld their fire until they had reached the *Clevelander* next to the bullpen. Zombies prowled the poolside restaurant like confused waiters. One tried to leap the pool and fell short, rising from the water sputtering and confused. The bodies of two fallen soldiers floated in the pool, testimony to the dedication involved in trying to save the civilians now herded into the bullpen.

Ginson concentrated their fire on the creatures above the survivors in the stands and clambering over the fence. The frightened civilians saw the muzzle flashes and heard the shots but couldn't see who was firing. After they had cleared a space around the bullpen, the rescuers entered the bullpen and began pushing the startled survivors toward the rear entrance. The survivors were understandably reluctant to leave the relative safety of their enclosure.

Ginson didn't give them time to argue. He kicked open the door with his foot and yelled, "Into the stadium." He grabbed the woman nearest him and shoved her bodily through the door. "Now!" he screamed at the others.

Either the timber of his voice or the frenzied sounds of zombies tearing at the fence broke the survivors' reluctance. They fought each other to escape the confines of the bullpen. The soldiers followed last, killing as many zombies as they could before evacuating the bullpen. As Kyle raced for the door, he glanced up toward the Legends Suites above home plate. A light blinked several times from one of the suites. He stopped long enough to check his cell phone but got no signal. *At least Rita's still alive,* he thought. He reached the door just as a section of fence collapsed into the bullpen, showering it with zombies. Walters slammed the door behind him, and then fired a burst through the door as it shuddered inward under the weight of pursuing zombies.

Ginson and half the men led the group of survivors down the corridor, while Walters, Kyle, and the rest of them piled anything they could find against the door to barricade it against pursuing zombies.

"It won't hold long," Walters warned. He produced a Claymore mine from a bag strapped to his belt and smiled. "Maybe this will even the odds." He quickly wired it to a fire extinguisher attached to the wall and strung a tripwire across the corridor about waist high, being very careful as he attached the wire to the pin of the Claymore. "There! That ought to slow them down. I wish I could see the look on their zombie faces when this baby blows."

The three-and-a half-pound device contained seven-hundred, one-eighth-inch steel balls, shooting them out in a sixty-degree arc at a muzzle velocity of almost four-thousand feet per second when detonated. Kyle had no doubt the device would play havoc with the leading edge of the zombies, but their immunity from pain and single-minded pursuit of anything living would hardly deter the others. "If we don't move, you'll get that chance," he said.

They caught up with the others waiting for them down the corridor.

"We have two choices," Ginson said. "We can go up and around back to the vehicles, or we can stay on the first level and fight our way through."

"Cutting across the field is a definite no," Walters chimed in.

"Rita is upstairs in the Legends Suites," Kyle reminded Ginson.

"Upstairs it is then, but we have to get these people out of here first. I saw two trucks out back. We'll use those." A look of sympathy crossed Ginson's face. "Look. If she's locked in, she should be safe for a short while longer. We'll get her out. I promise."

Kyle was eager to rescue Rita and fulfill his promise to her, but he couldn't dispute Ginson's logic. He glanced at the people gathered around them: children, some babes in arms; men and women of all ages. The only thing they had in common other than their white coveralls, some blood spattered, was the look of utter devastation on their frightened faces. In one short day, they had survived a zombie outbreak from within their midst and a near massacre by zombies from outside the stadium. Now they were in more danger. Most had been pushed to the brink of exhaustion, stumbling along blindly in the dark like automatons, propelled by fear. In the darkness, they couldn't see their surroundings, placing their trust in the soldiers helping them, even though soldiers had killed as many of them as the zombies.

Reluctantly, Kyle agreed. The survivors' safety had to come first. "Okay, but as soon as they're loaded and out of here, I'm going back for Rita."

"I'll come with you."

Through his Infrared lenses, Kyle could see his surroundings well enough to manage, but the civilians were blind. They huddled together with their arms extended, feeling their way along the wall.

"Why not use the flashlights so they can see where they're going?" he asked.

"Yes, please," a woman cried out. "I can't see." Several others agreed.

"No," Ginson said firmly, cutting off their protests. "Flashlights won't give us enough light to see trouble coming. The goggles will."

Kyle wasn't sure the advantage was worth it, but it was Ginson's show, not his. They moved up the frozen escalator as quietly as possible, but the scuffing of eight pairs of boots and the soft tread of fifty pairs of cloth shoes stumbling along in the dark echoed loudly in the enclosed space, announcing their presence to anyone ahead of them. Kyle grabbed one man's arm to keep him from falling headlong down the escalator as the man tripped over someone's leg. Behind them, the sounds of the bullpen door being forced urged them to increase their near frantic pace. Seconds later, the Claymore exploded, rattling the pipes overhead and shaking the building's walls. Several windows shattered. One of the women screamed in panic and bolted ahead of the group. She couldn't see where she was going, but her fear drove her blindly onward. One of Ginson's men switched on a flashlight. The sudden flare of light overwhelmed Kyle's night vision goggles, momentarily blinding him.

"Turn that damn thing off," Ginson growled.

"But the woman," the soldier protested.

"Leave her. I won't lose any more men for stragglers."

Kyle stared at Ginson, but Ginson turned away and kept walking. Was the loss of so many men affecting his decisions? *No*, Kyle thought. *Ginson is a better man than that.* Sometimes it was necessary to save as many lives as possible. Pursuing one woman could cost all their lives.

The soldiers redoubled their efforts and herded the survivors along like cattle, trying to keep them moving forward. A blast of hot air swept up the escalator bringing with it the scent of cordite and scorched flesh. The shotgun spray of tiny pellets would have killed the first wave of zombies, but would not slow the remainder.

Kyle caught a blur of movement ahead of them. At first, he thought it was the woman returning, but the solitary figure quickly morphed into several. Zombies! He tensed and raised the shotgun. He relaxed as a small spot of light played along the floor and wall, a penlight. The shadowy mass morphed into a group of five soldiers. One of the survivors saw the light and yelled. The soldier aimed his rifle down the corridor and played the light over the group of survivors. The intense beam blinded Kyle for the second time. He ripped off his goggles.

"Don't shoot," Kyle shouted as he rubbed his watering eyes. "We're not zombies."

The soldier relaxed. "Who the hell are you?"

"Sergeant Todd Ginson, Charlie Company. We have a group of survivors with us."

The soldier reached behind him and pulled a frightened woman forward by her arm. "Is this one of your stragglers?"

A sense of relief swept over Kyle as he saw that it was the lost woman.

"It's good to see you guys. We were trying to reach the field," the soldier explained. "I must have taken a wrong turn. We've been wandering these corridors for half an hour. I heard an explosion. Is it over?"

"Yeah, it's over, soldier," Ginson said. "There's no need to continue. These people are all that's left, except maybe for a few more stragglers like you. We need to get these people out of here."

The soldier looked stricken. "They're gone? All of them?"

"All of them. Now, snap out of it and turn off that damn flashlight. Do you know the way to the east parking lot?"

"We're lost, Sergeant. I don't even know where I am."

"Okay, we'll find it together. Get in the middle. We'll lead the way with the IR gear."

In the dark, the corridor seemed endless. It would be easy to miss a doorway or an exit or bypass a side corridor. The delay with the second group of soldiers had cost them their advantage. As the noise of pursuit behind them grew louder, panic increased proportionately. They would never make the exit before the zombies caught up. Ginson halted them.

"I need volunteers."

Walters stepped forward with a grin. "I'm up for it."

"Maybe you'd better ask what you're volunteering for."

"Hell, if it's killing zombies, I'm in."

Ginson ignored Walters' bravado. "I need four men to provide cover for the rest of us. We'll never make it with those things on our ass."

"I'm your huckleberry," Walters insisted.

The *Tombstone* movie reference brought a smile to Ginson's otherwise stolid face. No one else seemed eager to volunteer.

"I'll stay."

Kyle looked around to see who was speaking, only to realize that it was him. He took a deep breath. "I'll stay with Walters, but I want a flashlight." He removed his goggles and handed them to another soldier. "To hell with these things."

Ginson stared at him a moment before nodding. Two others spoke up, one of Ginson's men and the soldier from the second group.

"Okay, pass your IR gear to someone else." Ginson handed Kyle a flashlight. "We'll wait for you at the exit."

"Don't wait for us. Get these people to the airport. Leave us the Humvee. We'll be along later, after I find Rita."

Ginson held out his hand. "Good luck, Bane."

Kyle took Ginson's hand and pumped it several times, hoping it wouldn't be the last time he would see Ginson.

The pursuing zombies caught up with them only a few minutes after Ginson's group had departed. This time, four flashlights illuminated the corridor before them. Kyle felt better at being able to see his opponent without the hindrance of a ghostly green glow. The four of them took up positions on each side of a cross corridor. Kyle cowered behind a large garbage can. It stank of rotting hot dogs and nacho cheese and the buzzing of flies sounded like the murmurs of a distant crowd. Over it, the soft thumping of many feet grew nearer. They waited until the mass of zombies was only twenty yards away before opening fire. The noise was deafening. The M-249 SAW spewed a death blizzard of 5.56 mm bullets into the center of the zombie assault, while two M16s and Kyle's Beneli 12-gauge licked the edges. Walters handled the heavy twenty-two pound machinegun like a paint brush, adding daubs of red and crimson to the living mosaic of undead flesh. He held the SAW tucked under one arm while feeding a belt of ammo into it with the other. The horde advanced in spite of the withering fire, the zombies behind crushing the dying beneath them as they plunged unheeding into the deadly hail of fire. Each time the defenders reloaded, the zombies gained a few feet. Kyle reached into his pocket and pulled out his last four shells. He loaded the shotgun and aimed at the nearest creature. Its chest exploded as the 12-gauge tore a hole the size of a man's fist through it.

The SAW went silent. Walters cursed and dropped the empty ammo belt. One of the soldiers tossed him an M16 clip. He jammed it into the weapon and resumed firing. It sputtered death a few times before it suddenly went silent again. Walters banged it against the wall as a look of horror crossed his face.

"Jammed."

The M-249, designed to use belt ammunition at a high cycle rate, sometimes jammed when a standard STANAG M16 ammo clip was used. It was Walters' bad luck that it happened now. He looked lost without his weapon. Kyle tossed him his Glock, and then an extra clip.

"Here."

Walters smiled at his new toy. He dropped the useless SAW at his feet and started firing. The four of them continued pouring a stream of bullets into the creatures, but the time spent reloading allowed the creatures to edge within a few yards of them. Kyle picked his targets carefully with his remaining three shots. Then, his weapon, too, was silent.

Realizing that they were going to be overwhelmed, Walters yelled, "Duck." He pulled the pins on two grenades and lobbed them both down the corridor. Kyle pulled himself into a ball and hugged the floor behind the garbage can hoping the thin metal would provide sufficient cover. The twin explosions thundered in his ears even though he had cupped his hands over them. The trash can rang out as shrapnel peppered it, but none penetrated. The blasts showered the floor and ceiling with blood and gore. A wall of flame swept by only inches away from Kyle's face, singeing the hair on the back of his hands. He peeked around the corner to witness a scene of carnage and chaos. Shattered and smoldering zombies lay everywhere. The remaining zombies, deafened by the explosion and deprived of their sense of smell by the smoke, stumbled around blindly.

"Switch off the flashlights," Kyle warned, fearing the creatures would home in on the light.

Without the light of the flashlights to guide them or the smell of their prey to follow, the zombies acted as if a switch had been cut off. They stood immobile in the corridor moaning. Walters and the other soldier slipped across the corridor to join Kyle. In his hands was the useless M-249. He handed Kyle the Glock.

"Now's a good time to get the hell out of here," he whispered in Kyle's ear.

They crawled down the corridor on their hands and knees until Walters deemed it safe to switch on the flashlights. Then they ran. On the walkway ramp outside the stadium, the rain was blowing in sheets. It was warm but it felt good on Kyle's skin. He hoped the rain put out some of the fires plaguing the city. In their haste, they almost passed the broad stairway leading to the ground. Kyle came up short when he glanced down. Below them, hundreds of zombies made the concourse impassable. They thronged the entrance to the building and prowled the outskirts.

"What the hell ..." Kyle mumbled. "We'll have to find another way."

As he stood staring at the mass of zombies trying to decide their next move, a bright light flared around the corner of the building, quickly followed by a second. The zombies noticed the light and ran in that direction leaving the concourse clear. A lone figure appeared from behind one of the letters from the old Orange Bowl buried in the walkway as a memento. Kyle shone the flashlight on Ginson.

"I thought you had left already."

"I sent them on their way. I came back to help you find Rita." He pointed to a nearby jeep. To the two soldiers, he said, "Get back to the airport. You've done enough for one night."

"What about me?" Walters asked as he watched the two men eagerly comply with Ginson's order.

"You're a corporal now. It's time to earn your pay. You're coming with Bane and me."

Walters held out the SAW. "But my baby's dead."

Ginson pointed to three M16s and a bag of ammo clips lying on the ground beside the letter 'R' behind which he had been hiding. Walters smiled and handed the SAW to the two soldiers. "Take care of my baby," he warned, "I want it back when I come home."

"Walters and I can handle this alone," Kyle told Ginson. He pointed to the fresh blood staining Ginson's uniform. "You're leaking."

"What, this scratch? It's nothing. I stuck a Band-Aid on it. I'm good to go."

Kyle decided he would never win an argument with the obstinate sergeant and simply nodded. "Let's go find Rita."

Ginson tugged on his sleeve.

Kyle was frustrated by Ginson's delay. Rita needed him. "What is it?" he demanded.

"I radioed in a report to General Willows. He's ordered a missile strike on the stadium for 2000 hours. That's in about forty-five minutes."

Kyle shook his head. "More good news." He placed the Beneli empty shotgun in the jeep and picked up the one of the M16s. He pulled back the charging bolt, saw that the weapon was empty, slid in a fresh clip, and flicked off the safety. "Then we'd better hurry."

16

June 7, Marlins Park, Miami, FL –

Benoit's condition was steadily worsening. At first, the sedatives had eased his pain, but now he was pale, and his skin was cold and clammy. His pulse was weak and erratic. Her medical expertise was limited to children's colds, but Rita feared that the loss of blood had exacerbated a bad heart. She forced water down his throat to try to revive him. Benoit might have helped her determine his condition, but his moments of lucidity had become less frequent.

Benoit had been right about one thing. The siren and the shots drew zombies from all the surrounding neighborhoods. The few remaining soldiers, forced to fight in the dark, were quickly overwhelmed. One group took refuge in the Marlins dugout, while a second group fought bravely as they guided the few remaining survivors into the left field bullpen and secured its top with sections of chain link fence. Their battle lasted less than half an hour as zombies reached the stands and attacked them from all sides. The soldiers disappeared beneath a sea of bodies. The zombies then focused their attention on the hapless survivors now huddled in fear in the bullpen. Rita knew the fence would not hold long under the creatures' determined onslaught.

The creatures now roamed the stadium freely seeking out stragglers. Scattered shots and screams grew near, but then faded as time passed. She waited beside the door with only a chair as a weapon. The sounds of gunfire below diminished until only a handful of soldiers remained. The sound of renewed firing near the bullpen drew her attention. Hoping that Detective Bane had arrived, she tried the cell phone again, but got no signal. She signaled with the flashlight hoping someone, if not the detective, would notice it. She waited for an acknowledgement, but none came. However, the survivors disappeared into the stadium away from the creatures.

"They'll be here soon," she assured Benoit, but he lay silent on the bed she had made for him with two chairs. His chest rose and fell frightening slowly.

Several loud explosions shook the floor, followed by more gunshots, but then she heard nothing more for almost an hour. Her hope of rescue was growing dim. Something had happened, forcing them to leave her behind. She considered her options, but they each dismayed her. She and Tomas might make it out safely past the zombies, but she couldn't carry Benoit, and she wouldn't leave him behind. He would die without her, might die in spite of her help, but she wouldn't abandon him just to save her own life. She looked down at Tomas, asleep in a chair, and wondered if she would abandon a friend for his young life. The answer was still no. If the value of a person's life became so reduced that she would callously spend it for her own safety, what hope could there be for anyone? It would be better to die clinging to the values in which she believed, those which her father had instilled in her as a child. To do less would be to dishonor his memory.

Gunshots in the corridor outside woke Tomas and roused Benoit. Tomas began crying and Benoit managed to raise his head a few inches and open one eye before collapsing back onto his bed. Rita picked up Tomas and tried to calm him as she watched the door breathlessly, her heart pounding in her chest. Then the pounding came from the door.

"Rita! It's Kyle Bane."

Rita hugged Tomas to her chest and released her pent up breath. She laid Tomas beside Benoit and rushed to the door, frantically tearing at the barricade to remove it. As she flung open the door, flashlights blinded her as Kyle and two other men entered. She flung her free arm around him and kissed his cheek. He brushed his cheek where the mask had tickled it, looked at her, smiled, and said, "That was worth the trip."

"Is this all of you?" She surveyed the three men, disappointed by their small number; then noticed their torn uniforms, splatters of blood, and bruises and retracted her initial dismay. Their journey to rescue her had not been an easy one.

"The others had to carry the survivors to safety."

By the harshness of his tone, she was almost afraid to ask, "How many?"

"About fifty."

Her heart sank. Of the people she had known, eaten with, spoken to, most were probably dead. She fought back a wave of despair. She was alive, as was her son and Benoit.

"You came back for me," she said.

"I said I would didn't I?"

"Are you hurt?"

Kyle shook his head. "We had to slog our way through a few fungus heads, but no real injuries, except Ginson of course. He popped a stitch or two."

She pointed to Benoit. "This is Mr. Benoit. He was shot in the shoulder. I did all I could, but he's lost a lot of blood." In a quieter voice she added, "I think his heart is bad."

Kyle gave Benoit a cursory glance; then shared a look of concern with his two companions. She knew what they were thinking – how can they carry an injured man and still fight off zombies?

"Can he walk?" Kyle asked.

She shook her head in confusion. "He is barely awake. We need to nurse him back to health." She stared at Kyle. "Surely mores soldiers are coming?" When he didn't answer, she pressed him. "Are they coming?"

He shook his head. "No one's coming."

She suspected more that he wasn't revealing. "Why?"

"Because the army is going to blow this place to hell in less than twenty minutes."

She stepped back and stared at him. The tall, lanky soldier with the black mustache spoke up. "I can make a *travois* for him."

""What the hell is a *travois*, Walters?" Kyle asked.

Walters shook his head. "Don't you ever watch John Wayne movies? You have a serious education gap. It's an Indian litter. I can use these two curtain rods and drapes. One man can pull him. That leaves two to guard."

Kyle looked at Rita. "Three. Rita can shoot." He took Tomas from her arms and made cooing noises at him. "You'd better see to your friend. We have to leave now."

She busied herself with Benoit, trying to absorb the direness of the situation. Twenty minutes to escape through hordes of zombies seemed impossible. Even if they managed, could they get far enough away to avoid the blast?

Walters ripped down the two curtain rods and used his knife to slit a series of parallel holes about three feet apart in one of the curtains. He slipped the rods through the slits, and then secured broken chair legs at the top and bottom of his *travois* with strips of cloth. As Rita was changing Benoit's bandage, she noticed Sergeant Ginson holding his side where he had been injured at the courthouse. His hand came away wet.

"Is that fresh blood?" she demanded. "Why didn't you get that wound treated?"

Ginson shook his head. "I did. I'm okay. See to the old man."

Benoit stirred and opened his eyes. He focused on Ginson. "I'm not that old, Sergeant, though I feel it today. If you'll help me to my feet, I can walk."

"You just lay back and enjoy the ride. We'll do the driving."

The effort to speak had used almost all of Benoit's energy. Realizing how weak he was, he nodded his head and closed his eyes. Kyle walked over to her bouncing a giggling Tomas in his arms and watched her re-wrap Benoit's wound. She could tell by his expression that he didn't think Benoit could survive their escape, but he didn't say anything about it.

"Did you see my signal?"

"The light? Yes. But I couldn't respond. We were using night vision goggles. I was relieved to see that you were still alive. It looked bad when we got here."

"Benoit said the alarm sirens during the first outbreak drew them here. They … they crashed through the window wall. The soldiers couldn't stop them."

Kyle's face became grim. "The army will kill them all."

"But there may be others trapped like me."

"Probably, but we can't save them."

His being right didn't lessen the coldness of the idea of destroying Marlins Park. "We could search for them on the way out."

"Rita, we might not even make it out of here ourselves. We have less than twelve minutes. There are thousands of those things out there. The army won't pass up this opportunity. Frankly, I'm surprised they haven't destroyed the place already."

"But they know we're here, don't they?"

"Yes."

As she studied his face, she suddenly realized he wasn't wearing a mask. None of them were.

"Why aren't you wearing your masks?"

"We're the guinea pigs for a new vaccine. The job doesn't pay well, but it's steady work."

His attempt at humor didn't fool her. "If it doesn't work?"

"If it works, we might have a chance of surviving this Cordyceps Plague. If it doesn't ... then it's back to the drawing board."

"Finished," Walters announced. He laid the *travois* on the ground. He had included a harness for his shoulders.

"It's time to go," Ginson said. He pointed down onto the field. A fire had broken out in the Clevelander Restaurant near the Marlins signature homerun sculpture. Fed by a breeze through the broken window wall, the flames were spreading unchecked into the seats above. Smoke billowed up to the roof and pooled overhead like a threatening rain cloud. By the light of the flickering flames, the crazed zombies running around looked like a Seminole war dance. The sight of zombies thrashing in the pool was ethereal, like a scene from a horrible nightmare.

Kyle handed Tomas back to Rita. She placed him in her blanket sling and secured him to her chest. Kyle and Walters gently moved Benoit to the *travois*. Walters handed Rita his M16, slipped the makeshift harness over his shoulders, and lifted one end of the litter.

Ginson led the way with Walters, Benoit and Rita in the middle. Kyle followed, protecting their rear. She cringed when she saw the body she had stumbled over earlier. Ginson stopped just long enough to remove the dead man's dog tags. Just as they reached the non-working escalator going to the Vista level, a large man wearing the remnants of a tattered white coverall leaped at Kyle from the steps, bowling Kyle over. The zombie leaked blood from several bullet holes in his chest and side but ignored his severe injuries as he struggled in his madness to kill Kyle. The creature slammed a fist the size of a brick into Kyle's head, knocking him almost unconscious. His struggles lessened and the creature continued to rain blows into the detective's head.

Rita raised the unfamiliar M16 and pulled the trigger. Unaccustomed to the heavy recoil, the weapon sent her stumbling backwards. She caught herself against the wall to keep from falling on top of Tomas. Ginson rushed past her to Kyle's aid. When she recovered her balance, she saw the large zombie sprawled at an awkward angle on the escalator lying in a pool of blood, half his head missing. Her bullets, at least one of them, had found the target. Ginson pulled Kyle to his feet. His face was a bloody mess, and he reeled from the blows, but he was alive.

The noise would attract zombies. They wasted no time with stealth. Rita grabbed the rear of the *travois* to speed things up. The commotion had roused Benoit. He tried to sit up but Rita pushed him back down.

"You're heavy. Lie still before I drop you."

"Leave me here," Benoit gasped. "You'll never make it carrying me."

"I won't leave you."

"You're killing your child," he said.

His accusation hurt her deeply, but she knew he was just trying to make her angry. "Shut up and lie still."

Ginson had one arm around Kyle's waist supporting him, but he still managed to shoot a second zombie one-handed as it raced through the open door of a suite. The creature fell to its knees, but continued to struggle toward them, its hands clawing the air frantically. Ginson slid to a halt, still supporting Kyle, aimed his weapon at the creature's head, and fired. The head exploded, splattering Rita's cloth shoes with blood and gooey brain matter. She jerked her foot back instinctively, noticing that both her shoes were already soaked with blood from earlier.

She glanced through the door of a suite. The fire at the Clevelander had grown larger and had spread into left field seats. The mass of zombies crowding the field had doubled. They were attracted by the flames and stood swaying and moaning in front of the restaurant. Somewhere, a store of ammunition touched by the flames began exploding, adding to the confusion. The confusion played in the group's favor. Their shots drew few of the creatures their direction. They reached the outside ramps without running into more of the creatures. Just as it looked as if they would make it out of the stadium alive, the floor beneath them began shuddering. The glass around them began to shatter.

"My grenades or the Claymore must have damaged a support beam or two," Walters said.

Ginson shook his head. "It's probably the fire."

"Either way," Kyle said, "we don't have much time."

Before they took five steps, the floor groaned and began tilting downward. As she felt her legs folding, she stumbled and lost her grip on the *travois*. She swung Tomas to her chest and held on tightly to protect him. Everyone fell and tumbled downward. The *travois*, still attached to Walters by the harness, slid into him. Benoit's weight pushed him forward. The two of them landed on the first level in a tangled heap with her, Ginson, and Kyle, right behind them. The noise of the collapse drew the zombies' attention away from the fire and in their direction.

Rita struggled to get to Benoit amid the rumble but couldn't find him in the smoke and dust. Finally, she caught a glimpse of him ten yards ahead crawling down the concourse toward the approaching zombies.

"Benoit!" she yelled and started forward. The sharp rubble cut her feet through the cloth shoes but she ignored it. Walters grabbed her and dragged her back.

"He took one of my grenades," he said.

"But he's ..." she began.

"He's trying to save us. He's giving us time to escape."

She faced Walters with one fist balled, ready to fight him. She was in tears from anger. "We can't leave him," she pleaded.

Kyle grabbed the sling in which she carried Tomas and shook her. "We can't stop him. Think of your child. Let's go."

She looked at Benoit. Fifteen or twenty zombies were almost on top of him. She thought he smiled at her as he pulled the pin from the grenade in his hand, but it was too dark to be certain. She closed her eyes not wanting to watch him die. Kyle dragged her and Tomas to safety as the grenade exploded. She felt a hot wind brush her back, and then she was outside with the rain washing her face of her tears.

"Two minutes," Ginson called out. His eyes searched the sky.

Rita glanced up to see twin streaks of light approaching from the west, flying low beneath the cloud cover. The two jets roared over the stadium and circled. She ran as quickly as she could. Her rain-soaked, tattered shoes fell apart on the wet pavement. Kyle kept pace with her, but his face was an expression of agony. Sergeant Ginson fared no better with his injury. They were less than a twenty yards from Marlins Park, passing the west parking garage, when the jets began their final approach. She knew they weren't going to make it. They were still too close and moving too slowly.

"Hit the ground!" Ginson yelled as he ignited a flare and waved it over his head.

She fell to the ground with the others waiting to die. At first, she thought the pilots hadn't seen the signal, but at the last moment, they veered away.

"Come on!" Ginson yelled.

The jets wouldn't give them much time. They couldn't. Zombies were already spilling out of the entrance and through the broken glass wall. Ginson ran as he held the flare aloft to pinpoint the small group. They had only managed another sixty yards before the jets returned. This time she knew they would fire their missiles no matter what. The jets were approaching so low she was afraid they would crash. Eight bright streaks of fire lanced through the air toward the stadium just as the jets swooped upward. She fell to the pavement while protecting Tomas with her body. Two of the missiles struck the concourse in front of the stadium. Zombies disappeared in a ball of flame. Others became pieces of flesh shrapnel. Propelled by the blast, their body peppered zombies around them in a shotgun blast. Pieces of human bone punctured skulls, hearts and organs, killing dozens more of the creatures untouched by the blast itself.

The six remaining missiles penetrated the front of the stadium. The ground shook and the interior lit up six rapid times like a strobe light. Flames erupted from every opening and billowed skyward. With the sound of thunder, the retractable roof collapsed inward section by section, filling the interior with tons of steel, crushing anyone inside. The walls of the stadium began to collapse inward, as well as sections of ramp and parking garages. The entire structure folded in on itself.

The heat of the blast swept over the prostrate survivors. Large chunks of concrete and steel fell all around them, but thankfully missed them. A fine cloud of dust, turned into mud by the rain, settled over them. Rita sat up, staring back at the destroyed stadium, and Benoit. Only a handful of zombies, confused by the explosion but drawn by the flames, remained near the stadium. Around her, her companions got to their feet. For several minutes, they stared at the funeral pyre that had been Marlins Park. She knew they needed to leave before the light drew more of the creatures, but the flames were mesmerizing.

Only the roar of a helicopter broke the spell of the flames. She glanced up to see a large helicopter flying low over the parking lot, called in by the jet pilots. It landed a short distance away. With Tomas, who seemed unfazed by all the commotion, snuggled safely across her chest and one arm supporting Kyle, she joined Walters and Ginson in their walk to the helicopter. She didn't look back. Beneath the rubble and flames lay Benoit, her twice savior. She realized that she didn't know much about him except that he was a science teacher, but it was enough to form a lasting memory.

Someone in the Blackhawk offered her his hand and helped her into the helicopter. She snuggled with Tomas against a wall and closed her eyes as they lifted off. She and her son had survived.

17

June 9, MIA, Miami, FL –

Kyle's pummeled ribs felt as if they were grinding together whenever he moved, and the bruises on his face stood out like billboards for *Fight Club*. His right eye was swollen almost shut and his jaw ached, but he was still alive. And so far he hadn't succumbed to the Cordyceps Plague. In fact, Marli was so enthusiastic about the favorable results that she had forwarded the formula to the military for distribution to the country's pharmaceutical labs for immediate production. He was slightly perturbed that he hadn't seen her in over twelve hours. Upon his arrival, battered and bruised from the incident at Marlins Park, she had fawned over him until he had sent her away embarrassed by the special attention she was showing him. Now, she was so engrossed in her work that she ignored him completely. With her, it was always feast or famine.

Rita and Tomas had joined the other survivors inside the airport. Hotel rooms had been turned over to them, allowing a degree of badly needed privacy. Too late, as usual, the military had finally taken Marli's advice and sealed the airport buildings, filtering the air, and installing cleaning stations at all entrances, eliminating the need for uncomfortable masks or respirators. Ginson, after allowing the medic to re-suture his wounds, had reluctantly followed the medic's advice and taken it easy. Both he and Walters, now local heroes for testing the vaccine, lounged around on cots in the hangar allowing smitten female lab assistants to tend to them. Kyle suffered his share of hero worship the first day, but found the fawning a trifle annoying and insisted on carrying his own weight by reviewing Marli's projections. He had been at it all day.

The deadly graph lines were tending slightly downward. The rain had washed the air clean of the deadly Cordyceps spores, carrying them into drains and canals and on to the ocean where the high salt content rendered them harmless. It was good news but that didn't end the plague. Tens of thousands of infected still roamed the city spreading the spores. Other cities, unaffected by rain or not near salt water, still suffered greatly. Kyle knew that the new vaccine, provided it worked, wouldn't be a God send. With both production and delivery systems in turmoil, synthesizing the vaccine and it into people's hands would be difficult, and in some instances, dangerous. Even at fifty to sixty percent effective, the potent weapon in their arsenal did not involve bombs or purification by fire. It wasn't perfect, but it was a start. To Kyle, not quite a pessimist, but always wary of gift horses, things were going too well.

It didn't take long for the other shoe to drop. The quiet serenity of the hangar lab disappeared as the roar of dozens of low-flying helicopters shook the roof. Kyle glanced over at Ginson, sipping a glass of iced tea and raised an eyebrow. Ginson shrugged his ignorance. A few moments later, Ginson's radio burst into life. He rushed over to answer, spoke briefly into the receiver, and stood there looking dumbfounded.

"What's up?" Kyle asked, wincing s his jaw throbbed.

"It seems that the fire at Marlins Park has attracted an army of zombies. They're leaving downtown in droves and headed in this direction. We're going out to stop them."

"Doesn't the general realize you're still recovering," Kyle reminded him.

Ginson frowned. "I don't think he cares. He needs men with night vision experience as sharpshooters."

Walters sat on the edge of his cot with a slightly amused expression on his gaunt face. "I was getting too comfortable anyway. I could use some exercise. What about you?" he asked Kyle.

Kyle considered his options as his two friends stared at him. He hated to leave them in the lurch, but he suddenly realized that he had enough of dangerous sorties. It wasn't fear, though his close brush with death had installed a healthier respect for what the fungus heads were capable. It was a growing awareness that he was tired of killing zombies. The expedition to the court house and the one to Marlins Park had sated his appetite for death and destruction. He shook his head negatively.

"I'm sitting this one out."

His answer surprised Ginson, who cast a disapproving glance in his direction, but Walters smiled at him. "Finally got some smarts, eh, Detective," he said.

"This is a military operation. I'd just be in the way."

Ginson nodded. "Maybe so."

He expected Ginson to cajole him into going, but the sergeant accepted Kyle's refusal without a fight.

"I'm not good at following orders," he explained, trying to justify his decision; then realized he didn't need to validate his reasoning. He wasn't military. He was a cop on loan to the CDC. "I'm just tired. I've had enough."

Ginson stopped lacing up his boots and said, "Haven't we all?"

Kyle detected a slight edge of bitterness in Ginson's voice but ignored it as he realized that Ginson's remark wasn't directed at him personally.

"Good luck," he said.

"Thanks," Ginson replied.

After Ginson and his men had left, Kyle stared out the window. Fourteen Blackhawks, their rotors still spinning, sat on the runway. Squads of soldiers lined up beside each vehicle as squad leaders performed weapons checks in the growing dusk. Beyond the helicopters, a convoy of APCs and Humvees revved to life. This was to be an all out assault. The rain had stopped but the sky was pregnant with dark gray clouds. Nightfall was still an hour away but the day was rapidly growing dark. Fighting an enemy in complete darkness was always a dicey issue. Fighting one incapable of feeling pain and determined to kill would be next to impossible.

A momentary tremor of guilt swept over Kyle as he watched the unsuspecting soldiers queuing up for departure. It remained with him as Marli walked up beside him and placed her hand on his shoulder.

"I'm glad you're not going," she said.

He turned to her scowling. *Is she the reason I'm not going?* "You don't think I'm yellow?" he threw at her.

She jumped at his anger looked at him in surprise. "Yellow? Of course not."

"Then why do I feel like a coward?" His guilty conscience nagged at him like an itch he couldn't scratch. He had never walked away from a fight. What was it about this one that turned his stomach?

"You've proven your courage numerous times. This is a military operation. Besides, you can barely see out of your left eye." She reached out her hand to touch his bruise, but he flinched.

He pointed out the window where the last of the soldiers were mounting their vehicles. "Some of those kids out there have no idea what they're in for. A lot of them won't be coming back."

"Do you think one more gun will make a difference?"

He closed his eyes, hating her for her logic. All he had was emotion. He sagged against the wall. Did his pride make him believe that he could make a difference when hundreds of soldiers couldn't?

"No," he replied quietly.

"Then be proud of what you've accomplished and let the military take over. I still need you here."

"What more can I do here to help you? I'm all tapped out up here." He thumped his head with a forefinger, relishing the sharp pain it produced.

"*I* need you here," Marli repeated. She clasped his hand and brought it to her chest. Her heart pounded at his touch, and the skin below her neck flushed crimson. "I need you," she repeated.

His arms enclosed her in an embrace, pressing her so tightly he thought he might bruise her. Her lips sought his, warm and soft against his. The ache in his jaw meant nothing compared to the giddiness she produced in him. When their lips met, it was as if two old lovers, separated by time, had reunited at long last. All thoughts of leaving vanished from his mind, swallowed by her need, by his desire. He pushed her against the wall as his hands caressed her body beneath her lab coat. Her body responded by melting into his, fitting as naturally as if both their bodies had been formed as one piece. He felt complete, whole – satisfied. Nothing could spoil the moment.

Nothing except the sound of the Blackhawk helicopters revving their rotors for takeoff. How could he remain safely ensconced in the hangar lab enjoying life while his friends risked their lives? His bruises and aches couldn't pain him as much as Ginson's wound did him. He broke their embrace and pulled away. Marli stared at him, cocking her head to one side questioningly. Then, as realization dawned, her expression changed to one of disappointment, and then resignation.

"I have to go," he said.

She nodded, shaking a tear from her cheek. He expected her to ask him why, but she surprised him by saying nothing at all. She kissed him quickly and walked away. He watched her leave, unsure if he would ever see her again. Kyle hated himself more at that moment than at any other time in his life. Against overwhelming odds, two people had found each other amid the turmoil of a world gone mad, as Cordyceps' rising tide threatened to swamp the city, the entire country. Was he crazy to risk that love? Could he make a difference, or was it simply his male pride? He didn't know. He only knew that not going would make a difference to him, in him. He was a fighter by nature. That was the reason he had become a cop, to make a difference. Doing anything else was contrary to his nature.

He was bitterly angry with himself for his decision, but knew he could do nothing else. He returned to his cot and picked up his shotgun and Glock. He didn't see Marli, couldn't face her if he had. He exited the decontamination lock with his heart heavy from his betrayal of Marli, but pounding with excitement at the prospect of a fight. *Is this the kind of man I have become*, he asked himself, *a killer? Is there any love in me?*

As he crossed the runway, Ginson pulled up alongside him in a Humvee. A smile broke on Ginson's face, but then dropped as he noted Kyle's mood. Kyle hopped into the Humvee beside Walters.

"Let's go," he snapped.

He grabbed the roof to keep from falling as the driver hit the gas and the Humvee sped away, leaving Marli and his dreams behind.

* * *

Finding the enemy was not difficult. The area around the still smoldering Marlins Park was an island in a sea of zombies. The streets between the stadium and Downtown swarmed with thousands more. It looked as if every fungus head in the city were there. The military had destroyed the I-95 Bridge and all bridges crossing the Miami River to the south. Helicopters swept down from north of the city, herding the zombies ahead of them like cattle. Kyle and Ginson stared at the growing horde from atop the Dolphin Expressway overpass above 12th Avenue. It was a dark night. There was a quarter moon, but it was hidden by the clouds. The overcast sky threatened rain. The spotlights of the squadron of Blackhawk and Apache helicopters overhead dotted the moving mass below. The creatures swarmed over the bridges at 1st Street and at Flagler like migrating wildebeest. More still raced down the Expressway westward toward Ginson's position on the bridge. They wouldn't have to go to the battle. The battle was coming to them.

"Better still," Kyle muttered to himself. His anger at himself made him eager to face an enemy, any enemy.

Ginson glanced in his direction but returned his gaze to the zombies.

"Enough for everyone," Walters quipped as he threaded a belt of ammunition into his M-249 machinegun.

Ginson turned to the three trucks that had accompanied their small convoy and waved his arm. Sixty men leaped out ready for action. They quickly mounted .30 caliber and .50 caliber machineguns across the road. Three mortar teams set up their equipment, piling motor shells behind them within easy reach. The men moved with the expediency of training. If they were as afraid as their young faces revealed, their efficiency didn't suffer.

An Apache helicopter fired six missiles at the bridge across the Miami River on 12th Street. It disintegrated in a bright flash and tremendous explosion, sending its load of zombies cascading to the river below. Kyle stepped back as a blast of hot air and a cloud of concrete dust spilled over the Expressway. Bodies floated on the surface for only seconds before disappearing into the inky blackness of the water.

"Lights out," Ginson called out.

The vehicles doused their headlights as soldiers donned night vision gear. Their job was to close the Expressway and to act as snipers for the ground teams below. Kyle realized his shotgun would be of no use in such a fight, so he waited patiently, certain that he would soon be able to put it into action.

The snipers fired into the crowd first. Their targets collapsed onto the road, tripping other zombies racing on their heels. Through his night vision goggles, Kyle thought it almost comical to see the creatures stumbling and tumbling head over heels. The comedy was short lived as the creatures recovered and raced forward. Next, the mortars cut loose, creating small gaps in the mass that quickly refilled. By the time the machineguns engaged, the zombies were close enough for Kyle to pick out individual features. Women, men, children – except for the look of rage on their faces, they looked like any ordinary crowd.

Walters chided the zombies as they attempted to use abandoned autos as shields from his field of fire. "Oh, no you don't, asshole," he yelled as he cut a young man wearing swim trunks and sandals in half. "I got something for you. You, too, Mr. suit and tie."

The heavy fire took its toll on the creatures, but they did not stop coming. Feeling no pain, only rage, they had no compulsion to retreat. The leading edge was almost within shotgun range. Kyle readied his weapon. As he pumped a shell into the chamber, he found that his heart wasn't in it. He felt an unaccountable twinge of sympathy for the zombies. A week earlier and he might have been walking among them, ignoring them as just another face in the crowd. His idea of bad guys didn't include women and children, but he had no choice. They were deadly, and if nothing more, he would protect his friends. His heart raced and his pulse pounded in his temple. His finger gently caressed the trigger.

He watched with mild curiosity as two jets swept over their heads flying less than a hundred feet above the deck. The sky between him and Downtown suddenly ignited as their loads of napalm canisters landed, splashing eastward along the Expressway in a rolling ball of fire. The sudden flare burned his retinas through the goggles. He ripped them from his head and dropped them at his feet. The center and the rear of the zombie horde disappeared in a wall of flames, totally consumed by the blast of heat. Several of the creatures lucky enough to be on the edges of the group raced from the roaring conflagration with their clothing and hair on fire, their skin melting from the intense heat. Running through their companions, they ignited them as well, spreading the fire until their seared lungs refused to accept any more air; then collapsed onto the pavement still blazing. Kyle's gaze followed one flaming creature as it leaped over the side of the road and plunged into the river below. The water did not quench the flames but slowly disappeared as the creature sank. It did not resurface.

Kyle didn't bother firing his weapon. The mortars and machineguns quickly ended the threat of any remaining zombies. He took a deep breath in an unsuccessful attempt to erase the scene of mass destruction from his mind. He had been too exhausted and too stunned to contemplate the destruction at Marlins Park, but even that had been a building, not a mass of former human beings. He had not watched the creatures inside die, had not witnessed their deaths. He could not ignore this. His right hand began to tremble. He made a fist to hide it from anyone watching.

"Looks like we ain't got much of a fight left here," Walters complained. His goggles were attached to his helmet, but were presently swung away from his eyes. The flames reflected in the lens. The barrel of his M-249 SAW smoked from the heat of firing. Only a short piece of ammo belt remained unfired. A look of serenity marked Walters' dust-covered mien. He was proud of his handiwork. His job was killing, and killing he had accomplished.

Walters' glee sickened Kyle. He turned away in disgust. He refused to watch as the soldiers picked off zombies in the streets below from a distance of a few hundred yards like shooting clay pigeons. The thunder of jets firing their loads of missiles and the roar of helicopter gunships firing into the remaining masses of zombies interspersed the brilliant flashes of napalm, some so close he could feel the heat on his exposed skin and see the flashes through his closed eyelids. The soldiers cheered as a sea of napalm smothered the zombies gathered around the ruins of Marlins Park. More bright blossoms bloomed at various points in Little Havana. The military was taking no chances this time. Relying on superior firepower for large groups and clean up teams for small pockets of survivors, the battle lasted less than an hour. *No*, he thought, *this is no battle. It's a slaughter.* The odor of napalm and of burning flesh churned his stomach. He lurched to the rail and vomited. His blood lust withered like an autumn leaf. He had had enough. Why had he come? He sat down with his back to the rail, his fists clenched at his sides, and wept.

The fight ended quickly, but the fires lasted much longer. Already the flames raged westward at an alarming rate. Propelled by rising offshore winds, the flames enveloped whole neighborhoods heretofore untouched by the blazes that had already ravaged much of the city. Entire blocks disappeared in minutes, collateral damage. Left unchecked, the conflagration would last for days. Kyle wondered how many innocent lives would be lost.

Better than a nuke, he mused bitterly.

"You look sick," Ginson commented as he stared down at Kyle.

"I am," he growled, "I'm sick of this slaughter."

"I've lost enough men to these bastards. I'm for anything that gets the job done quickly."

Kyle looked up at Ginson. Ginson wore a sour look on his face, as if his words belied his true feelings. "Yeah, I know. It had to be done. It just churns my guts."

"We didn't get them all. If we don't find those Tertiaries and eliminate them, more people are going to become infected." He looked pointedly at Kyle. "Are you in?"

"No. This … this is it for me. I'll protect my friends; I'll protect myself, but no more wholesale slaughter. If I keep on killing, I'm going to forget who I am, a cop. I'm no soldier. I played at it, but that takes a different mindset. I don't envy you of your job. You'll do your duty here and then move on to another city and start over. I can't. Someday this city will need cops again. I want to come through this and still be there when it needs me. If I just keep on killing, I … I won't be any good to anyone."

Ginson's reply was curt, but Kyle thought he heard some sympathy behind it. "I'll get someone to drop you off at the hangar."

Kyle nodded. He hoped this didn't end his friendship with Ginson, but he had no choice. He couldn't risk losing who he was. "Thanks. I'll see you later." It was more of a question than a statement. "Good luck."

Ginson walked away to join his men. Kyle waited while he spoke to them. After a few minutes, one young soldier walked over to him.

"The sergeant told me to drive you to the airport. Are you ready, sir?"

Kyle got to his feet. His city was a blazing inferno. By morning, only ashes would be left. There was nothing for him here. "Let's go, son."

18

July 11, MIA, Miami, FL –

Rita liked her room. It was very much different from her small bedroom in her home, but the bed was soft, the sheets clean, and the water in the shower was hot. At least she had some privacy, sadly lacking at the FEMA facility. She had taken a long, languid shower when she had first been assigned Room 707 in the airport hotel. Along with the soot and grime, she had washed away Benoit's bloodstains. At the sound of a soft giggle, she glanced over at her son as he played with an ink pen she had found in the desk drawer, his only toy. He smiled at her as he sat illuminated by a dagger of bright sunlight spilling in through the window. The entire room was bright in spite of the heavy plastic sheeting sealing the window. She didn't mind. Her view from the window would only reveal death and destruction. She had witnessed enough of both.

From a hallway window facing east, she had watched the fires blossoming downtown and in her beautiful neighborhood. The park across the street from her home would be gone, the church one block over, the houses that lined the quiet street. Only rubble would remain, where once, people carried out their lives with no thoughts of ever leaving.

The military's decision to house the survivors from Marlins Park in the hotel came as no surprise. It wouldn't do to have them revealing just how many of the thousand people at Marlins Park had been killed by the soldiers. Perhaps her bitterness was misplaced. After all, a soldier whose name she didn't even know had saved her, Tomas, and Benoit during the confusion, and soldiers had rescued her from the stadium.

She saw her fellow survivors at meals and in the hallways, but most, like her, chose to remain cloistered in their rooms suffering in private as they tried to heal their emotional wounds. Hers would never heal. Too much death had tainted her, too much anger. In time, they would scab over perhaps, put forth the appearance of healing, but they would remain deep inside haunting her sleep for the rest of her life, just as they had troubled her sleep the previous two nights. Some moments she was ecstatic to be alive, giddy with delight at having survived all the death around her. At other times, she felt all torn up inside, as if some piece of her had gone missing, never to return. Benoit's death had scarred her. His selfless act had saved her life, given her a future. She would never be able repay the debt fully.

She fought back a tear. She was safe now, the general had assured her, but she knew she would never feel safe again. Now she realized just how much of her life was beyond her control. She had heard rumors that the plague was over for Miami, that most of the creatures had been killed. She had received the shot that they told her would protect her. Tomas had received his as well, but not as enthusiastically. He had cried for hours as she held his trembling body in her arms.

At a soft knock at the door, she turned away from Tomas. "Come in," she said. The door opened slowly. It was Detective Bane. "Hello, Detective," she said. She was glad to see him, but he looked terrible. His face bruised and his cheeks were gaunt and hollow. His cold eyes seemed lifeless. His voice was cold as well, but she knew his animosity was not directed at her but at himself.

"Are they treating you well?"

She shrugged. "Well enough. The food is good and we don't have armed guards standing over us. I'm clean for the first time in a week and I'm wearing shorts and a shirt from the shop downstairs, instead of white coveralls." She touched her head with her hand. "My hair is even brushed."

Kyle didn't even look at her. Instead, his eyes scanned the room as if he were searching for clues. "Where's Tomas?"

She pointed to the floor by the edge of the bed. Tomas recognized his name and clapped his hands together. "I want to thank you for …"

Kyle's cheeks reddened. "No need to thank me," he replied quickly as if her gratitude hurt him.

A tear ran down her cheek. "I heard about Little Havana. I guess I'm homeless now."

"You and half the city. Look, do you still have that photo of your husband?"

She reached into her shirt pocket and pulled it out. "Yes, why?"

"If you'll let me borrow it to make copies, I'll send it around to the other facilities and hospitals. Maybe someone knows where he is."

She clasped the photo tightly in her hand, fearing to relinquish it for even a short while. It was her only link to Ricardo. Her face became hard and cold. "You and I both know he's dead."

"Perhaps, but there's always a chance, isn't there?"

She nodded and handed him the photo. She didn't know why the detective had taken it upon himself to find her husband, but she appreciated the gesture. Perhaps he wanted to assure himself that he was still a cop. "Find him," she pleaded.

"I will."

She surprised him by hugging him and then kissing him on the lips. Then she pulled away. "Thank you again."

As he walked away, she felt lighter. She didn't know if he could find Ricardo or even if her husband was still alive, but Kyle had promised that he would try and he had so far kept his promises. There was nothing else to which she could cling except hope.

* * *

Kyle shoved the photo into his pocket after he left Rita's room. Seeing her again had been difficult. It brought back a surge of memories he had been trying unsuccessfully to suppress for the last two days. He stopped in the hallway and leaned against the wall. Glancing up at the row of lights in the ceiling, he saw once again the bright flashes of napalm. The soft chime of the elevator was the chatter of machine guns and the sound of sizzling flesh.

"Stop it!" he yelled, then glanced around to see if anyone overheard his outburst. He stood straight and waited for the door to open.

He had to keep it together. He couldn't save the city, but he could save one family. His life needed purpose again. Where would he start? The battle for Miami was over with no clear winner. Most of the zombies were dead, consumed in the napalm inferno in the Night of Fires as it soon became known, but there was no celebration. Thousands of non-infected had died as well, unable to escape the flames or killed by the escaping hordes of Cordyceps zombies. Large swaths of the city, including Downtown, Little Havana, and parts of Hialeah, lay in ruins, a blackened jumble of burned buildings, smoldering tree trunks, heat-bubble asphalt, and charred skeletons. A westerly wind arrived blowing the spores and the stench of death out to sea. The skies had opened up the morning of the tenth, quenching the rampaging fires and washing the city clean, or as clean as a graveyard could be. The army's mop up operations had gone well. Zombies still roamed the city or lurked in dark corners, but constant patrols would eventually shrink their number.

Surprisingly, survivors continued to show up at the remaining FEMA facilities. Thanks to Marli's intervention, the facilities now ran as true decontamination and relocation centers. The survivors were emaciated, frightened, and in shock, but they weren't beaten. Like Miami, its citizens were resilient and stubborn. It would take time, but both would recover. While production of the new vaccine was as yet just a trickle, Miami had been chosen as a test site. Marli spent much of her time making the rounds of the facilities and refugee camps administering the vaccine, which Marli now boasted had an eighty-percent effective rate. To Kyle, the remaining twenty percent seemed a defeat rather than a victory, but who was he to complain. The vaccine had so far worked on him, and his odds had been worse. Marli's colleagues had also developed a simple finger-stick blood test to determine infection. This allowed for rapid detection of the infected and their separation from the uninfected. Kyle tried not to dwell on the scenes of families being broken up as some members tested positive. So far, there was no cure.

Both Ginson and Walters had survived their night sorties, though Kyle had seen neither of them since the battle. He wasn't sure if Ginson would forgive him for not joining them, but it was a price he was willing to pay to retain his sanity. To assuage some portion of his guilt, he had helped in the cleanup operations around what had been Marlins Park. Dozens of massive pyres still smoldered where the corpses had been burning for two days. It was dirty, sickening work with the cloying stench of death permeating his skin, impossible to shower away, but the physical labor had allowed him time to take stock of his future. It also permitted him time away from Marli, who was much too busy coordinating the vaccination program to commiserate with him. He didn't blame her. He hated himself for his growing moroseness, but he still questioned his true motives for not accompanying Ginson. Fear was one factor, but he had faced his fears before. A sick-to-the-stomach uneasiness with the wholesale slaughter of what had once been human beings played a large part, but he had previously joined in the killing without reservations. No, the problem that plagued him was one of deep soul searching.

He had enjoyed killing fungus heads. They were like paper targets at the pistol range. He could vent his rage and his frustration on them for the interference they had caused in his life without recrimination. They were the ultimate bad guy, and he was the consummate dispenser of vigilante justice. Freed from the very laws he so carefully enforced, he had trod the fine razor's edge of a criminal and its song beaconed to him like a sweet Siren. He was afraid one more killing would push him over the edge. It was a theory he didn't want to test. He wanted to be a cop again, and he thought he might have found a way to be one.

He went to the general's new aide's desk hoping to use his copier. He was surprised to see Marli walking out of the general's office. He had been avoiding her, as she had most probably been avoiding him.

"Oh," she said, "I wondered where you were." A smile flickered briefly on her face, but she made no move to embrace him. Though the distance between them was just a matter of a couple of feet, it felt like a football field.

"I was visiting an old friend, Rita." Did he see a flash of jealousy in her eyes? At one time, he would have cared. Now, it only annoyed him. "I'm going to find her husband."

Marli smiled. "I hope you do."

He nodded toward the general's office. "What did you and the general discuss?"

"I suggested that we designate Dodge Island as a resettlement zone. It's isolated and there are several cruise ships at the docks and hundreds of empty homes that can be used as dormitories. It would be easy to resupply by ship."

"That's sounds like a great idea. The survivors need some semblance of order and a chance to feel like human beings again." He thought of Rita and suppressed an inner groan. Marli shuffled her feet, looking embarrassed. He didn't blame her. His glum cast a shadow over everyone around him. He stared at her, but her eyes refused to meet his. His training told him when someone was trying not to say something. "What else?"

"General Willows wants me to relocate to Philadelphia. They're trying to reestablish a CDC control center there."

Marli leaving? Could he stand one more loss? "Are you going?" He knew immediately by her expression that his reply had not been what she had wanted to hear.

"I really should."

She doesn't want to go. Am I the reason she's reluctant to leave? Perhaps there was hope after all.

"Can't you work from here? You have a lab."

"Do you ... want me to stay?"

She was laying it all in his lap. He surprised himself by saying, "Damn right I do. I'm stupid and slow, but I would have eventually gotten around to telling you how much I love you."

Her smile, tentative at first, but then exploding across her face, made his heart sing. He had no time even to think about what he had said before her lips were crushing his. He responded in kind, paying no heed to the soldiers who glanced in their direction. When she broke away, her face was more alive than he had ever seen it. He felt like a schoolboy on his first date, nervous but filled with glorious anticipation. Not all, but a portion of his despondency lifted.

"I can work from here. Doctor Ozay will stay with me. I have more good news."

"I don't know if I can stand anymore."

"Cordyceps infection is no longer rising. In fact, the infection rate is slowing in almost all major cities."

"That's great news," he said, but he was puzzled, "why?"

She shook her head. "No one knows. Maybe the disease simply ran its course or maybe conditions have changed. It really doesn't matter. Some predictions say new infections will end in six to eight weeks."

"Then it's over." Even as he said it, he knew it wasn't true. His instincts told him when a case was closed. This one wasn't.

"It appears so. Will you go back to your Special Investigations Squad?"

He hesitated. That was a question he had been avoiding. Chief Inspector Gilbert had asked him the same question only a few hours earlier. He had been unable to answer. He had no reason to remain with Marli other than his desire to do so. As Gilbert had reminded him, all civil authority would be needed to replace the military when they moved out, as he assumed they soon would, to cleanse other cities of the Cordyceps Plague.

"I don't know." He felt he needed to explain further. "I learned a few things about myself during the last couple of weeks, things I'm not proud of."

"If you mean about being a coward ..."

He stopped her. "No, not that. I'm no coward, but I don't know if I have the same edge I once had. I don't know if I can be a killer, but I can't be a paper pusher."

"I can find a place for you with the CDC – security."

"Same problem. I've lost the instinct. I might see anyone who isn't a crazed maniac as the good guy, and cost someone their life, maybe yours."

"What will you do?"

He shook his head. "I don't know yet."

"I want you around me."

He smiled at her. "That can be arranged."

From the corner of his eye, he saw soldiers running toward him. He stepped away from Marli, looked down the corridor and saw Walters. As he was wondering what the corporal was up to, Walters lifted his SAW and fired at the retreating men, killing two. A third fell wounded, bleeding from the leg. A frightened soldier raced by. Kyle grabbed him and spun him around.

"What's happening?"

"He's infected," the soldier yelled and broke away.

Kyle stared at Walters. The corporal had a look of rage on his normally easy going face. His chest heaved with exertion and his eyes roamed the corridor. Walters was a fungus head. The vaccine hadn't worked for him. His fifty-fifty chance had not paid off.

To Marli, he said, "Get out of here."

She didn't hesitate. She ran around the corner and down the corridor as quickly as she could. One sentry took aim at Walters and fired, but only hit him in the shoulder. Walters fired a burst from the M-249 that opened up the man's chest like a scalpel. Unlike the other fungus head zombies he had encountered, Walters still retained the knowledge to operate his weapon and he did so with deadly accuracy. How much of Walters remained? Kyle decided to find out.

"Walters," he yelled.

Walters turned to him. He leveled the SAW at Kyle's chest. Kyle held his breath, but Walters withheld his fire. There was no glimmer of recognition in the corporal's eyes, but the fact that he didn't immediately fire gave Kyle cause to hope.

"Drop the weapon, corporal."

Used to following orders, Walters' hand wavered. The barrel of the SAW lowered a few inches.

"Where's Ginson, Walters? Do you want to let him down?"

It was the wrong thing to say. Walters raised his head and howled. Then he pointed the SAW at the ceiling and pulled the trigger. He ignored the chunks of plaster falling on him and continued to howl. Kyle hoped he would keep firing until the ammunition belt was empty, but Walters released the trigger. The two men faced one another, Walters hesitant, and Kyle trying to ignite some spark of Walters' humanity. If Walters could change, so could anyone else who had taken the vaccine.

At that moment, drawn by the commotion outside his door, General Willows stepped out of his office. The motion broke the stalemate. Walters' mouth opened wide in a scream as he turned the weapon towards the general and pulled the trigger. Bullets raked the wall beside Willows, as Walters slowly brought the weapon to bear as if he was fighting the impulse from his enraged mind. Kyle didn't have time to think. Instinct took over. He pulled his Glock and fired two rounds at Walters' head, knowing any other target would not be enough. Walters dropped the SAW to the floor and stared at Kyle for a moment before collapsing to his knees. Kyle thought he saw a flicker of recognition in Walters' eyes before he keeled over dead. Kyle's heart went deathly cold. He had killed one of his few friends, a man he had come to love like a brother.

He stared at Walters' corpse as blood pooled around the body. Then he flung the Glock away from him in disgust. He stumbled over to Walters and knelt beside him, cradling Walters' shattered head in his arms as blood dripped down his arms. He felt Marli's arms cradling his head as he wept, but could not answer as she whispered repeatedly, "It's not your fault." It was his fault. Walters' blood was on his hands, figuratively and literally. The fact that he had killed Walters to save the general didn't matter to him. Walters, the person that he was, had been alive somewhere inside the creature he had become, fighting to get out. He hadn't given Walters the time to fight. How many other fungus heads had he killed that had been fighting to free themselves of their infection, how many peoples' last thoughts were of loved ones or friends?

He remained that way, clasping Walters, refusing to allow the medics to take away Walters' body until Ginson arrived and pried Walters' cooling corpse from his arms.

"You did the right thing," Ginson said. "He would have wanted one of us to stop him."

Kyle didn't reply. Whether Ginson was right or not, didn't matter. Walters was dead. He felt a sting in his arm and looked up at Marli.

"I gave you a sedative." Her voice was distant, receding even as she spoke. "You need rest."

He tried to protest but his lips refused to move. His entire body began to go numb. As his eyes closed, he wondered if he ever wanted to awaken.

* * *

July 12, MIA, Miami, FL –

Kyle awoke in his cot in the hangar with a pounding head, residue from the sedative. His mind was slightly clearer, but he still felt as if someone else inhabited his body. His hands were clumsy as he buttoned his shirt. It took three tries before the buttons properly aligned with the holes. The image of Walters collapsing had repeated in his head during his unconsciousness, until it had become a mantra that remained with him now that he was awake.

Someone had washed Walters' blood from him, but he could still feel it staining his hands. He couldn't tie his bootlaces, so he let them dangle. He panicked for a moment when he couldn't find Ricardo's photo, but someone had removed it from his pocket and laid it on his pillow. He shoved it in his pocket and slipped out of the hangar before anyone could stop him.

Things had returned to normal when he went to the office to photocopy the photograph. The floor where Walters had died had been moped clean of his blood, but for just a second, Kyle saw Walters' body lying there. He wiped the vision away with the palm of his hand. He made a couple of dozen copies of the photograph and scribbled his cell phone number and his name at the bottom of each one. Commandeering a jeep by the ruse of saying he was acting for the general, he left the airport.

His mind was still groggy and he shouldn't have been driving, but there was no other traffic on the streets. In fact, the city was a graveyard. Most of the smoke had dissipated, but its absence revealed a city blackened by fires and devoid of life. It reminded him of a Civil War photograph he had seen of Richmond after the Evacuation of 1865, chimneys standing like rows of sentries and walls that enclosed only rubble. A few stray dogs and cats wandered the empty streets. Fat buzzards and flocks of blackbirds filled the sky. He shuddered as he thought of what they were feasting on. He passed through numerous army checkpoints that gave him only a cursory glance and noticed armed squads exploring buildings block by block in search of zombies.

The same thing was happening in other major cities. Despite all nature could throw at them, mankind was slowly regaining control, but at a heavy price. Millions were dead, tens of thousands missing or homeless. It would be months before enough vaccine was available for everyone. The country was scarred, but a scab was forming over the wound. Like most wounds, it would slowly heal. He wasn't as sure about his own scars.

His first visit was to the Jackson Memorial Hospital near the civic center. He needn't have bothered. The hospital and the civic center were both gone, razed by the fires. Next, he tried the FEMA facility Charles Hadley Park near 46th Street. Forty large tents surrounded by double-layered chain link fencing held nearly eight hundred people. He spent over an hour passing through each tent, searching for Ricardo's face among the survivors. He questioned evacuees at random. He spoke to nurses and doctors with no results. No one had seen him.

He visited all five remaining FEMA facilities, showing Ricardo's photo to anyone who would look at it. He tried the surviving area hospitals with no better results. He left copies of the photo everywhere he went. By day's end, he was beginning to think that he would not be able to keep his promise to Rita. Finding her husband wouldn't erase Walters' death, but it would help move the balance of karma a little more in his direction.

Defeated and exhausted by the day's lack of results, he returned to the airport to face Rita. He wouldn't give up, but his hopes diminished. His concern rose when he couldn't find her in her room. No one seemed to know what had happened to her. He sought out the general. Willows met him at the door and ushered him in.

"Thanks for saving my life, Bane. Shame about Walters."

Kyle suppressed a wince. "Yeah. It could've been any of us."

"So right. It's something we'll have to live with for awhile. What's on your mind?"

"Rita Hernandez, one of the evacuees, is missing. Do you know anything about it?"

Willows smiled. "Sometimes in all this heartache and misery, a little ray of hope breaks through. It seems your photo safari paid off. Mrs. Hernandez's husband was found at a hospital south of here. He was unconscious when he was brought in almost a week ago. He's been there under a John Doe ever since. A nurse saw your photo of him when she came on duty. I sent Mrs. Hernandez and her son to his side a few hours ago. They said his prognosis was good."

Kyle was stunned. Relief flooded over him. Ricardo was alive. He, Rita, and their child were together. With all the destruction and loss of life, the reunion of a small family didn't mean much in the grand scheme of things, but it mattered to him a great deal.

"I'm glad."

"It happened only because you care, son," the general said. "Mrs. Hernandez told me what you had done for her."

Kyle didn't know what to say. "I … I promised her."

The general's face grew serious. "Doctor Henry tells me you've been impossible to live with these past few days, something about losing your identity. If you were one of my soldiers, I would tell you to buck up and do your duty, but you're not. In all honesty, you've done far more than your duty. All I can offer you is some sage advice. You may have doubts about yourself, but no one whose life you've touched has any doubts about you. Doctor Henry sets a great store by you. I think she's smitten. If I were you, I wouldn't let her get away."

"I won't."

"Good. Now go clean up. You look like shit."

He glanced in the mirror behind the general's desk. He did look like shit.

19

July 20, Dodge Island, Miami, FL –

Almost three weeks had passed since the initial outbreak. As Marli had predicted, fewer cases of infection were reported each day, but Walters' strange conversion had her puzzled. Had the ineffective vaccine caused him to retain some part of his personality, or had the Cordyceps fungus mutated? As far as the general was concerned it was a moot point. To Kyle, it was a bad omen. The medical center the military had established on Dodge Island had immunized over sixty thousand people so far. Another twenty thousand waited for fresh batches of vaccine to arrive. Less than one hundred thousand survivors in a city of two-and-a half million was a staggering death toll, but when compared to the countless dead of the other cities that had suffered through the plague, it was a mere pittance. Kyle didn't know how other cities of the world fared, but doubted they had done much better.

Ginson was gone. Walters' death had almost devastated him, but he refused to buckle under. He had volunteered for duty in Des Moines, trying to leave Miami far behind him. His parting with Kyle had been civil, but Kyle couldn't help detecting some animosity seething just below Ginson's composure. Kyle understood the sergeant's dilemma. He had killed the last survivor of Ginson's original squad. Now Ginson was utterly alone. He might not blame Kyle, but he still held him responsible. In a way, he was. His volunteering to test the new vaccine in his eagerness to rescue Rita had prompted Ginson and Walters to do so as well. It had failed Walters, perhaps even contributed to his death. Ginson felt survivor's guilt. Perhaps they all did to a degree. He hoped Ginson forgave him in time, as he was still trying to forgive himself.

Kyle was no longer a detective. That part of his past was gone. He had resigned SIS. There would continue to be crimes. Not all the survivors were good people. The criminals would always be around, but there was less opportunity for crime. There might not be a need for detectives, but the city would always need cops, and Dodge Island was back under civilian authority. The rest of the city, what was left of it, would have to wait. The survivors of the Cordyceps Plague needed time to rebuild, but first they had to rebuild themselves. Lives were devastated, families torn apart. There was nothing as fragile as the human psyche, but nothing so resilient. Ghosts from the past would haunt them forever. The trick was to allow the ghosts to walk among them in peace.

His own ghosts were held at bay by Marli's love, and his growing love for her. It was a healing process for both of them, but one at which he took great delight. Rita's reunion with her husband Ricardo had been one small step in the healing process. Theirs was just one family in millions, but he had been a part in making it happen. Small recompense for those who had not survived, but it sufficed for him. Saving just one family was enough to make it all worthwhile. Building another with Marli would be icing on the cake.

To everyone concerned, the Cordyceps Plague was over, yet the small tight knot deep in Kyle's stomach would not go away. If nature could unleash one plague, well why not another, more deadly one? As he walked his beat along the boulevard, watching the people of Dodge Island going about their daily lives, he worried that it had all been too much too soon. Plagues, like crime, happened when least expected. He remembered an old adage from his youth – You can't trust Mother Nature.

He watched another helicopter fly by overhead with its load of refugees destined for the relocation center. Their coming and going had become a routine affair, but this helicopter drew his attention when it seemed to jerk in the air as it hovered over the landing pad in front of the decontamination area.

"Rookie pilot," he muttered.

Some instinct made him glance twice as the chopper finally settled gently onto the tarmac. Instead of quickly disgorging its normal load of cowed people huddled together for company, the chopper sat on the field, rotors spinning, its doors curiously closed.

A soldier eager to get the chopper back into the air rushed to open the door. As he slid the door slid open, half a dozen zombies erupted from the chopper. To his surprise, several of them were carrying weapons. One creature landed on the hapless soldier and began pounding his head on the tarmac. The others spread across the field. Kyle drew his Glock at the sound of the first screams. Cordyceps was rising again.

END OF BOOK 1